An Affair of Hearts

An Affair of Hearts

The Ladies' Wagering Whist Society, Book 6

Meredith Bond

Copyright, 2020, Meredith Bond. All rights reserved.

No part of this book may be reproduced or transmitted in any form by any means—graphic, electronic or mechanical—without permission in writing from the author, except by a reviewer who may quote brief passages in a review.

Cover Art by QuarterbackTB,

https://qtbdesign.wixsite.com/qtbdesign

Logo by Anjali Banerji

Edited by The Editing Hall,

http://theeditinghall.com

Published by Anessa Books,
For more information please visit
http://anessabooks.com

Dramatis Personae

Christianne Ayres (previously Lady Norman): Founding member of the Ladies' Wagering Whist Society

Lydia Welles née Sheffield: member of the Ladies' Wagering Whist Society

Diana Crowther, Lady Colburne née Hemshawe: member of the Ladies' Wagering Whist Society

Claire Tyne, Lady Blakemore: member of the Ladies' Wagering Whist Society

Alys Russell, Duchess of Kendell: member of the Ladies' Wagering Whist Society

Mrs. Penelope Aldridge: member of the Ladies' Wagering Whist Society

Cynthia Montley, Lady Sorrell: member of the Ladies' Wagering Whist Society

Ellen Aston, Lady Moreton: member of the Ladies' Wagering Whist Society

Joshua Powell, Lord Wickford: owner Powell's Club for Gentlemen

Tina Bronley, Duchess of Warwick née Rowan: Christianne's natural daughter

Robert Bronley, Duke of Warwick: Tina's husband

Lady Margaret Bronley: Warwick's sister

Liam Ayres, Lord Ayres: Christianne's husband and Tina's father

John Welles, Lord Welles: Lydia's husband

Andrew Crowther, Lord Colburne: Diana's husband

Beatrice & Isabelle Kendrick: Lady

Blakemore's nieces

Edward Pike, Lord Conway: Bel's fiancé

Paul Adler, Lord St. Vincent: Bee's fiancé

Elizabeth Adler, Lady St. Vincent: Paul's young step-mother

James Douglass, Marquess of Rossburk: Lady Margaret's romantic interest, school friend of Joshua Powell

Charles Aldridge: Mrs. Aldridge's son, watchmaker and businessman

Chapter One

~April 21, 1807~

Everything sparkled. The chandeliers with their crystal droplets reflected the candlelight, the gilt-edged mirrors surrounded by wall sconces echoed the light, even the guests dressed in their finest glittered, laughed, talked, and danced with brilliance. Elizabeth, Countess St. Vincent, sighed happily as she turned to her friend and hostess for this evening's soirée. "You have done such a magnificent job this evening, Lydia," she said. Even Lydia was looking quite sparkling this evening with her bright green eyes shining, the color picking up the pretty green embroidery edging her pale blue gown.

"Indeed, Lady Welles, you absolutely have outdone yourself." Mrs. Aldridge, standing on Lydia's other side, agreed.

"Thank you," Lydia said, giving them both a bright smile. "Elizabeth, your dress this evening is lovely."

"Oh, thank you. It is one I brought with me from the countryside, but I think it's holding up quite well here in London," Elizabeth said. She'd only been in town for a month, but already she had a good feeling about this season, her very first since her disastrous come-out six years ago.

She had, of course, also dressed to impress, just like everyone else. Despite the fact she was still in half-mourning for her departed husband, her gown of pale violet with deeper purple ribbons and lace was in the latest fashion, even if the décolletage was a little lower than what she normally wore. It was still quite conservative for a lady of her age and stature, but Elizabeth, with her full figure, had always gone for a more demure look. Her dark brown hair was carefully tamed into a complicated coiffure with purple ribbons woven through and a few curls allowed to rest gently over her shoulder.

"I beg your pardon, Lady St. Vincent?" a footman asked, approaching Elizabeth.

"Yes?"

"Lord St. Vincent has requested your presence in the library," he said with a slight bow.

"Oh. Tell him I'll be right there," she said.

"Is everything all right, do you suppose?" Mrs. Aldridge asked with a look of concern marring her motherly countenance. She was a kind, well-respected older lady who was a member of a very exclusive club known as the Ladies' Wagering Whist Society, along with Lydia and six other prominent ladies of the *ton*.

Elizabeth didn't know exactly what the ladies of the Whist Society did. They claimed they merely played cards together every Wednesday afternoon, but so far, their influence seemed to be quite significant and growing. From what Elizabeth understood, they were responsible for no fewer than six prominent matches among the *ton*, including that of Elizabeth's own stepson, who had just requested her presence. They also held an annual party to raise funds for the people of the Rookeries that earned a significant amount as well as being one of The Events of the season.

The ladies of the Wagering Whist Society were, in short, what just about every woman of the *ton* desired to be—well-respected, well-known, influential. They made a positive impact, helping those who needed it without asking for anything in return. If they had been accepting additional members, Elizabeth would have been first in line. As it was, she was proud to call its members her friends.

"I can't imagine what St. Vincent wants. I'll just go and find out. If you'll excuse me?" Elizabeth gave the two ladies a nod and then went off to find the library.

~*~

"How very unusual," Penelope Aldridge said as she watched Lady St. Vincent make her way out of the drawing room. "Why would he be in sudden need of his stepmother?"

Lady Welles frowned next to her, also watching the young lady as she went. "I can't imagine, but I agree something seems off." She turned and caught the eye of the footman who had delivered the message.

He approached her with a slight bow. "Yes, my lady?"

"Who asked you to find Lady St. Vincent?" she asked.

"A gentleman, my lady. Lord St. Vincent, I presume," the man said.

"But he did not specifically say?" Lady Welles asked with a frown.

"No, my lady."

Lady Welles turned worried eyes to Penelope, who in turn asked, "Was he quite tall, young and handsome with blond hair?"

The man looked startled, perhaps at the preciseness of her description. "No, ma'am. He was short and rather rotund. I wouldn't think he was below thirty or perhaps five and thirty."

Penelope didn't like that at all! She shared another look with Lady Welles.

"That's not Lord St. Vincent," the younger lady said with a certainty.

"No, it's not. Thank you," Penelope said, dismissing the man.

"After you, my lady," Lady Welles said, indicating the way to the door.

Penelope followed Lady St. Vincent out the door in the direction of the library.

~*~

Elizabeth found the door to the library slightly ajar. Clearly her stepson wanted to make sure she found the correct room, although it was odd he would send a message in that way. She couldn't imagine why he might want to see her in private during a party. It must be something vitally important if he couldn't wait to speak with her at home tomorrow.

The room was oddly dark with the only light coming from the fireplace.

"Paul?" Elizabeth called out as she entered the room.

"'Tis I, my ravishing beauty," a man's voice said from just beyond the door. His voice was soft and higher pitched than Paul's.

This wasn't right. Elizabeth immediately turned to leave, but a hand grabbed her waist and pulled her back forcibly.

Her back met with a hard, rounded form of a man in a corset. The voice, the physique... she realized with horror it was Lord Rogan who had hold of her. He immediately bent his head and began to nuzzle her neck, even as his hands took a firm hold of both her breasts and squeezed.

"Unhand me!" she tried to yell. Her breath, however, felt like it was being squeezed from her lungs, and her words didn't come out as forcibly as she'd intended.

"Oh, my sweet, delicious, voluptuous Elizabeth," he murmured. "You are as enticing as I thought you'd be. I do like a full-breasted woman. Let me get closer—"

Elizabeth didn't think he possibly could get any closer until one of his hands dove straight down the front of her dress. Her stomach immediately revolted. She coughed, gagged, and attempted to scream all at the same time and simply ended up making a strangled noise.

"Lady St. Vincent!" a woman's voice said from the doorway, her horrified tones so well reflecting the revulsion Elizabeth herself was feeling.

"Excuse me," Mrs. Aldridge's voice cut from behind the woman Elizabeth hadn't yet identified.

The first woman turned and moved back into the hall, allowing Lydia to follow Mrs. Aldridge into the room.

"Get off her you brute!" Mrs. Aldridge began using her fan to rain blows down upon Lord Rogan, whose hand was now caught inside of Elizabeth's dress. Lydia ran straight to the fireplace and grabbed a multi-arm candelabra.

With the distraction her friends provided,

Elizabeth managed to tear herself free of the man, wrenching his wrist and ripping her own dress in the process. She may have won her freedom but so too did the contents of her stomach. She ran to the side of the room, helpless to stop it.

She was vaguely aware of Lord Rogan running from the room as she coughed and spit.

Gentle hands rubbed her back. "There, there, it's all right. He's gone now. You're going to be all right."

Elizabeth could do nothing but burst into tears. Never before had she felt so out of control. Her knees wobbled, but she managed to remain on her feet, leaning one hand against the wall for support. A handkerchief was pressed into her other hand.

She used it to wipe her mouth. Some voices whispered behind her, most likely Lydia and Mrs. Aldridge. A man's voice she didn't recognize joined them, but Elizabeth simply didn't have the courage to lift her face to see who it was.

There was the sound of footsteps retreating, and then Lydia came and gently directed Elizabeth away from the wall. "It's going to be all right, Elizabeth. You poor thing. Mrs. Aldridge's son has gone to fetch your carriage. You'll be home in a trice."

"Thank...thank you," Elizabeth hiccoughed. "I'm... I'm so..."

"No, no, don't even say it. I am appalled, no, mortified that this should have happened to you this evening. I cannot believe my own footman—" Lydia was so overcome, Elizabeth had the urge to comfort *her*.

"No, poor Lydia. I would...hug you, but I... I think I'm a mess," Elizabeth managed. She desperately was trying to keep her tears at bay. She was having trouble breathing for the sobs caught in her throat.

"My lady, your carriage is waiting," said the same man who'd been there a few minutes earlier, re-entering the room. He was well-dressed, clearly one of the guests. His light brown hair shone in the candlelight, even as his dark eyes looked at her with such concern. He came forward, averting his eyes in a gentlemanly manner, and placed her wrap around her shoulders, pulling it forward so it covered her ripped gown.

Elizabeth grasped it closed. "Thank you."

With barely a touch, he led her from the room, down a much too long hall, to the front door. He handed her up into her carriage and then gave her driver the go-ahead after securely closing the door behind her.

As the carriage pulled away, Elizabeth let go of the breath she hadn't even been aware she'd been holding and allowed herself to collapse into a fit of sobs and tears.

Chapter Two

~April 22~

Elizabeth didn't even remember how she'd gotten to bed that night. She awoke the following morning with the muscles in her stomach sore from heaving the previous night. She had absolutely no desire to bestir from her bed, not that morning nor any morning. She just wanted to stay where she was in the soft, comforting warmth, but something, she realized, had woken her.

A moment later her bedroom door was thrown open with such force it banged against the opposite wall.

"My God, Elizabeth, are you all right?" her brother strode into the room, followed by her stepson, Paul.

"Let her sleep," Paul was saying, but clearly Edward had no intention of listening to him.

She reluctantly pulled herself upright, dragging the covers over her shoulders. "I'm fine," she told her older brother. He perched on the edge of her bed, his deep blue eyes looking so worried for her.

"We just heard. It was Rogan, wasn't it?" Edward said, placing a gentle hand on her cheek and looking at her closely as if checking for bruises. To be honest, she didn't yet know if she had any.

His concern only made her tear up once again. She could only nod for fear of truly beginning to cry once again.

"I should have shot him when I had the chance," Paul growled. Elizabeth suspected he was referring to her first encounter with Lord Rogan at Lady Sorrell's soirée the previous month.

"I missed the opportunity as well and now regret it," her brother said from the foot of the bed, running his fingers through his straight black hair in agitation.

"That man has no shame," Paul said.

"No intelligence more like," Edward added.

The two men looked at each other, one fair and tall, the other dark and broad, both able to be terrifying and intimidating in his own way, and nodded. "We'll have to decide who gets the honor of killing him," Paul said.

Elizabeth took in a deep calming breath. The men's indignation gave her the strength she wished she'd had the previous evening. "Neither one of you will kill him because it would kill me and the Kendrick twins to lose either one of you," she said, thinking of the two girls who were engaged or about to be engaged to the two dearest men in Elizabeth's life.

They both were silent at that bit of wisdom.

On a thought, she added, "If you, either of you, call him out, it will be made more public than if we just left it alone. My reputation is already tenuous, don't harm it any more than necessary." She paused and looked from one man to the other. "Please."

"Then we go on as if it never happened? Who else was there?" Edward asked, clearly not liking this.

Elizabeth thought back, but all she could remember was Lydia, Mrs. Aldridge, and vaguely some gentleman assisting her to her coach. She had no idea who he'd been, so she simply said, "I only remember Lady Welles and Mrs. Aldridge."

"Good. They won't spread a false word about you," Paul said. "In fact, I have no worries at all about it staying within our own private circle. None of our friends would say a word against you or spread the tale outside of the group."

"Is that how you heard?" Elizabeth asked.

"Yes. Mrs. Aldridge stopped by to check on how you were doing. St. Vincent and I were together in the breakfast parlor when she came in," Elizabeth's brother said.

"She might still be here—we did rather run out on her," Paul admitted sheepishly.

"Oh, dear! Please check would you, and I'll be down as quickly as I can. I do want to thank her," Elizabeth said.

The men nodded and left together to see to the lady, and so Elizabeth could get up and dressed.

She was horrified to find bruising on her ribs and a horrible red mark on her shoulder where Lord Rogan had been suckling at her. She dressed in her most conservative morning gown, a plain gray dress with almost no adornment and then added a fichu to hide her shoulder.

~*~

Mrs. Aldridge was enjoying a cup of tea and the men's company when Elizabeth joined them in the breakfast room twenty minutes later.

"My dear Lady St. Vincent," Mrs. Aldridge said, immediately rising upon Elizabeth's entrance. She stepped forward and took her hands, her forehead scrunching in concern. "How are you, my dear?"

"Thank you so much for coming, ma'am. I'm doing better," Elizabeth said, giving her hands a squeeze.

"Can you eat? You must have some nourishment," the lady said, indicating that Elizabeth join them at the table as if she were the hostess instead of the other way around.

"Thank you. I'll have a piece of toast. I think that's all I'll be able to stomach just now," Elizabeth said.

"Add a boiled egg to that. You must have something a little more substantial, my dear, it will stand you in good stead," the woman said. She was so wonderfully motherly; Elizabeth just wanted to reach out and hug her.

She shared a look with her brother, who was laughing silently, his shoulders shaking ever so slightly with his mirth. "Mrs. Aldridge, you are an absolute dear," Edward said. "Our own mother was never so concerned for my sister's health as you are."

"What? Oh, I don't believe that for a moment, Lord Conway," the lady said, resuming her seat. "I'm sure she just showed it in a different way. Every mother is concerned for her children." She *tsked* her tongue.

"Mrs. Aldridge was just telling us all about the Ladies' Wagering Whist Society. In truth, I never realized how much those ladies have done," Paul said, resuming his seat as well. He never failed to stand when a lady entered the room. Edward did so for other women, but never Elizabeth, which just made her laugh.

"I must admit, when I joined the group, I never

expected to be part of such an influential group of ladies. To be honest, I thought we would play cards, nothing more," Mrs. Aldridge said, the lower of her double chins wobbling with the titter of laughter that followed.

"Do you know what their stakes are when they play cards?" Edward asked Elizabeth with a twinkle sparkling from his brilliant blue eyes.

"No," Elizabeth said, sitting back while the footman placed a plate with a sliced boiled egg and the toast rack in front of her. She reached for the butter as she looked to Mrs. Aldridge.

The lady giggled and leaned forward. "We play for secrets!"

"Secrets?" Elizabeth echoed.

"Yes. We all have secrets, of course. If you lose two games and have the lowest number of points, you must divulge a secret to the group," the lady explained.

"What sort of secrets?" Paul asked.

The lady laughed again. "Well now, that would be telling, wouldn't it? No, no, not one word, not one hint of anyone's secret is allowed outside of the group. And don't even ask, for I won't tell you who has, so far, divulged their secrets."

"No wonder it's such an exclusive group," Elizabeth commented after clearing her mouth with a sip of tea.

"Oh, yes. We certainly couldn't let just anyone in," the lady agreed, her chin set to wobbling again as she nodded her head vigorously.

Elizabeth had just taken another bite of her egg and toast when the door burst open and her son, Matthew, came running in.

"Mama, Mama!" the tow-haired little boy shouted. He threw himself onto Elizabeth who, if she hadn't dropped her toast and made a grab for the four-year-old, would have bashed his head on the table.

"Matthew, what have I said about shouting in the house?" Elizabeth said, reprimanding him.

His governess came panting into the room. "I am so sorry, my lady, he...he's much too fast for me. I just can't make it down the stairs as quickly as he can. I swear he must skip half the treads."

"It's all right, Mrs. Smithy. I don't quite know how he does it either, but he can certainly move more quickly than one would suppose for someone so small." Elizabeth pushed her chair back and lifted the child into her lap.

"Oooh, neg!" the boy said, his eyes alighting on her plate. He reached out and picked a piece of egg off her toast and stuffed it into his mouth.

"Don't you feed the child, Elizabeth?" Edward asked with a laugh as he watched his nephew make short work of the rest of Elizabeth's breakfast.

"He most certainly has eaten, my lord," his governess responded.

"But he's a growing boy," Elizabeth finished.

"A bottomless pit, more like," Paul added with a laugh. "I think he eats more than I do." He reached over from his place at the head of the table to ruffle Matthew's hair.

The boy giggled. "I'm growing!" he exclaimed. "I'm gonna be bigger dan you, Paul."

"Yes, I believe you are," said Elizabeth's stepson, giving his little step-brother a smile. Elizabeth looked from one to the other, awed at the family resemblance despite being from two different mothers. Her husband had thought it a matter of course that both of his sons would take after him, although he had been a little surprised that Matthew had gotten Elizabeth's blue eyes rather than his own, which were green.

"I didn't know you had a son, Lady St. Vincent," Mrs. Aldridge said, looking fondly at the child. "How old is he?"

"I'm four!" Matthew answered before Elizabeth could even open her mouth. He held out four little egg-dusted fingers just to be sure she understood. Elizabeth reached out and grabbed the little hand with her napkin and wiped it clean.

"Four years old? Oh my! You are a big boy, aren't you?" the lady said, laughing.

"I'm gonna be bigger than my brodder!" Matthew informed her.

Mrs. Aldridge looked over at Paul and then back to Matthew. "Well, in that case you'd better eat up because you've got a lot of growing to do!"

Dutifully, the child reached out and took the rest of Elizabeth's toast and started nibbling away at it.

Mrs. Aldridge laughed again, clearly delighted with the child. "He is a dear!"

"He is a minx!" Edward corrected.

Matthew looked over at his uncle. "What a minx?" he asked around a mouthful of bread.

"It's someone who is impolite and speaks with his mouth full," Elizabeth said.

He turned and looked up at her but didn't say anything until he'd chewed and swallowed. "No, it's not, Mama. You just made that up."

"Are you calling me a liar?" Elizabeth said with mock horror.

"No, you would never lie to me, Mama. I love you." He rested his cheek against her bosom, and it was all Elizabeth could do to hold on to the joy and love in her heart.

"And I love you, my sweet boy," Elizabeth said, giving him a gentle squeeze. "Now, is there a reason you absolutely had to see me this morning, or did you just want to steal my breakfast?"

He giggled. "I wanted to steal your breaffast. I was hungry and Mrs. Smithy wanted me to learn my letters."

"You *should* learn your letters, that's very important, but you should also have enough to eat," Elizabeth told him. She looked up at the governess, who was looking fondly at the child.

"If I'd known he was hungry, I would certainly have called for more food, my lady," the woman said as soon as she realized her employer was looking at her.

"I'm sure you would have. Why don't you take Matthew downstairs to the kitchen and see if the cook has another egg for my bottomless little pit."

Matthew climbed down from her lap, saying, "I wanna napple."

"All right. I'm sure Cook has an apple for you if she hasn't put them all into a pie for dinner," Mrs. Smithy said, taking the child's hand.

"Pie? I want pie! I want pie!" Matthew said, jumping up and down.

"Pie is for dinner. Let's see if we can find you an apple and then back to your letters," the woman said gently as they left the room.

"He is absolutely adorable!" Mrs. Aldridge sighed as the door closed behind them. She turned back to Elizabeth. "I can see now why it is so vitally important that you reestablish your good name as soon as you can. You can't have that sweet little boy growing up..."

"He will never know his mother ever had such a reputation," Elizabeth said with a certainty she wished she felt.

Mrs. Aldridge nodded her agreement. "Lord St. Vincent informed me that you are going to attempt to pretend as if last night's attack never happened."

"Yes," Elizabeth said, reaching for another piece of toast since Matthew had eaten hers.

"I think that is very wise, my dear. You want to avoid any talk and actively suppress any gossip if possible. Were you planning on making calls today?" the lady asked.

"Yes. I was thinking of going to Lady Hartfell's at-home," Elizabeth said.

Mrs. Aldridge nodded. "An excellent choice. She is well-connected and kind. Rarely do you hear an unpleasant word from the lady. And I believe her own garden party will be coming up shortly, won't it?"

Elizabeth shook her head. "I don't know. I haven't received an invitation if it is."

"Hmmm, no, neither have I," Mrs. Aldridge said. "Perhaps it's later in the season."

"That would make sense if it's a garden party, to wait until it's a little warmer," Edward commented.

"Yes, yes, it would," the lady said, nodding again. "Well, if you'd like, I can join you on your visit," she said, turning back to Elizabeth.

"That would be very kind of you, ma'am, but you needn't put yourself—"

"Oh, it's no trouble at all. To be honest, I was thinking of going myself, so it really makes sense for us to go together. And, well, I don't know how much clout I hold in society—probably very little indeed—but it couldn't hurt to have me by your side, now could it?" Mrs. Aldridge said.

"I think it's a brilliant idea," Paul said, giving them both an encouraging smile.

Chapter Three

Penelope was incredibly impressed with Lady St. Vincent's fortitude. She was certain that if she had been attacked when she was a younger woman, she would have kept to her bed for days. And yet, here was this strong young woman stepping out with her to face down society.

Penelope could only hope that the gossips—well, one in particular—hadn't yet had a chance to spread her horrid tales. Lady Findlater was renowned for saying the worst about people, and Penelope had had to push past the woman the previous evening to get into Lord Welles's library. How she had known to be just there at that moment, Penelope would never know.

After Lady St. Vincent had gone home, Penelope and Lady Welles had gone in search of the notorious gossip, but she was nowhere to be found. Now, there was only the desperate hope her tales could be stopped before they got out. Perhaps she and Lady St. Vincent could even give their own version of the events if anyone asked.

Penelope didn't hold out much hope, however, because they hadn't even entered Lady Hartfell's home when they met two other ladies just leaving. They took one look at Lady St. Vincent and turned their heads the other way in a most pronounced and disturbing manner. The cut direct!

Lady St. Vincent paused and watched the women walk away. "Maybe this wasn't such a good idea," she said quietly.

Penelope gave her a pat on her hand and said, "If you would prefer not to..."

But Lady St. Vincent was made of sterner stuff. She took in a deep breath and gave a shake of her head. "No. We should learn the worst." She then marched straight up the steps and rapped on the door.

Even the footman raised an eyebrow when Lady St. Vincent handed over her calling card, but he allowed them entrance and escorted them to Lady Hartfell's drawing room.

All talk came to a cold, dead stop the moment Lady St. Vincent's name was announced. Everyone turned to stare. There were seven or eight people in total, sitting around a tea tray on gold chintz sofas and chairs.

Lady St. Vincent froze, but Penelope was not going to allow the rudeness of a few people to stop her. She took Lady St. Vincent's arm and walked farther into the room. "Good afternoon, Lady Hartfell. How lovely it is to see you," she said, as if nothing was out of the ordinary.

The woman paled. "Good afternoon, Mrs. Aldridge. Lady St. Vincent, you have a great deal of nerve showing up here—or, in fact, anywhere today."

"Thank you so much for your concern, my lady," Lady St. Vincent said gently. "I thought getting out would make me feel better after my horrible ordeal last evening."

"Your..." the lady began to say, but then

paused.

"Lord Rogan's attack. I assume that is what you are referring to?" Elizabeth asked gently when the woman couldn't seem to be able to put her words together.

Lady Hartfell's eyes widened at Elizabeth's forthright language but pulled herself together quickly. "I beg your pardon, but it was my understanding that you welcomed Lord Rogan's attentions. Why, he said that you, yourself, were the one who asked *him* to meet you in the library."

"That's ridiculous!" Penelope snapped.

"He told you that *himself*?" Lady St. Vincent asked, clearly shocked.

"That's what Lady Findlater said he told her," a larger woman Penelope didn't know said from the sofa.

"He was obviously lying, and Lady Findlater should have known better. She was right there. She saw Lady St. Vincent go into the library where she was accosted by Lord Rogan," Penelope explained.

"Oh, no, that's not at all what she said. She said Lady St. Vincent went in and greeted Lord Rogan as if she fully knew he would be there waiting for her," another much-too-thin woman said from the other sofa.

"It was clearly a preset assignation," Lady Penderton said, joining in the conversation with a nod.

"But it wasn't!" Lady St. Vincent argued.

"Lord Rogan tricked her…" Penelope started, but her voice was drowned out.

"Lady St. Vincent, whether it was or not is not actually the main issue. I believe the point is that you have clearly done all you could to attract men to your boudoir. You did so when you first made your debut, and clearly you have returned to London to continue with your depraved conduct," the skinny, sour-looking woman said in the most forthright manner Penelope had ever heard.

"What you do in private is one thing, but to bring that out into society—" the first woman commented.

"But I have never, not now nor when I made my debut, ever done anything to—" Lady St. Vincent started.

"Maybe she can't help it. If I had a figure like that, I'm sure I would attract a great deal of men as well," the pinched woman said with a slight sneer.

"No, Marietta, even if you were built like that, men still wouldn't treat you that way. It's not just her figure, it's the way she smiles at them. It's *inviting. You* know better than to behave that way," said Lady Crowther who was sitting by the skinny one's side.

Penelope felt Lady St. Vincent shrink beside her. She wrung her hands in frustration. She so wanted to defend her friend, but these women were refusing to listen to anything she or Lady St. Vincent said.

"Ladies before this conversation can go any further, I think we must agree, with apologies to the lady herself, we simply cannot accept such behavior and therefore cannot welcome Lady St. Vincent—" Lady Hartwell began.

"But I haven't done anything wrong!" Lady St. Vincent said vehemently. "It's not my fault I'm built the way I am. I dress modestly! I *don't* invite—"

"Oh, come now, Lady St. Vincent, clearly you

do because men are taking you up on that silent invitation left and right," the first lady said. "Personally, I cannot stomach such behavior. I recommend a holiday."

"Yes," the pinched woman agreed. "If you simply left London—"

"I refuse to leave! It's not fair. It's not right!" Lady St. Vincent cried.

"Then prepare yourself for no one, and I mean no one, to invite you anywhere nor acknowledge you in the street. Why, I can hardly believe we have had the nerve to speak with you for so very long this afternoon," the pinched woman said.

"Indeed. We shall cease this immediately," the first woman said. She turned to Lady Penderton so that her back was to Penelope and Lady St. Vincent.

"I am very sorry," Lady Hartwell said.

"No, I don't believe you are," Lady St. Vincent said before turning and walking right out the door.

Penelope didn't think she could add anything to that smart retort, so she simply followed the lady out the door.

"I am so very sorry," Penelope started as soon as they were back in her carriage.

"No. I shouldn't have even thought that there wouldn't be such a reaction. I *should* have known better." The young woman swiped angrily at her cheek.

"My dear, I don't know—" Penelope started to say, but then she stopped herself because she did know precisely what to do.

"You have already done so very much, Mrs. Aldridge. Truly, I could not ask for a better friend," Lady St. Vincent said, grabbing her hands. "You were there. You and Lydia saved me from that awful man's clutches, and today you stood by my side as those women said awful, untrue things about me. I don't know how I can ever thank you." A tear slid down the girl's cheek.

"No, no. Do not even think of thanking me yet, for I have not even begun to do all I hope to do. No, you may thank me when your reputation is restored."

~*~

Elizabeth waved to her dear friend after being dropped off in front of her house, then slowly climbed the three steps to the door. Frank, the footman, already had the door open and was waiting for her.

She just felt so tired.

"Good afternoon, my lady. There was a delivery for you a short time ago. I put it in the drawing room," he said as he bowed her into the house.

Elizabeth paused as she handed him her wrap. "A delivery? I don't believe I purchased anything."

He just lifted a shoulder. "I didn't ask who it was from. It was delivered by a footman in livery, so I don't believe it was from a shop."

With a slight frown, she gave a nod. "Thank you, Frank. I guess I'll go see what it is. Oh, are my brother and Lord St. Vincent still here?"

"No, my lady, they left together soon after you."

As Elizabeth climbed the stairs to the drawing room, she wondered if they'd gone to see Bel and Bee Kendrick. She'd meant to ask Paul when and how he was planning on proposing to Bee, but in all the excitement so far, she'd completely forgotten. She felt awful for being so self-absorbed when he had such wonderful happenings in his life at the moment.

A most enormous bouquet of hot-house roses stood on the table in the center of the room. They were beautiful and perfumed the air in the loveliest manner. One of the maids must have seen the flowers and put them into one of her favorite crystal vases.

Elizabeth smiled, thinking they must be from that gentleman who'd seen her into her carriage the previous evening. He was so kind and considerate, she wouldn't be surprised, and now she would learn his name.

But as she approached the table, she noticed a box just in front of the flowers with a note sitting on top addressed to her. That was odd. He wouldn't have sent a gift; it was more than enough that he'd sent such a large bouquet. An icy warning tingled across the back of her neck.

Hesitantly, she picked up the note and unfolded it.

My dearest Elizabeth,

I am so distressed that we were interrupted last night. The next time we will have our rendezvous at my home where our privacy will be assured.

I'd love for you to wear this small token of my affection...and nothing else.

The flowers are my way of apologizing for a poor choice of location for our tête-à-tête.

Until then, my sweet, beautiful Elizabeth,

I am humbly yours...etc.

Rogan

Chapter Four

Elizabeth's stomach began to heave as she read the note, but she wouldn't allow it to overcome her this time. No, this time she would not be sick. She was much, much too angry. Fury over came her like storm. She let out a scream and lashed out at the roses staring at her, laughing at her stupidity for allowing this man anywhere near her. The flowers, vase and all, went flying to the floor, shattering with a satisfying crash.

But it wasn't enough. She wanted to do more, she wanted to hurt someone—preferably Lord Rogan himself. But there was no one, nothing she could do—so she stopped short of destroying her own home.

The box sitting on the table caught her eye. She grabbed it and tore it open. Inside lay an overly ornate mass of rubies of various shades of pink and purple, with a diamond in the center and emeralds on either side. It took her a minute to realize it was supposed to form the shape of a flower with leaves. It was hideous.

"My lady? Is everything all right?" a maid asked from behind her.

She spun around but couldn't take her anger out on the poor girl. "Yes. There was an accident.

Please clean this up and throw the flowers into garbage heap."

"Are you sure?" the girl asked, coming forward. She started delicately picking out the roses from amongst the broken glass. "I could probably..."

"Throw them away or keep them downstairs for yourself. I don't ever want to see them," Elizabeth said, cutting the girl off.

She looked up, worried, but nodded. "Yes, my lady."

Elizabeth looked down at the box again, noticing the name of the jeweler was carefully printed on the inside of the lid. It gave her an idea.

"I'll be going out," she said, striding to the door with the box. She went straight to the front door and then paused, considering her plan. Turning to Frank, who was standing ready to open the door for her, she said, "Call my maid. I need her to accompany me on an errand."

"Will you be needing your carriage, my lady?"

"No. I will walk," she said, accepting back her wrap from him.

He bowed and ran off. Five minutes later, she and Susie were walking at a brisk pace toward Bond Street.

Elizabeth only wished the walk were farther, getting her blood moving in a productive manner felt good. They arrived at the jeweler's in merely twenty minutes.

A bell rang as they entered the shop. A distinguished-looking portly gentleman with dark hair, graying at the temples, stood behind a glass counter. He looked up and smiled. "Good afternoon, madam, may I help you?" He would soon regret his cheerful nature, Elizabeth thought with some satisfaction.

"Yes." She placed the box in front of him. "I am Lady St. Vincent. I would like to return this."

His brows lowered, and he opened the box. They rose again immediately. "Why, this was purchased just this morning, my lady. Does it not please your ladyship? Would you care to find something more to your taste?"

"No, thank you. I simply need the money the gentleman used to pay for it."

"Oh! I don't know that I—"

"That money is meant for a good cause, I assure you, sir. One much better than..." She stopped herself from saying exactly how awful she thought the piece and instead softened her tone. "Please. I would be extremely grateful for your cooperation." She made a show of looking at other pieces of jewelry. "My stepson and brother both are soon to be married and will be looking to purchase items for their brides-to-be. I would be very happy to send them your way if you would be kind enough to give me whatever Lord Rogan spent on this piece."

"Really? Both..."

"The Earl of St. Vincent and the Viscount Conway," Elizabeth supplied for him.

"Oh! I see, yes, of course, my lady. Of course! If you would just wait one moment, I will get my book and see what Lord Rogan paid." The man bowed and stepped back into a small office behind him.

He returned with a piece of paper. "He paid with a cheque on his bank, naturally." He handed it over.

"Of course," Elizabeth said. She nearly gasped at the amount listed but swallowed it back and smiled at the man instead. "This will do. Thank you very much, Mr...."

"Swinely, my lady, Mr. Alfred Swinely," the man said with a broad smile.

"Thank you very much, Mr. Swinely. Good day to you." Elizabeth turned and started toward the door.

"You will send their lordships—" he called after her.

She paused at the door. "Naturally, Mr. Swinely. I will happily do so. Thank you, again."

He smiled and waved and Elizabeth turned and headed to Lydia's house.

~*~

"I'm very sorry, my lady, but her ladyship isn't at home," the footman told her after she knocked.

"Oh, well, is his lordship here?" she asked, eager to see this thing done. The longer she held onto Rogan's money, the more tainted she felt.

"Yes, I believe he is. If you would wait here just a moment, I'll check." The footman walked quickly back toward the library—a room Elizabeth would certainly never step foot in again. She desperately hoped Lord Welles wouldn't ask her to come back there to speak with him now.

She had been waiting, appreciating the quiet of the house for no more than five minutes, when Lord Welles himself came and greeted her. "Lady St. Vincent, how are you? Lydia told me about the horrid occurrence last night. Please accept my most sincere apologies..."

"Thank you so much, my lord. It wasn't your

fault. I assure you, you have nothing to apologize for," Elizabeth said as his words petered out in awkwardness.

He gave her a warm smile. "You are very kind, but indeed, everything that happens under my roof is ultimately my responsibility."

"Well, I was wondering if you could help me set things a little more right, in that case," Elizabeth said. She offered him the check.

He took it, looking at it in a confused manner. "What is this?"

"Lord Rogan had the temerity to send me a gift this morning. A piece of hideous jewelry with which, I suspect, he meant to buy my cooperation."

"My God!" Lord Welles exclaimed, as horrified as he should have been, Elizabeth noted with satisfaction.

"Yes. Naturally, I would not keep such a thing. I returned it to the store where he purchased it with that." She gave a nod to the cheque in his hand. "I'd like you to give that money to those who need it. I understand you have such connections?"

"Indeed, I do. This is very generous, my lady." He gave a little laugh. "I suspect most women would have simply thrown the jewelry back in Rogan's face and left him to recoup his funds."

"I don't think he deserves to get off so easily," Elizabeth said.

"I happen to agree with you, and this amount of money will go a long way to ease the suffering of others."

"Excellent! That is exactly what I was hoping," she said, giving him a satisfied nod.

He bowed to her. "Thank you, my lady, for your

generosity. I'm sorry Lydia isn't here to thank you as well. I know she was concerned for your well-being."

"That is very kind of her. Please tell her that Mrs. Aldridge was kind enough to look in on me today. That might ease her conscience as well."

"I'm certain it will."

~*~

Charles Aldridge was happily occupied in his workshop, experimenting with the mechanism on a new watch he was making, when his mother interrupted him.

"Charles, I wish to have a word with you," Mrs. Aldridge said, coming into the tiny room. It had once been a linen closet before Charles took it for his own little workshop. Watches weren't large objects, and the pieces that went into one were so small as to need hardly any space at all. Charles was content with his linen closet and had so far resisted his mother's insistence that he move to his father's old workshop in the back of the house.

Charles sat up and removed the magnifying glasses from his eyes. Rolling his head back and forth to ease the strain of being bent over his work for so long, he said, "Yes, Mother. What may I do for you?"

She came over and rubbed at the back of his neck with strong hands. She'd done the same for her husband when he'd been alive and had learned just where and how hard to press for maximum effectiveness. Charles let out a groan of contentment at his mother's ministrations.

"You should not stay bent over for so long. You're going to hurt yourself," she said, digging her fingers into his sore muscles.

"So you've said. Is that what you wished to speak to me about?"

"I think it's past time you began an earnest search for a wife," she said. "I was speaking with Lords Conway and St. Vincent this morning, and they are both extremely happy young men. Lord St. Vincent hasn't yet proposed to Miss Beatrice Kendrick, but he said he expected to do so within the week, and he believes she'll view his suit favorably. Lord Conway, as you might not know, has recently become engaged to Miss Isabel, Beatrice's twin sister."

"I did not know, mainly because I don't know who any of these people are," he said with a chuckle. He let his head roll to either side as his mother removed her blessed hand from massaging him.

His mother sighed heavily. "The Misses Kendrick are Lady Blakemore's nieces. Miss Isabel made her debut this season. I'm certain you must have met her. She's a redhead with a beautiful, clear complexion."

"Ah, well, since I haven't been out and about much this season, I couldn't have met her, now, could I?" he asked. He would have offered his mother a seat, only there wasn't one. If he offered her his, she would probably accidentally put her elbow on his workbench and disrupt the delicately balanced watch that was there. His conscious tinged only a little at his ungentlemanly behavior. If she'd wanted to sit down to talk to him, she should have asked him to come to her rather than the other way around.

Mrs. Aldridge frowned at him. "I'm sorry you haven't been in Town for the past month. You've missed the debuts of a number of very noteworthy and attractive young ladies."

He shrugged. He honestly had very little interest in the young ladies of the ton, noteworthy or not. "When business determines that I must be elsewhere, then I must be elsewhere."

This merely earned a scowl from his mother. "I don't understand why you don't just leave the running of your business to someone else."

"Because there isn't anyone else. Father had me to assist him. I have...?" He paused for a moment to drive home his point. "No one," he completed the thought.

"Which brings us back to my original point. You need to find yourself a wife."

"So that I may have a son who can help me run the business? Even if I married tomorrow, which obviously I can't, it would be a very long time before I have such a child," Charles pointed out with a little laugh. Honestly, his mother could be very amusing sometimes. He knew she was more intelligent than she let on, but sometimes... He almost wondered.

"I am very well aware of that," she said, frowning. Her lips, however, were twitching with suppressed humor as she tried not to laugh at herself. "But if you don't start now, you won't have that child for even longer, you know. You've got to get started as soon as possible."

"And you want to be grandmother?"

"I do!" There was a great deal more enthusiasm in those two words than Charles had expected.

He supposed he could do this to make his mother happy, and she *was* right—it was certainly time he bent his mind to marriage. He had just celebrated thirty-two years—past the age of most gentlemen married. "Very well, Mother, I will think about it."

"Don't just *think* about it! Go out to parties. You've got a stack of invitations in the library waiting for you. We should go through them together and decide which ones are more likely to have eligible young ladies present and which you can probably safely skip."

"You want to go through the enormous stack with me *this* evening?" he asked, a little horrified. He'd been hoping to have a pleasant, quiet evening tinkering with his watch. No matter how much he loved his mother, the idea of spending an evening going through society invitations and hearing all the latest gossip couldn't have been any less appealing.

"Yes. When else? I don't have any other plans," she said, widening her eyes at him.

"Oh, well, er, I'm afraid..." He thought fast. "I'm so sorry, but I do. I'm to meet Ainsby at the club for dinner. I do apologize. We'll have to do it another time." He pulled out his own watch from his pocket and flipped open the elaborately engraved gold cover. The gold hands were set just below a fine glass crystal that had the numbers painted directly on it. Below, he could see through to the watch mechanism in all of its beautiful intricacy. It was a piece his father had made for Charles's fifteenth birthday. "In fact, I should probably get going." It was not quite seven, but if he stopped off at his cousin's home, perhaps he could actually convince him to join him for dinner as Charles had claimed.

His mother clearly wasn't happy, but she nodded. "Very well. Tomorrow, then."

"Yes, tomorrow." He stood up and gave her a peck on the cheek and then ran up to his room to get changed for his new evening plans.

Chapter Five

Quinton, Lord Ainsby was in the middle of his toilette when Charles was admitted to his bedchamber.

"Cousin, a pleasant surprise, as always," Ainsby said, looking up from buttoning his breeches.

"Didn't mean to interrupt you, Quin," Charles said, closing the door behind him.

His cousin just shrugged. "Quite all right. You are always welcome to observe a master at work." He narrowed his eyes at Charles. "Might learn something. That neck cloth is quite a piece of work. What did you do, scrunch it up and then hope it would fall correctly?"

Charles turned and looked at himself in the tall mirror in the corner of the room. He tried to straighten his neck cloth. It *was* looking a little frumpy. He sighed. "I did my best. I don't have a Handwell to tie it just so like you do," he said, meeting the valet's eyes in the mirror.

"No, you don't and you can't have him," Ainsby said, allowing Handwell to help him into his waistcoat.

"Then don't complain about my neck cloth," Charles said with a laugh.

Ainsby just smiled and shook his head. He

sobered up immediately. "Do you know people are talking about you?"

"No, and I honestly don't care," Charles said.

"Well, you should!"

"Why don't we discuss it over dinner at Powell's," Charles offered. He truly had no interest in what the gossips were going on about, but if it got his cousin to join him, he'd happily use the excuse.

"Can't, sorry. Previous engagement," Ainsby said with his mouth mostly closed as his valet tied his neck cloth very carefully under his chin.

"Oh? With someone interesting, I hope?"

"No," Ainsby sighed. "Mother is insisting I go to Lady Melfort's. She's hosting a dinner and musicale in honor of her granddaughter who is making her come out this season.

"My condolences."

Ainsby burst out laughing. "Thank you." He nudged his chin down, creasing his neck cloth just so. "It will be an evening of charming pleasantries and excruciating noise that some might call music."

"And as boring as an evening can get," Charles added.

"Indeed! And what of you?"

"Me? Oh, I've got no plans."

"You're lucky your mother isn't nagging at you to marry," his cousin said with a sigh.

"Oh, no, she is! In fact, I escaped her nefarious plotting just now by telling her that we had plans."

Ainsby laughed. "Oh, ho! So, I'm your alibi, am I?"

Charles gave a little laugh and a shrug. "I just

have no desire to marry some chit whose best quality is that she comes from a noble family."

"So, who *do* you want to marry? The daughter of a watchmaker?" Ainsby asked, pouring a finger of port into each of the two glasses his man had just set out on his dressing table.

"Possibly," Charles said, taking one of the glasses. "I actually hadn't given it much thought."

"No time like the present," Ainsby said, lifting his glass in salute.

Charles lifted his likewise and took a sip, realizing his cousin was probably right. He *did* need to think about what sort of girl he wanted to marry. "Well, I suppose she should be pretty and clever enough to know that my business is important and will take a great deal of my time. I need someone who won't expect me to be constantly escorting her about to parties and such."

"Ah! So *not* a lady of society," his cousin said, laughing.

"No. You see my problem. My mother wants me to marry some nobleman's daughter. She wants me to become a part of society."

"But you don't."

Charles scoffed. "No! I'm a businessman. I've got responsibilities."

"A business to run. Watches to make," Ainsby put in.

"Precisely. I don't want to be waiting hand and foot on some girl, puffed up in her own self-esteem, who has condescended to marry me—probably for my money or because her penniless father forced her to do so."

His cousin chuckled. "Well, then, I would

highly suggest you *not* mention this to your mother."

"Goodness, no." Charles drained the last of the port from his glass. "And what about you? Are you going to toe the line and marry some girl who's going to drag you to parties every night?"

The smile faded from Ainsby's lips. "I don't know. I don't have the excuse you do."

"You've got an estate to run, your seat in Parliament."

"Yes. All the normal things a nobleman needs to look after," Ainsby said. "But, like you, I don't have a great deal of interest in spending my life escorting some pretty little thing to various entertainments."

Charles just shook his head. "There's got to be an alternative."

"I suppose I'll recognize it when it presents itself—or when *she* does." He put his now empty glass on the table. "Well, enough of this deep thinking. I've got to finish readying myself to have my hearing abused."

Charles laughed. "I suppose I'll head out to Powell's. Give my love to your lady mother, and best of luck to you." Charles said, putting his hand on the door handle.

"Oh, and Charles... Do be careful," his cousin said ominously. "Don't take the talk too lightly."

Charles just gave a shrug and left his cousin to finish dressing.

~*~

Charles walked into Powell's reading room and looked about to see if there was anyone he knew. He didn't mind dining alone, which was a good thing since he didn't see anyone he recognized.

He went back out and turned down the hall toward the back of building where the dining room was situated.

"Are you alone, sir?" the footman asked after he entered.

"Yes," Charles said, once again looking about for anyone he knew. The room was pretty full. It wasn't a very large room, only about ten tables, but nearly every one was occupied by at least two people.

"If you don't mind, sir, this is the only table available just at the moment," the footman said, indicating a table just next to the door.

"The others...?" Charles asked, indicating a few other empty tables farther away.

"They have already been spoken for, I'm afraid."

"All right, then. This is fine." Charles sat down facing the door. He could amuse himself by watching who came and went.

He ordered his food and then sat back to watch the others in the room. It was times like this that he did sort of miss not being active in society. If he were, he would surely know more people and have someone to eat with.

He was about halfway through his meal when two men walked in. They paused at the door and looked around, as most did. Oddly, when one of them spotted him, he nudged his friend and said something too quietly for Charles to hear.

His friend's eyes widened for a moment and then he headed straight for Charles.

"You're Aldridge, are you not? I don't believe

we've met," he said, holding out his hand. "I'm Hanslow."

Charles stood. "Aldridge. Charles Aldridge," he said shaking, he presumed, Lord Hanslow's hand.

"Pleasure. This is my friend, Viscount Swinton," Hanslow said.

Charles shook his hand as well.

"May we join you?" Hanslow asked.

"Please." Charles sat back down.

"Enjoying a quiet evening after last night's excitement, I suppose?" Swinton asked with a titter.

Charles tilted his head ever so slightly. "Last night's excitement?"

"Oh, you know, Lady Welles's party and all that," Hanslow said, picking up from Swinton.

"Ah, yes, the party. I'm afraid I left rather early. I was—" Charles started.

"Of course, previous appointment, I imagine?" Swinton said with another little laugh and, strangely, a wink.

Charles didn't know what he was referring to. "Er, no, I was tired. I'd just come back—"

"Of course you were, had to get, er, straight to bed, eh?" Hanslow said. He burst out laughing and gave his friend a nudge with his elbow.

Swinton too started laugh and gave Charles another wink.

"I don't know—" Charles began, now completely bewildered by the men's behavior.

"Hey, Touffington, Aldridge here was very tired last night," Hanslow called out to another diner at the next table.

Lord Touffington looked up from his dinner,

took in Charles, and burst out laughing. "I bet he was!"

The two other men at his table looked to be as confused as Charles, but Touffington leaned forward and explained something to them quietly. They too began to chuckle at whatever joke it was Hanslow had started.

"Listen, I don't know—" Charles began.

"Of course you don't, eh?" Swinton said, giving him another wink.

That was it. Charles had had it. He threw his napkin down on the table and stood up. "I don't know what you are going on about. Clearly, you're all sharing some sort of joke at my expense, and I don't believe I like it."

"Your expense? What? No! We're, er, happy for you. The widow St. Vincent is quite a handful, I imagine," Touffington said.

"Two handfuls," Hanslow said, laughing and holding up his hands at chest height. He pretended to squeeze something in front of him.

Charles suddenly realized he was referring to a woman's breasts, specifically those of this widow St. Vincent. Charles didn't know the woman, but he certainly wasn't going to stand for a lady being maligned in this way.

The other men were laughing uproariously at Hanslow's crude remark.

"I don't know any widow—"

"You don't know..." Swinton said, laughing even harder as if Charles had told a joke.

"Gentlemen, I'm so happy you're having a good time," Lord Wickford said, coming up to Charles, who most definitely was not enjoying himself.

"They may be, but I am highly offended, and I'm not even sure why," Charles admitted. "I believe they're indicating that I did something with someone, but I don't know..."

"Aldridge, surely you got the lady's name before you bedded her?" Touffington said with a laugh.

Charles now truly became incensed. "Before I *what*?" he nearly shouted.

Lord Wickford placed a calming hand on his shoulder. "Clearly, these gentlemen are of the belief that you had an assignation with Lady St. Vincent last night."

"But that's ridiculous. I don't even know anyone by that name," Charles said.

"You were seen escorting her from Lady Welles's party," Wickford pointed out. "You left together after the lady was seen having an amorous meeting the Lord Rogan."

Charles thought back to the previous evening. His mother *had* asked him to escort a young woman to her carriage, but she didn't seem to have just come from a pleasant interaction. If he wasn't mistaken, she'd just been sick and was extremely either ill or upset or both.

"I did escort a lady to her carriage, but she wasn't well. I didn't actually—" Charles started before he was once again interrupted.

"We don't need to know the particulars," another gentleman at Lord Touffington's table started.

"You may not, but I'd like to hear them. How big are they, Aldridge? Like good size apples? Melons?" Swinton asked.

"Bigger?" Hanslow added.

Charles was revolted. "You are—" he started.

"Now, now, such conversation is not appropriate," Lord Wickford said, interrupting him but looking at the other men. "We do not allow the disparagement of ladies in this establishment, gentlemen. If you want to have such a conversation, I suggest you do it elsewhere. This is a respectable club."

"Thank goodness for that," Charles said. "But you are all very much mistaken. I did nothing more than escort the lady to her carriage and see her off."

"Right, of course, you did," Swinton said, giving Charles another wink and a broad smile.

"Right, right. So glad to see marriage didn't ruin her. Wonder if she'll reopen her door to anyone or if it's just you—and Rogan, of course." Hanslow said, still laughing.

"I think we're going to have to ask her and find out," Swinton said with a titter.

"You wouldn't dare!" Charles said, shocked at the gall of this man.

"Well, why not? If she went home with you..." Swinton started.

"You say you have no claim to her," Hanslow said, picking up on his friend's train of thought. He gave a laugh as he stood. He gave Charles a slap on his back before moving to another table with his friend. "I think it's open game," he said to Swinton as they moved off.

Charles sat back down at his dinner once again, but he'd completely lost his appetite.

Chapter Six

"So, it's not true?" Lord Wickford asked, taking Swinton's seat.

Charles frowned. "No. It is absolutely not true! The lady was sick. I helped her to her carriage. That is all," he said as firmly as he could.

The club owner nodded. "I believe you. Sadly, the lady *does* have a reputation. Many of these men wouldn't find it too hard to believe that she went straight from an assignation with Rogan in the library to one with you in your bed."

"I can hardly believe any lady would do such a thing," Charles commented, picking at his food again.

"I'm of the same mind. I *do* know the lady, and she doesn't seem to be the sort to engage in such behavior. That doesn't stop the rumors, however," Wickford said, watching him.

Charles put down his fork. He couldn't eat any more. "It doesn't make sense. If she's not the sort to do such...things, how did the rumors get started?"

Wickford just shook his head. "I don't know. It was before my time here in London. All I know is what I've heard recently, and truly, it is all hearsay."

"But if these men think I slept with her..."

"They'll make some sort of inappropriate advance and hopefully her stepson Lord St. Vincent or her brother will be around to protect the lady's honor," Wickford said.

"Hopefully?"

"They're both rather preoccupied with their own romantic interests at the moment," Wickford explained.

"But the lady... They can't just leave her on her own to defend herself from the likes of those two," Charles protested.

"Not just them, others as well, I'm afraid," Wickford said with a frown.

"But that's not right! Nothing happened," Charles said.

Wickford shook his head. "It's the way of men and rumors, I'm afraid."

Now Charles felt well and truly ill.

~April 24 ~

"Hold that up so it doesn't drag on the ground," Elizabeth told Matthew as they crossed the street to the park.

The little boy dutifully held his brand-new blue paper kite up above his head—and nearly poked his mother in the eye with one of the spokes. She gently took the thin stick that had nearly hit her in her hand to protect herself.

"Careful, now," she said, giving him a smile.

It was early enough in the morning that there wasn't too much traffic, and the park itself was nearly empty. They headed out over the grass.

"We want to be well away from the kite-eating trees," she told her son.

He turned wide round eyes on her. They were the same brilliant blue as her own, but his hair was a much lighter brown, almost as if it had tried to be as blond as his much older step-brother but couldn't quite make it there. "The trees *eat* kites?" he asked.

"Oh, yes. They gobble them right up, just like you do a piece of cake. First, they grab a tight hold of them, and when you're not watching, they chomp, chomp, chomp them down to nothing," she said, snapping her thumb and fingers together like a mouth getting closer and closer to Matthew's adorable little nose. He giggled and pulled his face away from her teasing hand.

Before she quite realized what he was doing, he'd slipped his hand out of her grasp and started running away, his kite fighting the wind behind him.

"Matthew, stay close!"

"But I want to fly my kite, Mama!" he called back, not even pausing.

"Hold the string tight and let go of the kite," she called after him. She kicked up into a run as well to keep him in sight.

The boy did as she said, but the toy simply made a nosedive straight into the ground. The boy stopped and looked at it in disappointment.

"That's all right. Try it again," Elizabeth said.

He did so, running off, holding the kite up to try to catch the wind. Sadly, either the child couldn't run fast enough or there just wasn't enough of a breeze to send the kite sky-ward. Matthew ran and ran, trying to get it to fly.

They'd been at it for about ten minutes when a barking dog came bounding after the child. For a moment Elizabeth panicked, stopping to locate the dog and assess the threat, but then she caught sight of a little creature not a foot in height with long, floppy black ears, a black and white little body, and a long black feathered tail, yapping excitedly after the boy.

Matthew turned toward the animal, moving his kite safely out of the dog's way so it wouldn't get trampled.

"Duchess! Duchess! Oh, you naughty dog!" a woman called after the pup.

Elizabeth joined Matthew, who was now sitting on the grass, giggling, and trying to pet the dog, who wouldn't stay still long enough for the boy to do so. She turned, shocked to see Mrs. Aldridge panting up to them.

"I'm so sorry... Oh, Lady St. Vincent! I didn't know it was you," the woman said, clearly out of breath.

"Good morning, Mrs. Aldridge. Is this sweet little dog yours?" Elizabeth asked.

"Yes, yes, she is," the woman said. She smiled down at the dog and Matthew, who had finally managed to get the animal to stand still long enough to be pet. "Are you having fun this morning?" she asked the child.

He looked up at her. "I am." He then cocked his head and added, "You're the lady who was at breaffast."

"I do beg your pardon," Elizabeth said. "Mrs. Aldridge, may I present my son, Matthew Adler. Matthew, this is my friend, Mrs. Aldridge."

Matthew immediately popped to his feet and bowed properly. Mrs. Aldridge giggled and gave the child a nod. "I am very pleased to meet you, Master

Adler."

"What is your dog's name?" Matthew asked.

Mrs. Aldridge laughed at his forthright question. "Her name is Duchess."

"Oh, is she a duchess?" he asked, his eyes widening.

"She thinks she is," the lady responded.

The dog chose that moment to remind Matthew that he had been petting her, and she wanted him to continue. She rubbed up against his legs and stuck her nose into his little hand. He was very happy to comply and dropped down onto the ground once again to pet the dog.

"I am so happy to see you are getting out, Lady St. Vincent," Mrs. Aldridge said.

"Well, I do try to spend time with Matthew at least once a day. His step-brother just gave him this lovely new kite, so we thought we'd give it a try. Sadly, there doesn't seem to be enough wind."

"Oh, well, hopefully the outing wasn't a disappointment."

"How could it be when we got to meet you and Duchess?" Elizabeth asked. It was mornings like this when she could completely forget her cares and woes and just be happy. How could she possibly be sad and upset when there were little boys, kites, and puppy dogs?

~*~

"Are you sure you want to do this?" Edward asked Elizabeth one last time before they headed out the door that evening.

"Yes. Absolutely," she said without hesitation. "It's been three days. People should have stopped speaking about it. And the longer I don't show my face in public, the more guilty I'm going to look."

It hadn't been easy to come to this determination. She'd fretted about it for the whole day, going back and forth. She didn't *actually* want to go to this party. If people were still talking about Rogan's attack on her, she didn't want to be there. But if they weren't, then she most definitely did so she could get on with her life.

It was that desire—to move forward—that had ultimately helped make the decision. It would be ridiculous for her to come to London to reestablish her reputation and then turn tail the moment she faced any adversity. She wanted to get on in establishing a good reputation, in being a member of society. She wanted to go to parties, to be active in charity work, to be a contributing member, and not someone who just hid herself away in the countryside, chased out by the cruel gossips.

She was here, now, and she was going to go to this party.

With a lift of her chin, she led the way out of the house, her brother following in her wake.

The party was so crowded, Elizabeth didn't think her presence would even be noted. She wormed her way into Lady Emmerton's drawing room with Edward directly behind her. It was a little less crowded farther inside the room.

They found Paul accompanied by his future aunt-in-law, Lady Blakemore, as well as Lady Sorrell and Lady Moreton—all very notable, well-respected women.

"Elizabeth! You did come after all," Paul said, greeting her. Despite the fact they shared a house, they hadn't actually seen each other that day.

"I did," she said, beginning to have doubts that

it had been the right choice.

"I do hope you haven't run into any trouble so far?" Lady Sorrell asked.

"There were a few nasty gossips at the entrance, but we ignored them," Edward said with a frown.

"Lady St. Vincent, how is Mr. Aldridge?" a gentleman said, pausing just behind her. "I assume you left him well." He gave a laugh and then started to walk on.

Paul's hand shot out, and he stopped the man.

"St. Vincent, don't," Elizabeth's brother said quickly and quietly.

"Don't get angry with me," the man said, looking down at Paul's hand on his sleeve. "*He's* been going on about it at Powell's."

The mouths of all three women in front of Elizabeth dropped open.

"I can't believe Mrs. Aldridge's son would do such a thing," Lady Blakemore said.

"No, neither can I," Lady Moreton agreed.

"He must be mistaken," Lady Sorrell added.

"I don't even *know* the man!" Elizabeth said, trying to keep her voice steady and calm.

They were all silent for a moment. Lady Wraxley joined them just at that moment.

She didn't so much as join their group as approach Lady Blakemore directly. She also, Elizabeth noticed, didn't even look in her direction. Another cut.

"Lady Blakemore, I am shocked and appalled," Lady Wraxley said, looking down her nose at the woman she was addressing.

"I beg your pardon?" Lady Blakemore answered. She too could look down her nose at someone and did so now. It was almost comical, these two older ladies looking at each other like hens squaring off for battle.

"That you would knowingly associate yourself with a woman of *her* reputation. I had always thought you to be an upstanding member of society, honorable to a fault," Lady Wraxley said.

"And so I am," Lady Blakemore retorted. "I can tell you I choose my friends with great particularity, and I do not count *you* among them."

Elizabeth, herself, gasped at that one.

The woman strode off in a huff.

"My lady, please don't get into trouble on my account!" Elizabeth pleaded.

"I can assure you, I would not, normally, but first of all, you have been wronged, Lady St. Vincent. Secondly, I don't like Lady Wraxley, never have," Lady Blakemore said, not even looking in the direction the lady went.

Elizabeth gave her a grateful smile but then turned to her brother. "I think we should move on before we cause any more trouble for our friends."

"I have to agree. Come, let's take some air on the balcony. I'm sure you could use some," Conway said, taking her arm.

Elizabeth nodded to her friends and allowed him to lead her away.

It did feel good outside. The air was cool, but after the heated rooms of Lady Emmerton's home, it was lovely.

"How are you holding up?" Edward asked, running a hand down her arm affectionately.

"I'm—"

"Another one! My God, that woman knows no bounds!" a woman's voice said from behind Edward. She leaned forward ever so slightly. "Shame on you!" she hissed at Elizabeth.

Elizabeth spun around and faced her accusers.

"They should not have allowed her entrance," the woman's companion said in a matter-of-fact way.

"And just what do you think you know of the matter? Shame on you for listening to unfounded gossip," Elizabeth scolded the two women.

Their mouths dropped open at her temerity, and indeed, she was rather shocked herself. Perhaps Lady Blakemore's strength was rubbing off on her.

"It is not gossip when the information comes directly from two people who were actually there," one of the women said with a sniff.

"That's right. We heard an account directly from Lady Findlater *and* Lord Rogan."

"And what about *my* account of what occurred, does that not count for anything?" Elizabeth asked, grasping onto her skirt to keep her hands from shaking with her fury.

"No, it doesn't. It's your word against that of *two* respected members of society. I believe them sooner than I would you. You already had a reputation for lying and other inappropriate behavior. Come along, Jane." And with that, both ladies swept away in a cloud of hauteur.

That was it. That was the last straw. Elizabeth felt her throat tighten once again, and her eyes burn with unshed tears. They didn't believe her. No one believed her.

She turned toward her brother. "Why, Edward?" she whispered, her voice not able to get past the lump in her throat. "Why are they spreading such horrid tales about me? They're completely false, but there's nothing I can do... Nothing I can say..."

"Right, we're leaving. Let's go," Edward said. He didn't wait for her to agree or say anything at all. He simply took her arm and led her back inside the house. There, he didn't pause, but excused himself and Elizabeth as he led her straight for the door. They didn't stop to say a word to anyone, which was good because Elizabeth didn't think she would be able to find a kind thing to say.

The moment her carriage pulled away, Elizabeth took a breath. It came out in sob. She hadn't intended that to happen. Indeed, she didn't want to cry at all, but all of a sudden, she simply couldn't help herself. All her tension, all her hurt just came pouring out.

It wasn't fair! She hadn't done anything! But she was being blamed, as if this were all her fault.

Her dearest brother didn't say a word. He simply sat next to her on the bench, with his arm around her, and let her cry into his coat. He did hand her his handkerchief.

Chapter Seven

~April 25~

The following morning, Charles was dealing with accounts. It was his least favorite part of owning a business, although he did have to admit to a great deal of satisfaction when he tallied a column of figures and it came out exactly as he'd expected. It was even better, of course, when the column of income surpassed that of his expenses. He was happily staring at such a column when a footman knocked on his study door.

"I beg your pardon, sir, there is a Lord St. Vincent who wishes to see you. Are you at home?"

Lord St. Vincent? Wasn't St. Vincent the name of the woman he was being accused of bedding? Goodness, gracious, this must be a relative. Well, he supposed he shouldn't be surprised by this visit, only that it had taken the man so long to get here.

"Show him in," Charles told the footman. He'd face the fellow and explain everything. Hopefully, he was a reasonable man.

Charles stood and awaited his guest by the fireplace.

Lord St. Vincent was a great deal larger than Charles had expected. He was not only tall, but broad and looked to be a great deal more muscular than an average dandy. Charles was no delicate violet, but this fellow had at least one stone on him.

The man walked into the room, barely paused in the doorway to locate Charles, then strode straight up to him and whipped his gloves across Aldridge's face. "Mr. Charles Aldridge, name your seconds!"

Charles rubbed his face and shook his head. "I have to say, I was not expecting that."

"I said—"

"Yes, thank you, I heard you. May we discuss this a moment first?" Charles asked, determined to be calm and polite no matter what his guest did.

"I demand satisfaction," the man reiterated.

"I can imagine you would, and you shall have it—just, I'm not certain the dueling field is the right place."

"Where then? Shall I meet you at Gentleman Jackson's? I can assure you—"

"No, no. No need. I'm certain you could do me a great deal of harm there, and I would be happy to give you that satisfaction but not in Lady St. Vincent's name." He indicated the sofa and chairs that surrounded the fireplace. "Come, have a seat, please. May I offer you a brandy?" Charles asked.

"No! I'm not here to be chummy with you! You have bandied my stepmother's name about, made false insinuations, and—"

"I have done nothing of the sort," Charles said. He *would* keep calm, even if his guest would not, but he was also going to do so in comfort. He sat down.

"I have challenged you to a duel, and you sit down and want to share a drink?" the man asked incredulously.

Charles sighed and stood back up. "Lord St. Vincent, as I said, I would be most happy to duel with you *if* I had done anything, but I warn you now, I would delope. Do you really think killing or seriously wounding me, possibly forcing you to flee the country, would do your stepmother any good? Wouldn't dueling simply drag her name even further down into the mud?"

Lord St. Vincent paused to consider this. "Her name is already being spoken in the most inappropriate ways. I must do something! She is absolutely distraught at what people are saying. Honestly, I worry for her."

"So much so that you would put your own life on the line to clear her name," Charles observed.

"Absolutely and without hesitation."

Charles nodded. "Then there has to be another way because, as I said, I will not shoot you—certainly not for being noble."

The man in front of him seemed to deflate just a touch. He conceded to sit down.

"I must tell you, before two nights ago I had never even heard of Lady St. Vincent. In fact, I learned her name only when I was asked, in a very crass way I might add, how I enjoyed my evening with her. I informed those asking that not only was I unacquainted with the lady in question, but hadn't had any sort of relations with her, and they were mistaken." Charles frowned. "They didn't believe me."

"I was told you were bragging about your evening with Lady St. Vincent," his guest said.

"I assure you, it was quite the opposite. However, the more I protested that the accusations were false, the less they believed me. I finally just gave up and left."

St. Vincent nodded. "Some men are like that." He paused and then asked again, "You said nothing about having slept with Elizabeth?"

"I'm assuming you mean Lady St. Vincent? No, not a word. Why would I lie about such a thing? I don't know her, and I see no reason to harm a lady's reputation and many *not* to do so. I am sorry to say, but there seemed to be plenty of men too eager to jump in where I would not. Nothing I could say dissuaded them from their course."

Lord St. Vincent ran an agitated hand through his blond hair. His was similar to Ainsby's—and unlike Charles's own hair—in that it simply fell back into place when he did so.

"Word has it you were bragging about your relations with her and she, naturally, is devastated. She specifically came to London to reestablish her reputation. To become an upstanding member of society and now..."

"Now her name is being dragged through the mud," Charles offered.

"Yes."

"I am so very sorry."

"No more so than I." Lord St. Vincent stood and shook his head. "Well, if what you say is true, and you were not the one to spread the rumors, then I owe you an apology."

"Oh, no need. It was an honest mistake. I just wish I could do something to help the lady," Charles said.

"Well, if you can try to spread the word that you truly did not meet with her that evening..."

"Of course! I have done so already and will continue. It's the least I can do," Charles said, also standing.

He saw his guest to the door but was surprised when he found Ainsby standing on the other side of it, his hand in the air ready to knock.

"Ainsby, what a pleasant surprise," Charles said.

"St. Vincent, you here?" Charles's cousin said.

"Just leaving. Thank you for your time and understanding, Mr. Aldridge." He gave them a nod and went off.

"Well, if St. Vincent was here, then I suppose you've heard," Ainsby said, coming into the house.

"Sadly, yes." He led the way back to his study, his cousin trailing behind. "This is a real mess, and I can't help but feel I need to do something to fix it."

"I tried to warn you the other night, but you weren't interested. Now, I don't think you have a choice but do something," Quin said, heading straight for the sideboard in the library and the decanters of brandy and other spirits there.

"I know," Charles said, dropping back onto the sofa. "Pour me one too. I need it."

"I imagine you do." Ainsby came over and handed Charles a drink then joined him on the sofa.

"What am I going to do? I've tried arguing with my accusers. I've told them that I did *not* have relations with Lady St. Vincent and don't even *know* her. They laughed and thought I was dissembling to protect the lady."

"They're bloody..." Ainsby's words seemed to fail him in his anger.

"Maggots?" Charles offered.

"Contemptible!" Ainsby said vehemently.

"Yes, that too." Charles took a large swallow of his drink and almost wished it were something stronger. He had a decanter of Scottish whisky on the sideboard, but his cousin preferred the sweeter brandy.

"St. Vincent wanted satisfaction?" Ainsby asked.

"Yes. I didn't give it to him. Told him I'd delope."

"That's very gentlemanly of you, but I can't imagine he was happy."

"No, he wasn't. He's damned frustrated and worried about his stepmother. I don't blame him," Charles admitted before finishing off his drink and getting up to get the whiskey he actually wanted. He paused on his way to the sideboard, though, and turned back to his cousin. "Is Lady St. Vincent really his *stepmother*?"

Quin laughed. "Yes. His father married her just after her come-out... What was it? About ten years ago, I believe, possibly less. So, yes, St. Vincent's stepmother is just two or three years older than he is."

Charles shook his head as he poured his drink. "She looks younger—hardly out of the schoolroom."

Ainsby chuckled. "Well, you'd certainly win points with the lady if you told her you thought so. Speaking of which, I believe our mothers are now in cahoots."

"Oh, dear. Stepping up the pressure to marry, is she?" Charles asked. He turned around and leaned against the sideboard as he sipped at his whiskey. It burned with satisfaction all the way down his throat, leaving behind a lovely smoky taste.

"Yes," Ainsby said with a frown.

"I am sorry."

Something snapped into place in Charles's mind, however. He glanced at his glass, silently thanking the whiskey for clearing his head. "That's it!" He stood away from the sideboard and took the few steps over toward his cousin.

"What's what?" Quin asked.

"That's what I need to do! It would solve everything," Charles said, hardly able to contain his sudden enthusiasm.

"I have no idea what you're talking about, coz. What's that you're drinking? Has it addled your mind?"

"Whiskey, and no, it's done just the opposite. It's cleared it." He put his glass down and took Quin's empty glass from him. He splashed some whiskey into before handing it back.

Quin took a sip and nearly choked. "My God! That stuff will kill you!"

"Just the opposite, my friend," Charles said, laughing. He couldn't help it. He loved his cousin with all his heart, but the man was a little too refined when it came to some things—like good strong alcohol.

"So, what is it this swill made you realize?" Quin asked, putting his glass down on the table.

"I'm going to propose to Lady St. Vincent."

Quin choked—and he hadn't even been drinking anything. "You're insane! Wait, no, how many drinks have you had? Are you sloshed? Hammered?"

"Drunk?" Charles laughed. "No." He sat back

down next to his cousin. "Think about it. If I marry her, it will stop all the rumors. Her reputation will be restored—in as much as marrying a cit will restore it—and it will get my mother off my back as well."

"You're not a cit!" his cousin protested.

"I am, but that's all right. You don't mind, and I don't care about what anyone else thinks," Charles admitted.

Ainsby didn't argue. "You would be willing to marry a woman you don't even know to save her reputation?"

"Yes! She's pretty. I'm sure she's pleasant enough."

"She's very lovely, but don't you think you should... I don't know, court her for a little first?"

Charles gave a shrug. "Perhaps. But first I think I should propose. Even if she calls it off later, it should be enough to make people think better of her."

"And if she doesn't call it off?"

"Then I'll marry her. I don't think I'll mind, and my mother will be happy I'm marrying a lady of society. People have marriages of convenience all the time."

Chapter Eight

Elizabeth hated being helpless almost more than she hated being accused of something she didn't actually do. She felt this was all somehow her fault, but for the life of her she couldn't figure out what she could have done differently.

"I wasn't even wearing anything revealing," she commented to her brother, who was moping beside her. Well, perhaps he would have called it thinking, but to her it looked like he was moping.

He turned to her. "It wasn't your fault, Elizabeth. I've told you that."

"But it was. It is! Papa was right when he told me I was going to have to work very hard to keep men at arm's length. I just... I never worked hard enough at that. It's a failing of mine."

He took her hand and shook his head, but he didn't say anything. He actually wasn't given the chance because Paul came in just at that moment.

"I'm sorry, Elizabeth, I seem to have botched this," he said, dropping down onto the opposite sofa.

She sat up straighter and pulled her hand from her brother's. "What did you do? Or not do?"

"I went to Aldridge's home and challenged him to a duel. He refused. Said he'd delope and there wasn't any point," Paul said morosely.

"You challenged him to a duel? Why would you do that?" Conway asked.

"To restore Elizabeth's reputation!" Paul said, sitting straighter and frowning at him.

"But it would have done exactly the opposite! It would have dragged her name through the mud even more," her brother argued.

Elizabeth, sadly, agreed.

"That's what Aldridge pointed out. He also claimed he hadn't bragged about being with Elizabeth. He said others had accused him of being with her, and he'd protested, but they'd refused to believe him."

Elizabeth sighed loudly. "I believe him. He seemed like a very gentlemanly person the few moments I was with him."

"If he's right, and those accusing you of doing this don't believe either him or you, what are we to do?" Paul asked.

"I don't know," she said. Tears pricked at her eyes, but she wasn't going to give in to them—again.

"It's Rogan. It's all Rogan orchestrating this," Edward said with a growl to his voice.

"It doesn't matter who started it, it's all over town, being discussed in every drawing room, and we haven't got a clue how to stop those tongues from wagging," Paul pointed out.

Elizabeth leaned back against the sofa in defeat. "I don't think there is. Maybe I should do what I did last time and just turn tail—"

"No, you don't! That was the worst thing you could have done," Edward said vehemently. "I still can't believe our mother did that to you. She cemented that rumor when she did that. It was as good as admitting they were right, and you were guilty of lifting your skirt for anyone who so much as looked at you. If I had been here..."

Elizabeth reached out and took his hand, giving him a smile. "You are so good to me, Edward. I *do* wish you had been here. You wouldn't have allowed me to believe those horrid girls who told me I should allow men to touch me, that it was normal."

"Where were you?" Paul asked.

Edward frowned. "In Italy working at an opera company. I'd left just before Elizabeth made her come-out."

"What a shame," Paul commented.

"It was unfortunate timing," Elizabeth agreed. "But it's long past, so let's not worry about it just now."

Paul nodded his agreement. "We've got our current scandal to deal with. No use dredging up an old one as well."

"But it is the old one that started this one," Edward pointed out. "Rogan clearly remembered Elizabeth's past reputation and thought she was back for more."

"So how do we stop people from believing this?" Elizabeth asked.

"How do we get people to believe she's an innocent in all this?" Paul echoed.

"I don't actually want to leave Town," Elizabeth said, after a moment of silence in which they were all trying to think of a solution. "I'm not a coward, and if I leave, I think you'd be right, Paul. It would just confirm what everyone is saying."

There was a knock on the drawing-room door,

and then Matthew peeked his head around and peered into the room. When he saw his mother, uncle, and older brother, he came running in.

"Uncle Edward!" the child screeched. He ran to Edward and clambered up onto his lap.

"Matthew! What have I told you about the proper way to greet people?" his mother scolded.

The boy stopped, got down again, and bowed to his uncle. Then he proceeded to climb onto him. Edward laughed and helped the little scamp up. "And what are you up to this afternoon, Master Matthew?"

"I finished my lessons," Matthew said proudly.

"Very good," his uncle nodded. "And now?"

"I want to play," the child declared.

"Shall we…" He was interrupted by another knock on the door.

The footman, Frank, came in carrying a large bouquet of flowers. "I beg your pardon, my lady, these just arrived for you. Shall I have the maid put them in a vase?"

Elizabeth got up, frowning. "Who are they from?"

"The man delivering them said they were from Lord Rogan, who sent them with his warmest regards," Frank said, completely unknowing how much pain his words would cause.

Elizabeth took an involuntary step back. "Throw them out."

"My lady?" the footman asked, probably as confused by her harsh tone as her words.

"You heard the lady," Paul said, looking over at the man. "Throw them into the gutter. Stomp on them a few times if you like. They are worse than garbage." His voice held a touch of a growl that even made Elizabeth's skin prickle with fear.

"Can I jump on them?" Matthew asked.

"Yes, absolutely, my love. Frank, why don't you take Matthew down to the garden and allow him to destroy them as he sees fit." She turned to her son and gave him a smile. "Normally, you know, you are not to touch pretty flowers, right?"

He nodded solemnly.

"Well, these are an exception. You may tear these apart, jump on them, stomp on them, mash them into the dirt. Do whatever you like," she said, giving him an indulgent smile.

"Yay!" Matthew scrambled off his uncle's lap and went running over to Frank, who held his hand out for the child. They left the room with Matthew excitedly telling the man all he planned to do to the offending bouquet.

"The nerve of that man!" Elizabeth whispered as she sat back down.

"He's crazy," Paul said with a shake of his head.

"I know what we should do," Edward said as if he hadn't been paying a bit of attention to anything that had just occurred.

Elizabeth felt a spark of hope and turned toward her brother. Paul, too, sat a little straighter as he awaited Edward's idea.

"We should speak with Lady Blakemore. She's a very well-respected member of society. She knows just what's what and how to go on. I'm sure she'll have an idea," he said.

The spark in Elizabeth blossomed into full-blown hope. "Yes! You're absolutely right! She *will* know."

"Of course! Why didn't I think of that?" Paul asked, giving Edward a smile.

"The question is when we should speak with her," Edward said, still thinking it through.

"Yes. This evening is the Venetian Ball, so she'll probably be very busy getting herself and her nieces ready," Elizabeth commented.

"True. Oh, I should write Bel a note and tell her I won't be attending," Edward said, getting up.

"Yes. Can you ask her to tell Bee the same for me?" Paul asked.

"What? No! Absolutely not. I forbid it. You will both be attending," Elizabeth said. Just because she wouldn't be going didn't mean her brother and Paul shouldn't. In fact, there were too many reasons why they should go, why they *needed* to be there.

"But Elizabeth, it's not right for us—" Edward started.

"You stop right there, Edward," she said, holding up her hand. "Both of you are absolutely essential to tonight's plans. You *must* be there."

"They'll figure out a way—" Paul started.

"No, they won't, because they won't need to. Now, just stop this nonsense. You are both going, and that is the end of this discussion," she said with more authority than she actually held. Oddly enough, both men listened to her.

~April 27~

It took Charles two days to build up his nerve to carry out his commitment to assisting Lady St. Vincent.

The problem wasn't that he didn't know whether he would actually find the lady attractive— honestly, he'd hardly seen her the evening he'd escorted her to her carriage. She'd been ill, and he'd done the gentlemanly thing of not really looking closely at her pale face and mussed hair. He didn't even mind so much that she was a member of the *ton,* despite the fact he truly had no desire to become entangled in that morass of gossip and one-upmanship that so many members seemed to hold dear. And he didn't even consider her destroyed reputation because truly such things didn't matter at all to him.

No, his difficulty lay purely within his own silly fantasies and dreams. He couldn't count the number of times his mother had regaled him with all she'd given up to marry his father. She hadn't told him because she felt bad about what she'd given up—although clearly, she did somewhat since now she was insisting he become a member of the society she'd chosen to forego in order to marry. No, she'd told him in order to impress upon him just how much she loved her husband.

She'd gone against the wishes of her own family to marry Bertram Aldridge. She'd defied her papa and made her mother cry for days. But she'd done it because she was in love, and every single day of Charles's childhood, he'd seen that love. He'd felt it. And now, as an adult, he'd wanted to emulate it.

Yes, he was a little embarrassed to admit it even to himself, but he was a romantic. He wanted love. He wanted passion. He wanted to feel for his wife all that his parents had felt for each other and more, if such a thing were possible.

In proposing to Lady St. Vincent, he was going to be giving all that up. He was going to be throwing all his dreams right out the window.

Charles now paused outside Lady St. Vincent's

home and pulled out his watch to check the time. He almost expected to see that his watch had stopped or broken somehow because that was how his heart felt in his chest—broken. His silly childhood dreams were being shoved aside like so many spare gears, and now it was time to remake his life so it worked with more precision and less sentimental waste.

He took in a deep breath and re-pocketed his watch. His knock was answered almost immediately.

"Good afternoon, I was wondering if Lady St. Vincent was available," he inquired while handing over his greeting card.

The butler accepted it and bowed him into the house. "If you would wait here a moment, sir. I will see if the lady is at home."

Charles nodded, hoping she wouldn't take too long in deciding whether to see him or not. He'd heard these society ladies sometimes made a gentleman wait twenty minutes or more, only to turn around and send the fellow packing.

He was rather surprised when the butler returned within a few minutes to show him up to the drawing room. The room itself was pleasantly appointed. Naturally, everything was in the latest style, but it all seemed to be done with an eye toward comfort rather than show. The lady herself was a great deal more attractive than Charles had remembered. In fact, she was nothing less than jaw-dropping beautiful with her deep, rich brown hair, and a soft, feminine face with full lips and eyes of an intense blue. His own heart, which he'd imagined broken just a few minutes ago, stuttered and then began to pound so hard he wondered if she could hear it from across the room.

He paused to bow just inside the door as the lady came forward. She curtsied to him, her pale gray gown pooling prettily at her feet. While her dress was lovely, it was also the most modest gown he'd ever seen on someone so young. The collar sat just above her collarbones and a tall lace border climbed her long throat. Even his mother wore more revealing dresses than Lady St. Vincent.

"Mr. Aldridge, what a pleasant surprise, please do come in," she said, her voice soft and melodious.

"I do apologize if I'm interrupting anything," he said.

"No, not at all. I'm actually very happy for the company. You must think me horridly rude, though. I never got around to sending you a thank you for being so kind as to escort me to my carriage when I needed to leave Lady Welles's party early."

"Not at all. You were unwell," he said, accepting the seat she indicated with a delicate hand.

"I was, sadly. But you were a true gentleman seeing me off in that way."

"I only wish others were aware of what actually happened," Charles said, broaching the subject as delicately at he could.

She frowned and lowered her eyes to her hands clasped tightly in her lap. "Yes."

"I assume you've heard the rumors?" he asked.

"I'm afraid that not only have I heard them, but they have been thrown directly into my face."

"My God, I *am* sorry!" he said, shocked that anyone had the nerve to accuse her directly.

"Not nearly as sorry as I, I can assure you."

"Naturally."

She looked up at him. "And I believe you have received somewhat the same treatment, only from the male perspective it was less an accusation and more in the form of congratulations?" The pain in her eyes was obvious and belied the polite little smile on her lips.

Charles frowned at the lady. "Unfortunately, there are some men who are rude and crass beyond the pale. I attempted to relay what actually occurred but was laughed at, my explanation dismissed out of hand. The more I argued, the less I was believed."

"How very unfortunate," she agreed on a sigh.

"I don't care what others think of me, and I could honestly care less what they think I might or might not have done. However, the same cannot be said for you from what I understand," Charles said.

"I wish I could be so carefree," Lady St. Vincent said, turning her head slightly to gaze out the window behind Charles.

"Well, perhaps the reason I'm here will help restore that feeling," he said, his stomach clenching a little with nervousness.

She shifted her gaze back to him and waited for him to continue.

"Lady St. Vincent, in light of what has occurred, I would be honored if you would agree to become my wife." There, that wasn't as hard as he'd anticipated. Strangely enough, the words came together and slipped off his tongue without any hesitations or stuttering at all.

Her brows came together, and she leaned forward a touch. "I beg your pardon?"

Chapter Nine

Charles cleared his throat. Maybe that hadn't come out as well as he'd thought. "I said, I'd be honored if you would—"

"You are proposing to me? Because our names have been linked," she clarified.

"Because your reputation has been harmed due to my…" He couldn't say it was his fault; all he'd done was escort her to her carriage.

"Because of the idiocy of others who see what they want to see, not what actually occurred," she said, with a touch of anger to her voice. He didn't blame her one bit for being angry about it.

"Well, yes, but there it is. Your reputation has been damaged and I'm proposing to—"

"Fix it by marrying me," she finished for him, sounding even more angry.

"I believe such things are common enough, my lady," Charles offered. He couldn't understand why she was getting upset at him. He was trying to be a gentleman about this.

"Yes, yes they are, when an innocent young lady has been compromised. I am not innocent or young. I am a widow who was married for six years, sir."

"But your reputation—"

"Is my own to see to, thank you. I do not need your name to make it right again," she said, her voice calming ever so slightly.

"Are you certain of that?" He couldn't help but ask.

That made her pause for a moment. "To be honest, no, I'm not. But there has to be another way. Please do not take this personally, Mr. Aldridge, but I cannot marry you simply because other people have accused us of...of being intimate."

"My lady, I am merely presenting you with an easy solution to this difficulty," he explained.

"I appreciate that, sir, honestly, I do. Have you considered the fact that if we married it would merely confirm what people have been saying?" she asked with a slight tilt of her head.

That stopped him. "No. I hadn't thought of that."

She nodded grimly.

"Then it would have been as bad an outcome as Lord St. Vincent's idea of challenging me to a duel," he said, thinking out loud as he put it all together.

"Exactly. In both instances, my reputation would not have been any better off than it is now. My goal, sir, is to become respected by society, not to confirm their misconceptions," she said, standing.

He stood when she did. "Of course, that makes perfect sense."

"I am glad you understand. Once again, I appreciate your attempt to do something to aid me in this dilemma, but I don't believe marriage is the answer. I will find another way."

She held out her hand to him. He stepped forward and took it, thinking he would brush his lips lightly across the top of her knuckles but something strange happened when his fingers came into contact with hers. There was a a tingling sensation. Heat ran from her fingers straight up his arm and into his chest. He looked into her deep blue eyes. Had she felt it too?

He couldn't tell, but he thought maybe she had because her eyes widened ever so slightly, and her lips parted as if she were about to say something.

He caught hold of himself and did as he'd originally intended, only perhaps he might have allowed his lips to linger a fraction of a second longer than was strictly polite. There was something about her that felt good. That felt right. That felt...like something he'd never felt before.

Maybe it was the delicacy of her hand. Maybe it was the lightness of her touch. Maybe it was that she was so much smaller than he. Whatever it was, it made him want to hold her and protect her. Now, without a moment's hesitation or thought, he completely understood what had driven St. Vincent to call him out. Suddenly he wanted to hurt everyone and anyone who had dared to cause this beautiful woman harm.

For a moment, he was rendered speechless, but then he pulled himself together and forced himself to turn away from her. It was the hardest thing he'd had to do in a very long time.

~*~

Elizabeth bit her tongue as she watched Mr. Aldridge leave her drawing room. It would have been so tempting to call him back, maybe discuss his proposal a bit further. It would certainly have been a great deal more pleasant than sitting here alone once more.

Sadly, what she'd told him had been absolutely true. Marrying him wouldn't have quieted the gossips, but only emboldened them further. Elizabeth couldn't help but feel a loss in that truth.

At first, when he'd proposed, she'd been too shocked to think straight. And then, for some strange reason she'd become furious that this man should think he could just waltz into her drawing room and solve all her problems by asking her to marry him. She didn't want some strange man taking over her life.

She'd done that once already, and she certainly wasn't ever going to do it again. When she'd married St. Vincent, they'd both known he was her only option, and he'd taken full advantage of that for a good three years before he'd settled down. He had looked down at her, treating her like the green girl she'd been, and she'd hated every minute of it.

Granted, she didn't know if Mr. Charles Aldridge would do the same, but it wasn't out of the realm of possibility. To be absolutely honest, she didn't know the man from Adam, so she had no idea what he might or might not do were they to marry.

Which was another reason why she'd turned him down without a thought. But then, of course, her brain had clicked into gear. She had come up with a perfectly good, reasonable explanation why she shouldn't marry him, which was good because he did seem like the sort who would appreciate logic over emotion.

She had won the point, but now she was

wondering at what cost.

Something had happened when he'd taken her hand. She'd offered it out of friendship and appreciation for his kind offer, but then.... He'd touched her and fireworks had gone off inside her fingertips, quickly executing some happy little dance all the way up her arm and straight into her stomach, its pretty little sparks sending light and happiness into her head.

It made no sense.

How could she be made to feel so happy, so comforted by the lightest little touch of his hand against hers? Oh, but then he'd bowed over her hand, kissed the back of it, and those happy little sparks had turned into a burning inferno making her cheeks burn and fire fall into parts of her no one had touched since her husband had fallen ill.

My goodness, and here she was a good five minutes later, still standing staring at the door he'd just gone through. How ridiculous she was.

She gave herself a good mental shake and resumed her seat. She even went so far as to pick up her book, but she didn't read. How could she, when all she could see in her mind's eye was that handsome man, his elegant, slender nose, and high cheekbones? His dark blond hair falling ever so slightly into his dark green eyes. How was she ever going to concentrate now?

~April 29~

Penelope arrived at Lady Ayres's home as close to on-time as she could. Duchess, Penelope's King Charles Spaniel, hadn't made it easy, taking her time on the walk she always took just before the Whist Society meeting. Penelope could never understand why everything had to be so thoroughly investigated by the pup's cute little black nose, but finally the dog had conceded to moving on. The moment she could, Penelope had picked the dog up and taken her off to the meeting.

"Mrs. Aldridge, how lovely to see you," Lady Ayres said, giving her a smile as she came into the room. The lady was sitting on the sofa flanked by Lady Blakemore and Lady Moreton. Ladies Welles and Colburne were sitting across from them, happily munching on biscuits, and giggling over something.

"Good afternoon, ladies," Penelope said. She did so love being a part of this group. Every time she arrived for an afternoon of whist and camaraderie, she thanked her good luck to have been included in Lady Ayres's invitation to a fashion party the year before.

She put Duchess on the floor. The dog immediately went to Lady Colburne to receive the pets the lady always had for the dog. Of course, Duchess loved getting attention, but even more she loved the treats that lady would slip to her as well.

"Have you seen Lady St. Vincent recently?" Lady Blakemore asked. "I don't believe she attended the Venetian Ball, did she?"

"I have not seen her," Penelope said, accepting a cup of tea from Lady Ayres. "I do hope she's all right. I heard she had a difficult time at Lady Emmerton's last week."

"Ugh, it was awful!" Lady Welles said. "Some people can be so incredibly cruel."

"Unnecessarily so," Lady Moreton agreed.

"Thank goodness Lord Conway was with her. He whisked her straight out of there as soon as he could. Poor thing was completely distraught," Lady

Blakemore said.

"So, you have seen her?" Penelope asked, a little confused.

"No, but Lord Conway and Lord St. Vincent have, naturally. The latter came to me to specifically ask what could be done to stop all of this horrid gossip and reestablish her good name," Lady Blakemore said.

"That is precisely what I was hoping to discuss this afternoon as well," Penelope said to all the ladies gathered for an afternoon of whist and solving problems. She ignored Duchess, who'd put her paws up on her knee to beg for a treat. She'd seen Lady Colburne had already given her one, and while she loved her little spaniel, she knew she shouldn't eat too many sweets. Instead, she rubbed behind Duchess's adorable long, black ears. The dog rubbed her face affectionately on her knee.

The Duchess of Kendell joined them before anyone could suggest anything. She was immediately followed by Lady Sorrell, who came in full of apologies for being late.

"No worries. We were just discussing Lady St. Vincent's plight," Lady Ayres said.

"Oh, that poor woman!" the duchess said with a sad shake of her head. "I do so feel for her." She paused to scowl down at the spaniel who had come up to greet her, jumping up and putting her paws on the lady's legs. Somehow Duchess knew the lady didn't like her and did everything she could to gain her affection.

Penelope clicked her tongue to call for the dog. The duchess already didn't like Penelope very much; she didn't want to antagonize her any more than necessary. When the dog didn't immediately obey, she broke off a piece of the biscuit she'd been eating and offered it to the pup. Duchess was by her side within seconds, munching away at the treat.

"Lady Blakemore, do you have any suggestions on how we can help Lady St. Vincent? I truly believe we should do something to help her," Lady Welles said.

"I do agree," the lady said, frowning. "I'm just not sure what we can do. She needs her reputation restored."

"She needs to prove she isn't the woman she's accused of being," Lady Ayres said.

"You mean she needs to prove she hasn't had relations with either of the men people are saying she met," Lady Sorrell said, clarifying things in her usual forthright manner.

"Yes, especially since one of those men is my son, and I know for a fact he did nothing of the sort," Penelope said vehemently.

"You do know that?" the duchess asked a little skeptically.

"Absolutely!" Penelope answered with certainty. "Charles was as shocked and horrified by the allegations as the lady herself."

All the women nodded in understanding and sympathy.

"So, we need to prove that Lady St. Vincent is an upstanding member of society," Lady Welles said, clearly thinking aloud.

"How do we do that?" Lady Moreton asked.

An idea hit Penelope. "By showing the world *we* believe it to be true. By showing society that a number of gentlemen think so as well. By showing her being treated the way we want others to do so, no?"

Everyone turned toward her with widened eyes or nods of approval.

"Of course!" Lady Welles said, giggling and clapping her hands. "We will have a campaign to show that she is respected and respectable."

"How?" Lady Colburne asked.

"We shall all be seen with her in public," Lady Blakemore said, nodding her approval.

"But even more than that, we need some gentlemen to do so, to prove she *doesn't*, in fact, have relations with such men," Penelope added.

"Do you believe if she is courted by a number of upstanding gentlemen, the gossips will stop talking about her?" Lady Sorrell asked.

"Don't you think that would work?" Penelope asked the group at large.

"I think it most certainly *would* work," Lady Blakemore said.

"But then we need to find some gentlemen to court her," Lady Ayres pointed.

"Lord Roseberry and Mr. Hershawn?" Lady Colburne suggested.

There was agreement all around, for they were certainly two of the most eligible, upstanding gentlemen of the season.

"What about Mr. Aldridge and Lord Ainsby," Lady Welles suggested, looking to Penelope.

"Do you think it wise to include my Charles? He has been accused..." she said, feeling no need to complete that sentence.

"I think it *especially* important that he be seen with her behaving in a polite and proper way," Lady

Blakemore said.

Penelope nodded to her superior knowledge. "Then I will inform both my son and his cousin."

"Perhaps we can ask all four men together," Lady Sorrell suggested.

"And perhaps Lord Wickford as well? He is especially important as the owner of Powell's, don't you think?" Lady Colburne asked.

"Yes, absolutely," Lady Ayres agreed. "He knows everything going on and perhaps could put in a good word for her at his club, or at the very least, stem the gossip among gentlemen."

"It is agreed," Penelope said with a nod. "I will invite all the gentlemen to my home tomorrow and ask them if they would be willing to assist us in this endeavor."

"And the lady, naturally," Lady Moreton added.

"Naturally," Penelope agreed, making a note to herself to send the invitations that afternoon.

Chapter Ten

Warden Henry Archer called to order the meeting of the Worshipful Company of Clockmakers just as Charles slipped into the back of the room. He hadn't expected traffic to be as bad as it was at this time on a Wednesday evening.

"Order! Order!" the warden called.

Slowly, the room quieted and Charles found a seat next to a rather rotund older gentleman, who he vaguely remembered being introduced to some time ago. He nodded to the man who nodded back genially, giving Charles a near toothless smile.

"May we have a reading of the minutes of our last meeting, Mr. Shelton?" the warden asked the gentleman standing just behind him.

A slender man came up to the lectern and read through the minutes of the last meeting at record speed.

"Thank you, all in favor of approving the minutes?"

There was a round of 'ayes.' The warden banged his gavel, and the minutes were approved.

"Thank you, now on to new business."

Charles sat up straighter but found himself forced to listen to the head of the watch and clockmakers guild drone on about grievances from the springer subdivision of the guild. A representative of the subdivision got up to plead their case and then a vote was taken. While he supposed the issue was of some import on a purely political level, it didn't affect his business whatsoever.

Other matters were discussed, voted on and approved or not, but the one issue Charles had come to hear about didn't seem to be on the agenda, which made him more than a little unnerved.

Finally, the warden banged his gavel, calling out, "And that brings new business to an end unless there are any motions from the floor?" He peered out at the audience.

Charles stood up. "I have an issue, Warden," he said loud enough to be heard.

All eyes turned around and focused on him.

"It has come to my attention that a great number of inferior watches are being imported to our shores and sold for very low prices, and I'd like to know what the Company of Clockmakers is planning to do about it."

The warden frowned. "Inferior watches? Imported? From where? How? When?"

"From Switzerland, sir. I don't have particulars on the how and when, but I can assure you, good English watchmaking is being undercut by the cheap copies, some of which even bear the mark of British watchmakers but not the quality," Charles stated.

His words caused a ripple of discussion around the room.

The warden banged his gavel down once again.

"What are you proposing we do about this, Mr. er, Mr...."

"Aldridge, sir. Charles Aldridge," Charles supplied for him. "My father was Bertram Aldridge."

"Oh, yes, yes. He, er, passed a few years ago, now, didn't he?" the warden said, looking appropriately distressed.

"Yes, sir. I have taken over the business."

"Excellent. Glad to hear it."

"Thank you, sir, now about these watches from Switzerland?"

"Yes, yes. It sounds as if we'll need a committee to examine this matter. May I have volunteers, if you please?" the warden asked, looking around.

"I've heard of this," another gentleman spoke up. Charles recognized him as John Harris. He'd been a friend of his father's. "I'll join the committee with Aldridge."

"Excellent. One more, if you please, gentlemen," the warden called out.

"You can count on me," James Foreman said, raising his hand. He was a brilliant watchmaker. Charles had admired his work for years.

"Very good. Mr. Aldridge you have your committee. I expect a report at our next meeting." The warden banged his gavel. "Any other new business?"

There was silence around the room, and Charles sat, pleased that there would be some action even if he had to head the committee himself.

"No? Very good, then. Would someone like to make a motion to adjourn?" the warden asked.

Someone up front raised his hand. Another seconded the motion, and the meeting was officially ended.

Charles got up but stayed where he was, waiting for Mr. Foreman and Mr. Harris to come toward the back of the room. As he waited, a number of other men stopped to give him a word of support.

"So glad someone spoke up. Good job, Aldridge," Mr. Browning said, giving him a friendly pat on his arm before moving off. He had been another of his father's close friends, and Charles had rather been hoping he would have volunteered for the committee.

Mr. East, another friend of his father's, stopped in front of him, chasing away his disappointment in Mr. Browning. "Your father would be proud, Charles," he said.

"Thank you, sir. I felt it was important to look into this," Charles said.

"I agree. I agree most whole-heartedly. Although I didn't officially volunteer, I'd like to join your committee if you don't mind," the man said, peering at him from under large liberally salted eyebrows.

"I would appreciate that, sir." Something occurred to Charles. "Mr. East, am I mistaken in remembering that you have a daughter?"

The man's eyebrows rose. "No, you are not mistaken. My little Suzanne has just past the age of twenty." He lowered his brows again. "You wouldn't happen to be thinking of marriage, now, would you?"

"As a matter of fact, I am. My mother thinks it time," Charles admitted.

"Your mother?" the man either guffawed or coughed, Charles could quite tell which. "Doesn't she want you to marry from the nobility?"

"*She* would prefer that," Charles admitted. "I dare not set my sights so high. I'd rather the daughter of someone I knew and trusted." He gave the man a friendly smile.

"Well, then, we'll have to have you over for dinner some time," Mr. East said, returning his smile. "I'll speak with Mrs. East about it. You'll be hearing from us." He gave Charles a nod and moved on.

That was easy enough, Charles thought to himself. He repeated his efforts with another few gentlemen he knew, including Mr. Foreman who he remembered also had a daughter of marriageable age. His queries weren't always met with success. Some gentlemen claimed that their daughters were already married or courting someone else, but he thought he might have at least two dinner invitations coming his way, perhaps more.

Not bad for an evening's work, he thought as he rode in his carriage home. He felt a slight pang when he remembered the extraordinary feeling he'd gotten just from touching Lady St. Vincent's hand, but she had turned him down.

No, doing this, meeting girls from his own social class, was the most pragmatic thing to do—and who knew, maybe one of them would also send sparks of happiness through him. At the very least he had to try. The only thing he had to do now was make sure his mother didn't find out.

~April 30~

Elizabeth accepted a cup of tea from Mrs. Aldridge but wished she could have been drinking something stronger. She didn't know why she'd been invited to the lady's home, but the fact that she was joined by no fewer than four men—no make that five, she thought, as Lord Ainsby joined them as well—she was beginning to get a little nervous about this.

"We just have one more gentleman to await, and then we'll get started," Mrs. Aldridge said, smiling around the room.

There were a few other ladies in attendance aside from Mrs. Aldridge. Lydia and Lady Blakemore were both there. If it weren't for their presence as well, she would be truly curious and perhaps even a little worried.

"Do you know why we've been called here?" she asked Lydia quietly.

"I do," she said, giving Elizabeth a broad smile. "You'll find out soon enough, I promise. We just need... Ah, here he is." She rose and curtsied to Lord Wickford as he paused by the door, took in the assembled crowd, and bowed to everyone.

Elizabeth rose as well to greet him, but Lady Blakemore stayed seated and merely nodded to the club owner.

"Please do come in, Lord Wickford. May I offer you some tea?" Mrs. Aldridge asked, lifting the pot in front of her.

"Thank you, ma'am," Lord Wickford said, giving her a warm smile. He accepted his cup and then found a seat.

The lady, however, did not resume her seat. Instead, she cleared her throat and waited for Mr. Hershawn and Paul to turn their attention to her.

"Dearest friends, thank you all for coming today. I, Lady Welles, and Lady Blakemore have asked you here today to come to the aid of Lady St. Vincent. As you all are surely aware, her name has been blackened by the actions and words of Lord Rogan, in addition to the gossip begun by Lady Findlater who saw one thing and then reported a very different story to the rest of the *ton*."

"I do beg your pardon, ma'am, but are you saying that what is being circulated about Lady St. Vincent's behavior is not strictly correct?" Mr. Hershawn asked delicately.

"I am shocked and appalled," Lord Wickford said blandly with obvious sarcasm.

Elizabeth gave a little laugh and shared a look with Lydia, who was doing her best to hold back her own giggles.

Mrs. Aldridge frowned at Mr. Hershawn. "Lady St. Vincent was lured into Lord Welles's study under false pretenses, then rudely attacked by Lord Rogan who was there lying in wait for her."

"Really? That's not what—" Lord Roseberry stopped speaking immediately upon receiving a number of unpleasant stares from various people. His pale cheeks turned pink. "But perhaps I have been misinformed," he added more quietly.

"You have. I can only think it is a deliberate campaign by Lady Findlater and others of her sort who find great pleasure in destroying the reputations of otherwise upstanding members of society," Lady Blakemore said succinctly.

"Because we are all friends with Lady St. Vincent, I am hoping you will join me and the other ladies of the Wagering Whist Society in clearing Lady St. Vincent's good name," Mrs. Aldridge continued. "May we count on you to do whatever you can to aid us and her?" She looked around in particular at the gentlemen present.

"Naturally, we all would be very happy to do so," Lord Wickford said. "I am assuming you have plan in mind, Mrs. Aldridge?"

"As a matter of fact, I do, although it is not fully formed as yet because I wanted to leave much of it up to all of you." She folded her hands across her ample stomach. "The ladies of the Wagering Whist Society will, with discretion, go about society speaking of Lady St. Vincent in glowing terms. We will talk about her excellent philanthropic leanings, the committee she is on to help the people of the Rookeries, as well as what a pleasant and respected lady she is in general."

"How embarrassing," Elizabeth whispered more to herself than anyone else. She was certain her cheeks were burning red.

"Perhaps, but it is all true," Lydia said quietly, giving her arm a friendly pat.

"Gentlemen, I will call on you to be so kind as to escort the lady out and about. We believe that if she is seen with upstanding gentlemen such as yourselves, opinion will shift. Now, how you wish to carry out this request is, naturally, up to you. I would, however, appreciate it a great deal if you were to be seen driving in the park, dancing at parties—"

"I would be happy if Lady St. Vincent would join me at the opera next week," Lord Ainsby said, giving Elizabeth a nod of his head.

"I would be very happy to go for a drive or a walk down the Serpentine with her," Mr. Aldridge said.

"I believe you can certainly count on Roseberry and I to dance with the lady at parties," Mr.

Hershawn added.

"And I will guide conversations at my club in her favor, in addition to taking the lady for a drive down Rotten Row," Lord Wickford offered.

"You are *too* kind," Elizabeth said, nearly overcome with emotion. "Truly, I..." She couldn't even finish her sentence, only dig into her reticule for her handkerchief to stem the tears that were threatening to fall.

"There, there, now, Lady St. Vincent, you are too good to suffer at the hands of Lady Findlater and, well, it is not very lady-like of me to say this, but I would love to see her get her own comeuppance. Naturally, what we are planning will not lead to anything dramatic, but at least she'll see that she is not the be-all and end-all of society," Lady Blakemore said.

"Actually, my lady, I believe what Lady Findlater will quickly learn is the power of the Ladies' Wagering Whist Society and that it best to leave them and their friends well alone," Lord Wickford said with a broad smile that emphasized his very white, straight teeth in contrast to his darker complexion.

Mrs. Aldridge laughed. "Indeed, I do hope she will learn to leave us and ours alone."

"If she has any intelligence at all, I'm sure she'll get the message," Paul agreed.

"Well, then, it is a plan," Mrs. Aldridge said with a broad smile for everyone.

Elizabeth could only hope it worked!

Chapter Eleven

~May 2, 1807~

Elizabeth needed a few moments of quiet and support from Paul before she could bring herself to enter the soirée two nights later. The invitation to Lady Fostler's party had come just before the attack, and she hadn't heard that it had been rescinded. She could only hope there wouldn't be any unpleasantness.

"You *are* going to be all right," Paul told her before they exited their carriage. It was more of a command than a question.

"Yes, I am. I am not going to listen to what anyone says, but keep to my friends," Elizabeth said, taking in another deep breath.

"That's right. You have a number of very good friends, Elizabeth, stay with them."

"I *do*. I have excellent friends," she said, giving him a smile. On that happy note, they went into the party.

Just standing by the door, Elizabeth was pleased to see Lydia with her husband, speaking with Lord and Lady Colburne and the Duchess of Kendell and Lady Margaret. She was about to suggest they go over to meet them when Mr. Hershawn and Lord Roseberry sauntered up.

"Good evening, Lady St. Vincent, my lord," Roseberry said, giving them a bow.

"Evening, Roseberry, Hershawn," Paul acknowledged them both.

"How lovely you look, my lady," Mr. Hershawn said, bowing over her hand.

Elizabeth gave a little laugh. "Thank you, sir. Is that your father I saw you with just now?"

Mr. Hershawn turned to look toward the Duchess of Kendell who was just being led away from her group by his father, Lord Gorling. The two had their heads together and were already laughing over something.

"Yes, indeed," Mr. Hershawn said, turning back to smile at her.

"They always seem to be laughing together," Elizabeth commented with a shake of her head.

"Well, my father is a rather funny man," Mr. Hershawn said with a laugh of his own.

"He is quite amusing," Paul said. "Especially when he's trying to convince Parliament to switch to a more 'democratic' way of doing things. He thinks the Americans have the right of it, and we need to change and move with the times."

Lord Roseberry gave a little laugh. "From all I hear of his goings on in Parliament, it almost makes me want to take my seat just to see the raucous he's causing among the stodgy old members."

"It has been quite a scene," Paul said, laughing.

"Well, we certainly don't wish to cause a scene, my lady," Mr. Hershawn began, "but we do wish to apologize for being so stupid as to begin to believe the horrid things that were being said about you."

"Indeed, we feel completely ashamed," Lord

Roseberry added.

Elizabeth smiled at them both. "It is quite all right. You didn't know better."

"But we *should* have," Mr. Hershawn insisted.

"So do, please, accept our apologies," Lord Roseberry said.

"And know we are extremely honored to have been among the chosen to pull your name from the mud," Mr. Hershawn added.

"And quite look forward to spending time with you," Lord Roseberry said.

"Thank you, both," Elizabeth said. Movement behind his lordship caught her eye, and she smiled as she saw Lydia and Lady Margaret coming up to join them. As much as she appreciated the gentlemen's apologies, it was a little embarrassing.

"Good evening, Lydia, Lady Margaret," Elizabeth said, turning toward the two women.

Lord Roseberry and Mr. Hershawn turned around to greet them as well. At some point during the gentlemen's apology, Paul had excused himself and disappeared.

"Good evening," Lady Margaret said, giving them a little curtsy. "Lord Roseberry—"

"Good evening, Lady Margaret. I don't mean to be rude, but will you please excuse me?" Lord Roseberry gave them all a quick bow, turned around, and walked off.

"What was that?" Lydia asked. She shared a look with Lady Margaret and then Elizabeth, who was as confused as any of them.

"I, I can't say," Mr. Hershawn said. He was unsure of what his friend was up to as well. "If you'll excuse me, I'll see if I can't find out." He too gave them a bow and went off after Lord Roseberry.

"That is the oddest thing I think I've ever seen," Elizabeth said, watching the men go off. She turned toward Lydia and Lady Margaret. "Neither of you have quarreled with Lord Roseberry, have you? I mean, I can't imagine you would have."

"Even if we had, he couldn't be enough of a gentleman to face us?" Lydia asked.

"I wonder..." Lady Margaret began, but then didn't go on.

"What? Do you know something?" Lydia asked.

"No. It's just... I wanted to speak with him because I think he might be the gentleman I danced with at the Venetian Ball. If he is, then maybe he's avoiding me so I don't learn of his identity. Is that too farfetched?" Lady Margaret asked.

"I heard you spent the evening with just one gentleman. You think it was Lord Roseberry?" Elizabeth asked.

"I don't know, but..."

"Oh, yes, we discussed this at the last Ladies' Wagering Whist Society meeting. You were left with handkerchief with the initials JR, weren't you?" Lydia asked.

"Yes. I asked the duchess to inquire whether the ladies could think of any gentlemen of the ton with those initials," Lady Margaret said.

"JR?" Elizabeth repeated, wondering who she knew with those initials.

"The only men we could think of was Lord Roseberry and Lord Ranelagh," Lydia added.

"Yes, but I'm certain it isn't Lord Ranelagh," Lady Margaret said.

"The only other person I can think of is Lord

Redenton," Elizabeth said, knowing that wouldn't really help.

"Isn't he about eighty years old?" Lydia asked with a giggle.

"Sixty, but yes, he is an older gentleman," Elizabeth gave them a smile.

"I don't think he could have danced as much as the gentleman in question did," Lady Margaret said, giggling too.

Elizabeth laughed. "No. I don't suppose he could. Well, then, perhaps you're right, Lady Margaret. And it looks like you might have a bit of a difficult time pinning the man down, oddly enough."

There was a commotion at the door just then, and they all turned to see what it was about. Paul seemed to be quickly making his way toward it.

Lady Margaret gave a laugh. "I believe it's your stepson, my lady."

Elizabeth nodded. "Yes, he must have gone to greet Beatrice and Bel. I think those girls are going to cause a stir wherever they go for some time," she said with a laugh. "Oh, and there's Lord Roseberry again." He'd just walked past, looking like he was trying to hide from Lady Margaret. Elizabeth couldn't imagine why.

"Thank you! If you'll excuse me." She strode off, trying to get the attention of the gentleman.

"Why do you think he's avoiding her?" Elizabeth asked Lydia, who was left standing with her.

"I have no idea. It's the oddest thing. I wonder if he really is the gentleman she spent the evening with, and he's trying to keep it a secret for some reason," Lydia said, watching them.

"Lydia, I did so want to thank you, Mrs. Aldridge, and Lady Blakemore for coming to my rescue. The plan you came up with is brilliant, and well, it truly touched me to think I have such good friends," Elizabeth said. She was *not* going to cry again. She was determined, she was not.

Lydia reached out and took her hand. "Of course! I have just been feeling so awful that such a thing should happen to you in *my* home!"

"But it wasn't your fault! You had nothing to do with it. It was just coincidence where it happened," Elizabeth argued.

"I know, but still... And you are, indeed, a good friend. Lady Findlater and her ilk just annoy me to no end. I'm of the same mind as Lady Blakemore. That woman needs a taste of her own medicine or, or, or something!"

"I'm certain she never will get her comeuppance, but it's enough that you all are being so good and helping me to restore my reputation," Elizabeth said.

Lydia might have said something more, but just then Lord Ainsby came up and said, "Good evening, Lady St. Vincent, Lady Welles. I do hope you will excuse this intrusion, but I believe a dance is forming. Lady St. Vincent, I would be honored if you would stand up with me," he said with a bow.

Elizabeth curtsied in reply. "Thank you, my lord, I would love to dance." She gave Lydia a wink as she went off with the gentleman.

True to their word, each of the gentlemen present at Mrs. Aldridge's meeting stood up with Elizabeth. After the third dance, another gentlemen Elizabeth had never met before asked her to dance, and with that, she hoped her reputation *was* in fact on the mend.

~May 3~

Charles picked up Lady St. Vincent at precisely three on Sunday afternoon. Everyone who was anyone would be out in the park on a Sunday afternoon. It was an excellent time to be out if you wanted to be seen.

"Do you mind if we walk?" he asked as the lady's maid handed her a parasol.

"Not at all! It's a lovely day," she said, smiling up at him.

Charles had wondered whether this would be awkward, considering what had occurred the last time they had been alone together. She seemed to be quite at her ease, however, so he gave her a smile and escorted her out the door.

He offered her his arm and felt stupidly happy when she tucked her hand around it. "I'm so glad you aren't harboring any ill feelings from our last meeting," he said, deciding that being forthright would probably be the best way to go.

Her eyes twinkled as she looked up at him. "Did you think I would be angry because you proposed a way out of my difficult situation?"

"Well, I did suggest a rather drastic solution," he admitted.

"You did," she agreed. "Although I was rather taken aback by it at first, I realized you were merely trying to do the gentlemanly thing and did not intend to cause any insult."

"I most definitely did not," he agreed rather emphatically. "Truly, considering that your stepson was willing to put his life on the line, I thought my proposal was the very least I could do."

"And I appreciate that, truly—a great deal. It is the most awkward situation to find oneself in," she admitted.

"Indeed. Although, may I be so bold as to ask why the opinions of women as petty as Lady Findlater and others of her ilk mean so much to you?"

"Oh, I don't really care about Lady Findlater. It's more that everyone in society is believing her lies. From what I understand, it's not even just the one lady spreading these tales, but Lord Rogan himself."

"To what end?" Charles asked. He truly did not understand the point of all this.

"To harm me and my reputation? I honestly don't know. I can only think this is a continuation of what happened to me when I first made my debut six years ago," she said.

"*Six* years ago?" Charles asked, shocked. "Would someone really hold a grudge that long?"

"I can only presume so from what he's said to me," she said.

They passed Hyde Park corner and proceeded down the walking path along Rotten Row. There were, as expected, a great number of people out walking, riding on horseback, and in open carriages. Ladies carefully propped their parasols so they could both be protected from the sun and yet not hidden from view. Gentlemen were constantly lifting their hats to ladies as they passed by.

Charles and Lady St. Vincent joined the throng, walking silently for a little way and taking in all the sights.

"May I ask what you were accused of at that time?" Charles asked after a few minutes, once they were past the initial crowd and sure their conversation would not be over heard.

"The same as now," Lady St. Vincent admitted with a slight frown. "At that time, I didn't know any better and got into some trouble by following the advice of those who meant to destroy my reputation. I'm sorry to say that some girls can be exceedingly cruel, and I was a complete innocent and didn't realize they meant me harm."

"I am sorry. I'm sure it must have been difficult for you, but again, you were—and are—worried about what others think of you. Why do you care?" Charles asked.

The lady paused and looked up at him curiously. "Do you not care at all what others think of *you*, Mr. Aldridge?"

"No, honestly, I don't. They can say whatever they want—and I can assure you there are some very cruel things said about me in the halls of society. I simply don't care," he said with a shrug.

"Would it be horrid to ask what people are saying of you?" she asked, resuming their amble.

Chapter Twelve

"Not at all. In fact, if you are working to rebuild your reputation with society, I might not be the best person for you to be seen with. My reputation may taint your own in a completely different way," Charles admitted. She clearly had nothing to say to that, so he continued, "I am called a cit," he told her and then gave a little laugh. "It is true too. I am a businessman and not of noble blood. My mother has been labeled a mushroom because she is trying to insinuate herself where she, presumably, doesn't belong."

Lady St. Vincent frowned and then slowly nodded. "I have heard such accusations. But your aunt is married to a nobleman, isn't she?"

"Yes. She is our 'in' to society. My cousin, Ainsby, is a viscount. My maternal grandfather was a gentleman farmer who, although he held no title, was quite accepted in society. Based on that, he expected both his daughters to marry into the nobility."

"Lady St. Vincent, Mr. Aldridge!" a voice called out from the bridle path. Charles turned to see Ladies Welles and Colburne, along with another young lady he didn't know. They were all mounted on fine-looking horses.

"Ladies, how delightful to see you this afternoon," Charles said, leading Lady St. Vincent to the rail to greet her friends.

"It's a beautiful day to be out," Lady Welles said, smiling at them.

"Indeed," Lady St. Vincent said with a little laugh. "Everyone seems to have decided to enjoy this lovely weather."

"How fortunate it is," Lady Colburne said, with a twinkle in her eye. She clearly knew of the plan to rebuild Lady St. Vincent's reputation.

"I cannot but agree," Lady St. Vincent said. "Lady Margaret, were you able to catch Lord Roseberry last night and find out what he was up to?"

"I was," said the young lady Charles wasn't familiar with. "I will happily tell you about at another time, though. I'm not certain this is the best place..."

"Ah, no, if I'm not mistaken you are being requested to continue along," Charles said, noticing a carriage just behind them looking to move around.

The three ladies looked behind them, and then with a nod, a laugh, and a wave, they continued their ride.

They walked along for a moment before Lady St. Vincent continued with their previous conversation. "Your aunt did marry well, then, but your mother did not?" she asked, clearly still caught up in his story.

"Yes," he said, going back to the tale. "My grandparents were furious, but she and my father were very much in love, so they married against my grandfather's wishes," he said. "I am quite proud of them, to be honest. Neither of them cared a whit for what anyone said, they only wanted to be together, and so that's what they did." He turned to her, giving her a warm smile. "I was raised in a very warm, loving home."

She returned his smile. "And you learned your lesson that the opinion of others shouldn't affect what you do so long as you are happy?"

"Precisely," he agreed.

"I can understand that reasoning. Sadly, it's not the world I live in. I don't have someone for whom I would give up my social standing, in fact just the opposite. I want to be respected. I need to be an active member of society," she explained. "I have a son whose social standing may very well depend on my own. He will have a hard enough time, as it is, being a younger, untitled son from a second marriage. I simply could not bear to see him tainted by my actions."

"I didn't know you had a child. How old is he?" Charles asked. He had to admit he was surprised to hear she had a son, then immediately thought that it made sense since she was a widow, after all. She was just so young and beautiful; he couldn't imagine her a mother.

"Matthew is four."

"Then he is still much too young for you to worry about, don't you think?" he asked.

"Yes, but it still means I need to do all I can to assure my reputation is secure by the time he enters school."

"And being labeled a loose woman does not fit into all of your honorable goals," he said understanding.

"No," she said, staring straight ahead. "Truly, Mr. Aldridge, respect is all I require. Just a little respect."

They had come to the Serpentine River where there were a number of other couples walking arm in arm.

"Well, then, while walking along the river would be lovely, perhaps we should turn around and walk back along Rotten Row to be sure you are seen. We can only hope my presence will be of some benefit rather than the opposite," he suggested.

"I truly don't think your reputation as a cit will harm mine. You do have your cousin, and your mother is a very highly respected member of the Ladies' Wagering Whist Society," Lady St. Vincent commented as they turned back the way they'd come.

"I do hope you are right," he said, smiling down at her and offering her his arm again.

She took it, and he wondered why having her holding onto him made him feel good. It gave him a warmth and feeling that he could protect her from anything that might come their way. He had no idea whether that was true, but it made him happy to think so.

~*~

Penelope waited for a good twenty minutes after Charles left to pick up Lady St. Vincent before putting her dog, Duchess, onto her lead and going out for a walk to the park. She knew her son was going to walk with the countess to the Serpentine and along Rotten Row. They wanted to be sure they were seen by as many people as possible, and she wanted to be one of those people—only she needed to do so without Charles seeing her.

It was despicable, and she knew it—spying on her own child. But she did so want to see how Lady St. Vincent reacted to him, how they got along, and the reaction of others in society to their being out together.

The park was very crowded, however, and Duchess so excited to be out walking amongst so many people that she had a hard time seeing much of anything or anyone. Normally, she took the dog out when the park was empty early in the morning, but at this time of the afternoon, there were enough people about to make Duchess overly excited. Instead of taking her dog for a walk, Penelope had the distinct feeling that it was Duchess who was taking *her* for a walk.

After the dog attempted to jump on a few unsuspecting people, Penelope gave up trying to walk along the path and opted for the grass instead. That turned out to be a bad idea because Duchess kept trying to run and tugged even harder at her lead. Penelope wondered if the little dog was looking for little Matthew Adler, Lady St. Vincent's son, since this was exactly where they'd encountered them the other day.

"Duchess, stop!" she finally said to the dog, protesting. To her shock, the dog did so.

Duchess came to a complete stop. The sweet little thing sat and looked up, her tongue lolling out of her mouth. Penelope paused to catch her breath and loosened her tight grip on the lead. Then, without warning, the dog suddenly took off, and Penelope lost hold of the lead entirely.

"Oh, no! Duchess! Duchess! Stop!" she cried. She tried to run after the dog, but at her age and—

goodness gracious—size, she simply didn't have the wherewithal to actually run.

She knew she was being stared at, but she didn't care. She had to catch her dog. It was with relief that the pup reached what she'd been running toward—no fewer than *four* spaniels of the same breed.

They were all sitting very well behaved on their leads. Holding them with a laugh on his lips was a most handsome older gentleman. He wasn't much taller than Penelope, and she was what her husband had very sweetly called "adorably short." This man was clearly in much better form than she, who had allowed age and, she had to admit, some gluttony to become quite plump.

She panted up to the man and his dogs. He very kindly shifted all four of his leads to one hand and picked up the end of Duchess's to hand to her. "I believe you lost this?" he asked with a little laugh.

"Oh, yes, I do apologize for my Duchess's atrocious behavior," Penelope said, still trying to catch her breath.

"No worries. No worries at all," he said with a chuckle. "They can be quite challenging to keep hold of when they've spotted another of their breed."

"Oh, yes," she said, as if she knew all about this. To be honest, she had never been with the pup when she'd seen another spaniel. "She is such a friendly little thing."

She smiled at him, but her attention was claimed by two of his dogs who, now that they'd had a chance to smell Duchess, wanted to greet her as well. One sweet little puppy face rubbed up against her legs, another gave a little bark.

She bent down and rubbed behind each of their ears. "Aren't you so beautiful? Yes you are, yes you are," she cooed at them. Two were tri-color dogs like her own, the other two were all black.

"Such social little creatures, aren't they?" the man asked, giving Duchess a little scratch behind her ears.

"Indeed. Speaking of which…" She smiled and held out her hand. "I am Mrs. Penelope Aldridge. I don't believe we've met."

He took her hand and bowed over it. "Bolton." No lord, no Mr., she noticed. Just Bolton. How very odd.

"This is Duchess," Penelope said, leaning down and giving her own dog a pat on her head.

"Duchess, my, my," he said with a broad smile. He bowed to her. "Your Grace, it is an honor to make your acquaintance." The dog seemed to smile up at him, her mouth slightly open.

He then turned to his dogs. "And this is Nighty, Tiger, Fluff, and Harold," he said, pointing to each of the dogs in turn.

"They're beautiful, but how do you tell them apart?" Penelope asked with a little laugh.

"Oh, easy!" he said, also chuckling. "Fluff has the fluffiest tail—has since she was a pup. Tiger isn't all black, he's got a bit of white stripe on his head. Er, it was more pronounced when he was younger. Nighty is entirely black. Her name was originally Midnight, but we've shortened it, and she is rather naughty as well," he said with a laugh. "And Harold, well, he's just Harold," he finished with a shrug. "My daughter named him."

"So, two girls and two boys?" Penelope asked.

"Yes."

"Do you breed them?"

"I do! I do my best to ensure they breed according to color," he said, turning slightly pink at the indelicate conversation.

Penelope just nodded. "I find Duchess to be a very loving, affectionate dog who adores attention. I can only imagine how much work it would be to have four of them!"

"Ah, well, yes. I do try to give them equal attention, but I think they get a lot of affection from each other as well as from me, you know."

"Ah, that does make sense. Because I only have the one dog, I suppose she needs more human attention than one who has others of her kind," Penelope said, almost wishing she'd thought of giving Duchess a doggy companion.

"But she seems to be a very happy pup," he said, watching her as she attempted to pull the other dogs into a bit of play.

They looked as if they would have been happy to run around with her except for the leads they were all on.

Penelope laughed at the dog's antics. "I would let her off her leash, only I'd be afraid she'd run away and not come back. We had a little mishap along those lines only last week where she nearly toppled a little boy. Luckily, he turned out to be the son of one of my friends," she said with a little laugh.

"It is a valid fear, sadly. Perhaps walking would be easier. Would you care to join us?" he asked, holding out his elbow for her to take.

Penelope hadn't held onto a gentleman's arm

for so long butterflies began to flitter about in her stomach, but she took his arm, and they proceeded to amble along. His dogs quickly caught on to the fact that their walk would be continuing. After a few minutes, Duchess began to emulate the good behavior, but not until she'd made a few more attempts at playing with the others.

"You seem to have trained your dogs quite well," Penelope commented. "Duchess is the first dog I've ever owned, so I'm afraid I haven't done so well with her."

"Really?" he said, sounding quite surprised. "Well, then, I'd say you've done an excellent job!"

"Truly? Do you think so?" Penelope asked, looking up at Bolton.

"Indeed. Why, look at her walking along so nicely," he said, nodding at Duchess who had finally calmed down a bit. "How old is she?"

"A little over two years old," Penelope said.

He stopped and turned to her. "She's only *two*? Well, then, I think you have a great deal to be proud of. She is doing extremely well. At two, most of my dogs were still quite rambunctious."

"Oh, I'm so glad to hear that. Honestly, I don't know what I'm doing with her. On the other hand, I had no idea how to raise a child either, and I seem to have done pretty well in that area," she said with a laugh.

Just mentioning her son reminded her that she'd come to the park to watch him as he walked with Lady St. Vincent, but it was so much more pleasant walking with Lord Bolton. Mr. Bolton? How she wished she had the nerve to ask, but sadly, as he had only introduced himself by the one name, she presumed he didn't wish to share what his title was. She should honor that, she decided. It wasn't going to be easy, but there it was.

His pleasant company more than made up for the frustration his name was causing her.

Chapter Thirteen

As they neared her home after their walk, Elizabeth turned to smile at her companion. "Thank you so much for a lovely walk, Mr. Aldridge. I don't know if it did my reputation any good, but it certainly did a great deal toward lightening my mood."

"Well, I am very glad to hear that," he said. He paused for a moment, looking at something beyond her. "It looks like someone else is determined to make you happy as well."

Elizabeth turned to see a footman approaching her door, carrying a bouquet of flowers. She frowned and turned back to Mr. Aldridge. "Actually, that is just the opposite, I'm afraid. Those are from Lord Rogan. He sends me a bouquet every single day, and every single day I throw them into the gutter."

"Rogan? But isn't that the fellow who—"

"Yes, it is. I don't know if he's trying to apologize or merely annoy me, and frankly, I don't care either way."

Mr. Aldridge turned and frowned at the man delivering the flowers, but Elizabeth had an idea. She'd never actually been present when the flowers had been delivered, but now that she was, she was going to take advantage of the fact.

"Excuse me," she said, approaching the young man who was standing on the step, waiting for the door to be answered.

He turned.

"Those are from Lord Rogan, are they not?" she asked.

"Yes, ma'am," he said, coming down a step. The door behind him opened, and Frank stood there watching but not saying anything.

"Are you his man?" she asked.

"No, ma'am. I work for the florist," he answered.

"Oh, very good. Could you please tell me the name of your employer, in that case?"

"It's Mr. Harley, ma'am. He's got a shop on Pall Mall."

"I see. Thank you. I'll be over there later today to speak with him, in that case. You may return to Mr. Harley with those flowers and tell him... Tell him to please give them to Mrs. Harley if such a lady exists," she said, giving the man a smile.

His eyes widened at her odd request. "To Mrs. Harley, ma'am? But they're for Lady St. Vincent. I was told to deliver them to her."

"Yes, I know. I am Lady St. Vincent, and I am requesting you go back to your employer and tell him that I will be by later today," Elizabeth said, understanding she'd completely confused the young man.

He turned toward the footman, still standing in the door. Frank gave him a nod to confirm her words. "All right," the man said, coming back down onto the footpath.

Elizabeth gave him a nod and then turned back to Mr. Aldridge.

"Are you going to tell the florist to stop delivering the flowers?" Mr. Aldridge asked Elizabeth.

"Yes and no. I'm going to ask him to stop delivering the flowers, but to keep accepting Lord Rogan's money. I want him to keep half, and I'll give the other half to Lady Welles, whose husband supports the people of the Rookeries," she explained, giving him a smile.

His eyes widened. "I wonder what Rogan will say to that," he said with a little laugh.

"Oh, I don't expect him to learn of it. That's what the florist will have to do for his half of the money."

"Lie to his lordship and tell him that the flowers were delivered?"

She gave a little shrug. "It will be worth his while, and we'll all be happy. Lord Rogan will think he's sending me flowers, the florist will get paid for saying he's delivering them, and the people of the Rookeries will get a little more money for whatever they need."

Mr. Aldridge shook his head. "That's quite devious, you know."

"Whatever it is, I don't see anything wrong with it, do you?"

"No! Not at all. I think it's quite clever, actually." He started to bow to her, but she reached out her hand toward him. She didn't know why, she just had to touch him.

He took her hand, giving her warm smile. "Lady St. Vincent, it has been a pleasure. I do hope we'll have an opportunity to do this again soon."

"As do I, Mr. Aldridge," she said, enjoying the warmth of her hand in his and the sweet tingles that shot through her fingertips. "It has been wonderful getting to know you better."

~*~

Charles was greeted warmly by Mr. and Mrs. Foreman as he entered their drawing room that evening. He'd known Mr. Foreman for quite some time, since he and Charles's father had had a friendly rivalry for as long as Charles could remember.

Mr. Foreman pulled out his pocket watch—a very handsome piece with a silver-etched cover. "Right on time," he announced. "I do like punctuality."

"Thank you, sir. I always try, although London traffic doesn't always allow for it, sadly," Charles said before bowing over Mrs. Foreman's hand.

"Traffic is just awful, isn't it?" she asked, with a warm smile. She then turned around and dragged forward a rather reluctant young lady.

Miss Foreman was extremely pretty, taking after her mother with her rich, light brown hair that curled just so and big, brilliant blue eyes set in a softly rounded, delicate face. Sadly, she looked as if she were terrified rather than pleased to meet him. She curtsied, however, and did her best to give him a smile when her mother nudged her.

"Pleased to meet you, Mr. Aldridge," she whispered.

"This is our daughter, Honoria," her father said, giving the girl a frown since she'd clearly gotten the order of things wrong.

Charles bowed. Smiling, he said, "It can be so

very difficult to meet new people, sometimes, can it not?"

She gave him a more honest smile. "Yes."

Her mother gave him a grateful smile. "Please join us for a drink before dinner."

He was led farther into their drawing room. It could have rivaled that of any lady of society for its elegance. He happily accepted the glass of brandy his host offered and sat down to do his best to engage the Foreman's very shy daughter and do his best to remove the image of Lady St. Vincent from his mind's eye.

"Have you always lived in London, Miss Foreman?" he asked.

She gave him a wide-eyed nod.

"Do you enjoy the city?" he tried.

"Yes?" she said as if she were asking a question rather than answering one.

He smiled politely and asked, "What do you like most?"

"The park."

"Oh, do you ride?" he asked, hoping to finally pull out a conversation from this awkwardness.

She shook her head.

"Honoria is a little frightened of horses," her father offered.

She looked to him and then back at Charles, nodding her agreement but not saying a word.

"I see. Then you walk in the park?" Charles asked. Honestly, he was beginning to wonder about a girl who couldn't even hold a normal conversation.

"Yes," she answered.

For the twenty minutes before dinner and then well into the meal itself, the girl didn't say more than two words together. Charles was practically exhausted from attempting to draw her out by the time dinner had been served. Thank goodness, once they'd moved into the dining room, Mr. Foreman had taken the control of the conversation and broached the subject of the watches from Switzerland that were flooding the English market.

Charles happily discussed the situation with him, or rather, unhappily because it was a rather disturbing new phenomenon. It could have a serious impact not only on his own business, but that of all the English watchmakers.

They were deep into discussing possible solutions—everything from discounting their own products, to trying to make an even better, thinner watch, to starting an all-out campaign to try to convince the populace that the imported watches were vastly inferior to English-made timepieces—when Miss Foreman suddenly blurted out, "Papa makes watches."

Charles turned to her and then back to her father, who'd suddenly turned beet red.

Her mother smiled at the girl and said kindly, as if to a small child, "Yes, that's right Honoria, Papa *does* make watches. So does Mr. Aldridge, don't you, sir?"

"Er, yes, yes I do," Charles said. He was beginning to wonder about this girl.

"Pretty ones like Papa's?" the young woman asked.

"Yes, indeed. I do my best to make very pretty watches," Charles answered.

This seemed to make the child—woman?—

happy. She smiled and then went back to eating her dinner.

Charles began to wonder. "Miss Foreman, would it be very rude of me to ask how old you are?" he asked, hoping his question wouldn't be taken amiss by her parents.

She looked up at him and tilted her head a little. She put down her fork and then held up three fingers on her right hand. "And twenty."

"Three and twenty?" he asked.

"Yes," she nodded before picking up her fork to continue eating.

"I see." He turned to look at his host, whose coloring was still rosier than normal.

"Honoria is a, er, a special young lady," he said, his voice sounding slightly strained.

Charles nodded. That explained a great deal. "I understand. You are lucky to have such a special and, er, sweet child."

"Yes," Mr. Foreman said, dropping his gaze to his own plate. He didn't eat any more, but instead picked up his wine glass and drained it.

It was clear to everyone—except perhaps Miss Foreman—that Charles was not going to be offering for Miss Foreman's hand.

After dinner, the ladies returned to the drawing room, leaving Charles and Mr. Foreman to enjoy a glass of port.

"She's really a very sweet girl," Mr. Foreman said soon after the door closed, leaving them alone.

"I can tell," Charles said, accepting a glass of liquor.

"Not too much upstairs, of course, but very biddable," his host went on.

"That must make life easy for you and your wife," Charles commented, not really knowing what else to say.

"She would—"

"Sir, I could not marry your daughter. I'm sorry. I'm looking for someone with whom I can share my life on an equal footing."

"Some men like a sweet, innocent..." Mr. Foreman started. "You know, someone who would look pretty sitting at the head of their table every night."

"Some men would indeed like that. I'm afraid I'm looking for someone with whom I could hold an intellectual conversation."

"She most certainly can converse," Mr. Foreman said quickly. "Once she gets to know you a little better. Granted, I don't think she could discuss the finer points of the current political situation, but then I doubt many women could," he said, giving a little laugh.

"I actually know quite a few who could," Charles said. He'd had an extremely pleasant walk with one just that afternoon. They hadn't actually discussed politics, but he had no reason to believe she wouldn't be able to if he queried her.

"Oh, yes? Well, you are a fortunate man, then," Mr. Foreman said awkwardly.

"Yes." Charles drained his own glass and then stood. "Thank you so much for your hospitality, Mr. Foreman. I do believe that our committee will be able to discover some way to combat this problem of the Swiss watches. I'll contact you when we decide to meet."

"Yes, yes. Please do," Mr. Foreman said, standing. "Er, you'd like to say your farewells to the ladies, I imagine?"

"Yes, thank you."

He did so and then went home feeling oddly sad and empty.

Chapter Fourteen

~May 5~

"It simply seemed to be too cruel to invite you to the opera and not ask Lord Conway and Miss Kendrick to join us as well," Lord Ainsby explained as he handed Elizabeth from his carriage after they'd arrived the following evening at the theatre.

She laughed. "You are too good, Lord Ainsby, and clearly you know my brother all too well."

"I actually haven't known him for very long, but I have to say, we've had some fascinating conversations at Powell's," Lord Ainsby said, escorting her up the stairs and into the building.

They continued up to his box.

"Are they joining us here?" Elizabeth asked.

"Yes. I believe there was a family dinner or something of the sort at the Blakemore's home. Lady Blakemore, Miss Beatrice, and Lord St. Vincent are attending Lady Hallburn's soirée this evening," he explained.

"My goodness! The twins are going to separate?" Elizabeth asked, laughing as she entered the box.

"You might not believe such a thing is possible, would you," Edward said, moving away from the front of the box to greet Elizabeth. Bel stood next to him with a bright smile on her face.

"I do apologize. I didn't know you were here," Elizabeth said, feeling her face heat with embarrassment.

"Oh, no, it's perfectly all right. It's really very rare that Bee and I separate for an evening," she said, giving Elizabeth a smile. "In fact, apart from our forced separation at the beginning of this season, we never have been apart. We've decided, however, that it might be a good thing for us to get used to."

"I can't say I disagree, I'm afraid. You will soon be living in two different homes," Edward said, giving Bel a loving smile.

"Have you decided on a date for your wedding?" Lord Ainsby asked, while indicating they all take their seats. It was well known that Miss Bel Kendrick and Edward were engaged, but the engagement of her sister and St. Vincent was still a family secret. It would have been awkward to come up with an explanation for how the two had known each other before Miss Bee's recent arrival in London. Of course, Elizabeth had been let in on the secret.

"It will probably be this autumn," Bel said. "It'll be easier for my father to hold it after the harvest."

"And I'm sure it'll be beautiful up north in September or October," Elizabeth said.

"Oh, yes!" Miss Kendrick agreed.

"Ladies, while I know this is a riveting conversation, the opera is about to begin," Edward said, again indicating they all take their seats.

Elizabeth gave a little laugh and said quietly to Lord Ainsby, "We will probably be the only people present actually listening to the opera."

"I heard that," her brother said, his voice deep with a mix of disapproval and laughter.

She just giggled, sharing a smile with Lord Ainsby.

They sat through the first half with Elizabeth studiously keeping her gaze on the stage and absolutely refusing to look about the theatre to see what—or rather, who—other people were looking at.

Lord Ainsby wasn't as determined as she. He stole some looks around, even raising his opera glasses a few times to view the occupants of some of the other boxes.

When the curtain came down for the intermission he asked, "Shall we brave the censure or would you rather stay here? I would be happy to bring you a glass of ratafia, if you'd like."

Elizabeth gave him a warm smile. "I appreciate that, but no, the point is to see and be seen. The only way to do that is to leave the box. On the other hand, Bel, please don't feel you—"

"Don't be ridiculous, Elizabeth, I'm going to be with you and the gentlemen, of course," Bel interrupted her.

"Let's just hope we don't run into any difficulties. I haven't practiced with my pistols for some time," Edward said with a wink. He meant it as a joke, Elizabeth was sure, but it was simply too close to the truth for her to find it amusing.

"I do hope Lady Findlater isn't here," she commented as they filed from the box.

"Not that I've seen," Lord Ainsby said.

The notorious gossip herself may not have

been present, but there were a few of her cronies. Sadly, one of them was Lady Wraxley, who never felt the need to curb her tongue.

"I suppose they're keeping it all in the family, although I didn't realize cousins shared mistresses," they overheard the woman say to her companion.

Bel gasped and Elizabeth could just barely make out a growl coming from deep within her brother's throat.

"We do not pay any attention to snide comments of lonely, nasty, old women, Bel," Elizabeth said loudly enough for Lady Wraxley to hear.

Bel's eyes widened in shock, and she quickly covered her mouth with her hand. Elizabeth couldn't tell if she were merely surprised or laughing at her comment. From the corner of her eye, she caught the gentlemen exchange a look of surprise and mirth.

"Well, well," said a man's voice. Merely the sound of it made Elizabeth's skin crawl, and she resisted the urge to run.

She paused to look directly into the eyes of Lord Rogan before deliberately turning her back on him.

"I merely wanted to ask if you were having a pleasant evening," he said to her back. "I noticed that Miss Kendrick looked to be enraptured by the performance." His voice sounded much too normal and kind for Elizabeth. He was a monster and didn't have the right to actually be pleasant and polite.

She heard her brother say, "If you know what's best for your health, Rogan, you will keep your distance."

"Is that a threat, Lord Conway?" the man asked loud enough to draw the attention of other people standing about.

"Yes. Yes, it is. Good evening to you." Edward gave him a slight nod before joining Elizabeth and Bel.

"I can't believe he had the nerve to address you," Lord Ainsby said quietly.

"If I never see or hear from him again in my life, I might be satisfied," Elizabeth commented.

"If only that were possible," Edward said. "It's difficult when the *haute ton* is comprised of such a limited number of people."

"But he is not good *ton*," Elizabeth pointed out.

"Maybe not, but he's still received everywhere," Lord Ainsby said.

"He was remarkably pleasant just now," Bel said with an apologetic note to her voice.

"Do not be fooled, my dear. He is a snake in the grass," Edward told his fiancée.

"Why can nothing be done?" Bel asked. "After what he did, you would think people would spurn him."

"Sadly, it is the way of the world that a man in this situation is merely patted on the back consolingly, while the lady is blamed for the entirety," Elizabeth said.

"What? Are you saying that people blame *you* for the fact that *he* attacked you?" Bel asked.

"That is exactly what I'm saying. That is why no one will speak with me, and my reputation is so severely damaged," Elizabeth said.

"But that's not fair!" Bel cried softly.

"It is wrong in the extreme, and yet, that is the way of the world," Lord Ainsby agreed.

~May 7~

After seeing how well behaved Bolton's spaniels had been, Penelope was determined that her little Duchess should learn to behave that way as well. She had never taken the time to do any sort of training with the little dog, but she didn't see any reason why she shouldn't do so now.

To that end, she took Duchess out once again on her lead to the park. Surely if she were a little firmer, the dog would get the hang of walking this way and stop trying to drag Penelope rather than staying beside her and moving at a reasonable pace.

In the hopes that staying on the path would encourage the dog to walk properly, she avoided the grass. Sadly, instead of staying by her side, the pup once again began to drag her along. She did her best to control the dog, then was absolutely mortified when Duchess caught sight of a man coming in the opposite direction. Duchess crossed in front of Penelope, nearly tripping her, and jumped up on the man's legs.

"I beg your pardon!" Penelope said, pulling the dog back on her lead.

"Really, madam, you should learn to control your dog," the man said, bending down to brush the muddy tracks the animal had left behind on his white stockings.

"I am so sorry. I'm attempting to do that right now." She was so embarrassed, she hurried off, dragging Duchess along and keeping a tight hold of her leash.

"Most unfortunate," a kindly voice said from behind her.

She paused and looked back to find Bolton and his four dogs approaching.

Duchess went wild seeing the other dogs again. She began to bark with excitement and ran back to greet her new friends, dragging Penelope with her.

"Oh, Bolton," Penelope said. She was both horrified that he had witnessed her dog's horrendous behavior and quite thrilled to see the gentleman again. "I'm so embarrassed," she admitted.

He just laughed. "Not your fault. The pup just needs a little training, that's all."

"Yes, I know. That's why we're here," Penelope admitted. "Normally we would stick to the grass so she can't accost any strangers, although she has been known to escape from me even there."

"As she did the first time we met," he said with a twinkle in his eye. "I have to say it wasn't such a bad outcome. But perhaps it is a good thing we happened along. I would be more than happy to assist."

She gave him a grateful smile. They began to walk side by side with the five dogs happily trotting along in front of them. Penelope could only shake her head in wonder. There was no pulling, no dragging, just proper walking. "I don't know what it is, but Duchess always seems to be able to walk so nicely when in the company of your dogs," she commented.

"I think she knows that any other sort of behavior would be frowned upon," he said, jovially.

"But how does she know this?"

He leaned a little closer to her. "Perhaps you haven't noticed, but Fluff has given her a nip every so often when she's gotten out of line."

Penelope looked down at the dogs. Indeed, Fluff was walking by Duchess's side and seemed to be keeping a close eye on her. "Perhaps that's all that she's needed—an older dog to teach her how to behave."

"She'll need a little guidance from you as well, but I'll show you how to teach her." His smile warmed her straight to her toes, and Penelope was certain she was about to have a much more pleasant afternoon than she'd anticipated.

Chapter Fifteen

~May 8~

Elizabeth walked into Lady Ayres's drawing room, doing her best not to show just how nervous she felt. The last time she'd paid morning calls, she'd learned she was being blamed for Lord Rogan's attack of her and that her reputation was completely ruined.

Today would be different. She knew that, so really, there was no reason to be nervous. This was yet another piece of the ladies' campaign to rebuild her reputation.

"Good afternoon, Lady St. Vincent, how lovely to see you again," Lady Ayres said, rising and giving her a nod and a smile. Elizabeth paused and curtsied to the older lady.

"Good afternoon, my lady. Oh, and Lady Blakemore, what a pleasant surprise. I didn't know if I would be seeing you here today." Elizabeth said, giving both women a smile. With these powerful ladies here, she wouldn't have any troubles, she was certain. They were both eminently respected. No one would say anything against her with them here to defend her, surely, and maybe even some of the respect they commanded would rub off on her. She could only hope!

"Well, well, don't you have some nerve!" another lady said from the other side of the room.

Her good feelings immediately dropped from her heart to the pit of her stomach where it cramped. "I don't believe we've met," Elizabeth said, forcing her lips to stay curved in a slight smile.

"Lady St. Vincent, may I make you known to Lady Petersley," Lady Ayres said. "But I don't believe I understand your comment, my lady," she said, turning back to the woman.

The woman's eyes narrowed. "Of course you do, Lady Ayres. Unless you've been completely absent from Town—and I know you have not—you will know that Lady St. Vincent here has been behaving a way most unbecoming to a lady of society."

Lady Ayres's eyes went wide. She turned from Lady Petersley to Elizabeth, giving her a little wink, which did little to calm Elizabeth's clenched stomach. "Lady St. Vincent, do you know what Lady Petersley is referring to?"

Elizabeth had no choice but to play along. She too widened her eyes, trying to look as innocent and confused as she could. "I do beg your pardon, Lady Ayres, but I fear she might be referring to some rumors which have been circulating, perpetuated by those who somehow get pleasure by making entirely false statements about others. Is that correct, my lady?"

"You can just stop this charade, ladies," Lady Petersley said. Clearly, she had no sense of humor.

"Oh, you wouldn't happen to be referring to that patently and ridiculously false rumor that began when Lord Rogan attacked Lady St. Vincent at Lady Welles's party a few weeks ago?" Lady

Ayres asked.

"She must be, Lady Ayres," Lady Blakemore said, joining in the conversation.

Elizabeth suddenly realized that everyone in the room had quieted to listen to the exchange. There weren't many people there, but certainly enough to pass along whatever was said.

"But anyone who knows Lady St. Vincent would know that those rumors are entirely untrue," Lady Blakemore said as if it were obvious.

"I strongly doubt that, my lady," Lady Petersley said. "Why I heard it from Lady Yarworth, who heard it from—"

"Stop right there, Lady Petersley. Are you saying that you are accusing a woman of an absolutely heinous crime based on hearsay?" Lady Blakemore asked.

"Not hearsay!" Lady Petersley protested.

"But did you not just say you heard it, what was it, secondhand? Thirdhand, perhaps?" Lady Ayres asked, joining in again.

"Well, yes, but—"

"But what, my lady? Are you so incapable of thinking for yourself that you are willing to believe third-hand gossip over the word of the lady involved in the incident herself?" Lady Blakemore asked with a lift of one eyebrow.

Lady Petersley opened her mouth to speak but clearly could find nothing to say.

"Right. Well, Lady Petersley, I would like to suggest you stop believing everything you hear and, instead, attempt to determine the truth for yourself," Lady Ayres said. She then turned to Elizabeth, who was feeling as unbalanced as Lady

Petersley seemed to be. "Lady St. Vincent, did you *invite* Lord Rogan to make his inappropriate advances?"

"No! Of course not! They were repulsive to me," Elizabeth said vehemently.

"And what about the man who it was said you went home with? Mr. Aldridge," another woman asked with some satisfaction as if she'd gotten the better of Ladies Ayres and Blakemore.

"Mr. Aldridge was kind enough to see me to my carriage when I was ill after Lord Rogan's attack," Elizabeth said. "He did nothing more. In fact, I didn't even know him then, and I only had the pleasure of meeting him after this all occurred." She wondered just how many times she would have to explain this same thing. Actually, she thought, she would explain it as many times as necessary—five times a day, even—just so long as people began to believe her rather than the nasty rumors.

"There you have it," Lady Ayres said as if that took care of that. She sat back down on the sofa where she'd been when Elizabeth had come into the room. "Would you care for some tea, Lady St. Vincent?" She smiled up at her with true friendship.

Elizabeth returned her smile. "Thank you, my lady, I'd love a cup." She wanted something much stronger, but it wouldn't do to say so. Instead, she accepted the tea that was handed to her.

"I don't suppose anyone else would like to question this poor innocent and much maligned woman?" Lady Blakemore asked, looking around the room.

No one seemed to even be willing to meet the lady's eyes much less argue with her.

"Well then, let's move on to a much more

pleasant conversation. My niece has decided upon a wedding this autumn. Have you heard, Lady St. Vincent?"

"Yes! I imagine it's going to be quite magnificent—if I know my brother," Elizabeth said, beginning to feel her heart calm for the first time since she'd walked into the room.

"Is he going to have a hand in the arrangements?" Lady Ayres asked, sounding quite shocked.

"Oh, no!" Elizabeth said, laughing. "I simply mean he has given Bel leave to spend whatever she deems necessary to make it the most beautiful event."

"What a shame it is that it won't be held in Town," Lady Blakemore said. "I could just see them walking down the aisle at St. Paul's."

"But it will be ever so much more exclusive this way. I'm certain my brother will sing," Elizabeth said with a bright smile, happy to be a part of something that so many would love to witness.

"Lord Conway has an incredible voice, doesn't he?" Lady Ayres said, nodding.

"Better than some of the so-called professional singers on the stage, if you ask me," Lady Blakemore commented. She turned back to Lady Petersley who was still watching Elizabeth closely. She didn't say anything because she was too genteel, but she had a sparkle of laughter in her eyes when she turned back to Elizabeth.

~May 9~

Charles had never been to Gentleman Jackson's Boxing Salon. Given all that had been happening in the past few weeks, he was more than happy to entertain his cousin's suggestion that they meet there and literally take a jab at each other.

Ainsby was already there when Charles arrived. He'd stripped down to his breeches and was standing bare-chested, winding a cloth around his hands.

"You look ready to do some damage," Charles said, laughing at his cousin.

"I feel ready. I imagine you do as well?" Ainsby asked, smiling at him.

"Most certainly," Charles agreed readily. He began to strip and was soon half-naked like his cousin. Someone handed him some gloves to protect his hands. He was in the process of putting them on when Lords Hanslow and Swinton, the men who'd been the first to accuse Charles of sleeping with Lady St. Vincent, walked in. He stopped what he was doing.

"What is it?" Ainsby asked, looking over toward the door.

"I'm sorry, but I see two men who I'd much rather throw a punch at than you. Is it all right if I go and ask if one of them would be willing? I don't know the etiquette here."

"Who is that? Hanslow?" Ainsby asked, squinting across the room.

"Yes, and Lord Swinton."

"Can't say I have any fondness for either of them. Yes, let's," he said, and started across the room. "Hanslow," Ainsby said in greeting.

"Ainsby and Aldridge," Lord Hanslow said, beginning to disrobe.

"I was wondering if you'd be interested in sparring with me, Hanslow?" Charles asked. What he'd really like to do is beat the man bloody, but he supposed that was frowned upon in this establishment. It was supposed to a gentlemen's sport, and apparently, Mr. Jackson did all he could to keep it that way.

Lord Hanslow sized Charles up, probably figured he had a good stone or two on him and then smiled. "Happy to."

"Swinton?" Ainsby asked, turning to the other man.

Lord Swinton was a rather slender fellow, but he gave a shrug. "So long as we keep it friendly, Ainsby."

"Of course! Wouldn't consider anything else," Ainsby said with a smile that Charles knew belied his words. Growing up, Charles had seen that particular smile a good number of times just before his slightly older cousin bested him in whatever they were playing.

Charles shared a look with Ainsby, giving him a smile and a nod. "How about if we warm a bit while the two gentlemen prepare themselves?"

"Excellent idea!" Ainsby turned and stepped into the nearest ring and put up his fists.

As he and Charles threw a few light punches at each other, Charles said, "Don't hurt him too badly, eh? I wouldn't want your reputation to suffer any consequences. These men are gossips of the worst sort from what I understand."

Ainsby chuckled. "Oh, don't worry about me. I know where to hit, where not, and just how far I can push a man."

"Before he breaks down into tears?" Charles asked with a laugh, dodging his cousin's fist.

Ainsby burst out laughing. Charles saw from

the corner of his eye that the other two men seemed to be ready and so left his cousin to seek his new partner.

He and Hanslow moved into the next ring. Charles waited patiently while the fellow threw a few punches into the air to warm himself up. When he was given a nod, he approached.

As Hanslow's fists were already in position, he didn't hesitate but immediately went on the attack. Hanslow attempted to defend himself but wasn't particularly adept. Charles was faster and, perhaps because he had no training but was merely going with his gut instincts, put his punches where Hanslow seemed least likely to expect them.

"My word, Aldridge," Hanslow objected, already winded after just a few minutes. He gave a slight laugh. "Give a fellow a chance."

"Why should I do that?" Charles asked. "Did you give me a chance when you attacked me at Powell's last week?" He jabbed at Hanslow's abdomen. "I don't believe you did. No, no, in fact, I distinctly remember that whenever I tried to defend either myself or Lady St. Vincent, you cut me off and didn't allow me to get in a word." He threw a right-left combination that caught Hanslow completely off-guard, again leaving him panting and slightly doubled over.

"I... I didn't..."

"Oh, you most certainly did. And I have to say you were quite creative in your accusations, something which I can't say I appreciated one bit." Charles took a slight step back to allow the man to breathe for a moment. He didn't give him much time, however, before he stepped forward and began his attack again.

"I didn't make up..."

"Oh, no? Then who told you I'd gone home with Lady St. Vincent?"

"Rogan. It was Lord Rogan," the fellow said, attempting to protect himself from Charles's onslaught.

"Rogan wasn't there. He wouldn't have known what I did or didn't do," Charles informed him as he landed another blow to Hanslow's side.

"You should take that up with him. I was just repeating—"

"I suggest you stop repeating things which you have no knowledge of," Charles said, landing one final blow just below the man's ribcage. Hanslow doubled over before dropping to his knees, not able to breathe for the moment.

Charles just left him there. Ainsby joined him as he was getting dressed. Charles glanced into the ring where Swinton was hanging onto the ropes, circling the ring, panting. "You know, Ainsby, I am very glad you invited me here this afternoon. This was a great deal more enjoyable than I'd anticipated."

His cousin gave him a smile. "I always feel so much lighter, more relaxed afterward."

Charles gave a little laugh. "Yes! Yes, that is precisely how I feel. Shall we get something to eat?"

"An excellent suggestion. Powell's or someplace else?"

"Oh, let's go to Powell's. I like their flattened duck."

Ainsby burst out laughing, and they finished getting dressed in excellent accord.

Chapter Sixteen

~May 10~

The home of Mr. and Mrs. East couldn't have been any more different from the Foreman's home, Charles thought soon after he walked in and was greeted by his host and hostess. The Foreman's drawing room had been done in the latest fashion, looking almost as if everything had just come from the most exclusive shops. The East's home, however, was more settled and well-worn. To Charles's eye, it actually looked a great deal more comfortable.

"We're so happy you were able to join us this evening," Mrs. East said after they'd been introduced.

"I am honored to have been invited," Charles said, smiling. Oddly, it didn't look as if their daughter was yet present.

"You're probably wondering where my daughter is, eh?" Mr. East asked with a little laugh. "The girl likes to make an entrance."

"Mr. East," his wife scolded in a good-natured way.

He just gave Charles a shrug and a wink.

"Why don't we sit down and have a drink while we're waiting for Lucy to join us, shall we?" Mrs.

East said kindly.

Charles was happy to do so, but couldn't help but wonder at a girl who arrived late to her parents' own dinner party.

Finally, about a quarter of an hour later, a young lady came into the room in a flurry. "I do *so* beg your pardon for being tardy," the girl said. She was waving a lace fan in front of her face, making it difficult for Charles to see exactly what she looked like. He did catch a glimpse of thin pink lips, rouged cheeks, and deep brown eyes all set in a very slender face surrounded by carefully arranged blonde curls.

"My maid…" she turned to Mrs. East. "Mother, you really should turn her off, she takes so very long to do something as simple as putting up my hair."

"We'll discuss it later, my dear," Mrs. East said gently. "Let me make you known to Mr. Aldridge. Mr. Aldridge, my daughter, Miss Lucy East."

Charles, who had stood as soon as the girl came through the door, now bowed. "It is a pleasure."

The girl curtsied deep enough to be welcoming the Prince Regent. She did so very elegantly, but it really wasn't appropriate for Charles who had no title at all, let alone a royal one. Her mother was clearly embarrassed by the show and said hesitantly, "Why don't you get yourself a glass of wine, my dear, and join us."

Miss East gave her mother a nod and Charles a rather saucy smile before slinking off to the sideboard where the wine and glasses were.

After starting to watch her bottom sway provocatively as she walked, he quickly turned back toward the girl's father who had simply closed his eyes, as if he couldn't bear to see what his daughter was doing.

The girl joined them a minute later, taking the seat directly next the Charles, who was sitting on the sofa. "Mr. Aldridge, my father tells me that you are a very busy man," she said, smiling warmly at him.

He gave her a polite smile in return. "Indeed. Like your father, I am a watchmaker."

Her eyes grew wide. "Oh, how very... But you do more than that! He said you were also invited to just about every society party." She looked at him so expectantly, he almost hated to disappoint her.

"I am invited to *some* parties, Miss East."

"And your mother? Isn't she a member of society?" the girl asked with a tilt of her head.

"Er, yes, I suppose you could say that. She does attend a good number of parties and has quite a few friends who are members of society," he said.

"You must tell me all about it!" she said, leaning closer.

"I do believe dinner must be ready," Mr. East interrupted, much to Charles's relief. The man jumped up and held out his hand to his daughter. "Come, Lucy, let us proceed to the dining room, shall we?"

It was an unusual arrangement, but Charles invited Mrs. East to take his arm as they went into the dining room. He would have thought that Mr. East would be eager for him to escort his daughter, and he rather wondered why he wasn't.

Miss East turned out to be as loquacious as Miss Foreman had been silent. She chattered constantly throughout dinner, asking Charles all about society parties and, more specifically, all the people she read about in gossip pages of various newspapers.

"You are exceedingly well informed, Miss East," Charles said after she'd asked him a very specific question involving people he'd never even met.

"Well, as someone who plans on becoming a member of the *haute ton*, I believe it's my duty to know absolutely everything that is going on. I would be sadly remiss not to be up on every bit of news about people with whom I expect to become quite close," she said, blinking at him.

Her absolute certainty that she would somehow soon become a member of society was quite baffling, so Charles asked, "And how are you going to become a member of the *haute ton*, if you don't mind my asking?"

She widened her eyes at him and then giggled. "Why, through you, you silly one!"

Charles was just taking a sip of his wine when she said this and nearly spat it straight out again. He coughed for a moment, trying to catch his breath.

"Are you all right, sir?" Mrs. East asked.

"Yes, yes. Just went down the wrong way. Please excuse me," Charles said, still choking a little. "Er, I do beg your pardon, Miss East, but how, and more importantly, *why* do you think I would introduce you to society?"

"What? Why, after we are married, of course," the girl said in all honesty.

Luckily, this time Charles wasn't drinking when she came out with this outrageous statement.

"My dear, it is customary to allow the

gentleman to propose, not the other way around," her father said, laughing.

Charles was happy that the gentleman was finding the girl amusing. He certainly wasn't.

"Oh, I know, and you must excuse me, Mr. Aldridge, for being so forthright, but I am so certain you will ask me that I'm merely anticipating the delights to come," she said, fluttering her eyelashes at him.

"You seem to have a wonderful imagination, Miss East," Charles said. It was the only polite thing he could think of to say.

~May 11~

Elizabeth couldn't help the smile that came to her face as she entered the auction room and recognized absolutely no one. She breathed a sigh of relief and headed to an empty seat toward the right side of the room.

She'd woken up that morning feeling exhausted from all the politicking she'd been doing and could only imagine that a good number of her friends felt the same way. She just needed a day to herself, so when she saw the advertisement in the paper about the auction, she knew immediately it was precisely what she should do.

She'd never actually been to an auction before, so she was looking forward to the experience. She did know enough to have come with an idea in mind as to what she wanted to purchase, but aside from that, she was open to possibilities.

"Lady St. Vincent, what a surprise!" a gentleman's voice pulled her from her happy thoughts. Immediately, she felt her spine stiffen and her stomach clench, but then she turned and found Mr. Aldridge smiling down at her and she relaxed again.

"Mr. Aldridge, a surprise indeed," she said, smiling at him. "Would you care to join me or are you meeting someone?"

"I would be honored. I am alone this afternoon."

She moved over one chair, and he took the one she'd been sitting in at the end of the row.

"So, what brings you here today?" he asked with a warm smile.

"I'm interested in purchasing a vase, actually," she admitted. "I have something in mind, but I'd like to see what's on offer here."

"You wouldn't just go to a shop for such a purchase?" Mr. Aldridge asked.

"I could, I suppose, but something out of the ordinary would be so much more interesting. I was thinking of a Chinese cloisonné or perhaps a Japanese painted enamel."

"That sounds fascinating and most unusual."

"I understand all the pieces today are going to be various types of enamel," she said. "Although I don't know a great deal about the art form, I have always found it to be very pleasing to the eye."

His smile grew warmer still, making her heart skip a beat. "I cannot but agree with you."

"What are you here to purchase—if anything?" she asked.

"I'm actually here to get ideas for watch covers. There is some very fine enamel work being created here in England. Before I hire artists, I'd like to see what there is on offer and perhaps get ideas for designs that might be popular," he told her.

"Oh, for your business! You're a watchmaker?"

she asked. She'd always known he was a businessman, but she'd never knew what sort of company he owned.

"Yes, I am." He pulled out the most beautiful watch from his pocket and flipped it open with just a touch of his fingernail to the lid. As he did so, it began to ting ever so softly. "Precisely two," he commented. "I expect they'll get started soon."

"That is a most interesting watch," she said, looking at it more closely.

He held it out for her to see. "My father made it for me. It's a repeater. It chimes on the hour."

"How fascinating! I don't know that I've ever seen a pocket watch do so," she said, smiling up at him.

"It's not a very popular design, but I like it. I can know the hour without even having to pull it from my pocket."

"Yes, I can see how that would be very useful. So, you are interested in enamel covers for your watches. I've seen quite a few, and they can be quite beautiful."

"Yes, indeed. If at all possible, I'd like the ones on my watches to be distinctive." He seemed as if he were going to say more, but a man strode up onto the stage and banged a gavel for everyone's attention.

"Ladies and gentlemen, without further ado, I'd like to get started," the man said. As he did so, three men came from a back room and placed the first lot of items on the stage.

Three hours later, Elizabeth had purchased two vases, and Mr. Aldridge had bought some interesting enamel-work pieces as well.

After Elizabeth arranged to have her vases delivered to her home, Mr. Aldridge gave the man an address where he wanted his items sent.

"Are they not going to your home for you to enjoy or study?" Elizabeth asked.

"No. I'm sending them to the artist I plan to hire so he can see the sorts of designs I'd like him to recreate," Mr. Aldridge said as he accepted his receipt.

"I see, that's very clever," she said.

He placed a very light hand on the small of her back to direct her away from the table so the next person could arrange for their items. "Would you care to join me for an ice or a cup of tea?"

She looked up at his very pleasant, friendly countenance and said, "I couldn't think of anything I'd rather do more. It would make a perfect end to this lovely afternoon. Thank you."

His eyes twinkled with happiness, and he led her outside and toward his carriage. She paused to give directions to her own coachman and then joined him.

They were lucky and found a table inside the shop when they arrived at Gunter's. Elizabeth was pleasantly surprised.

"I think we've missed the worst of the crowds," Mr. Aldridge commented.

"What's the time?" she asked with a broad smile, certain he was always happy to pull out his beautiful pocket watch.

Indeed, he gave her a brilliant smile as he did so. "It's nearly half past five," he said, briefly consulting his timepiece.

"Ah, so most people have gone home to get

dressed for the evening," Elizabeth said, with a nod.

"Oh! Do you need to be off to do the same?" he asked, beginning to stand back up.

She reached out a hand and placed it on his arm. "No, not at all. I am looking forward to a quiet night at home this evening. I'm in no rush at all."

He settled back down again. "Good. I'm glad," he said, and then looked a little unsure of himself. "I mean, I'm glad you have time to have an ice, not that I wouldn't want you to go out."

She giggled. "I think I understood your meaning."

A waiter approached, and she ordered her favorite, a lavender-flavored ice.

"That sounds fascinating, I'd like one as well," he told the man.

"They're better than the usual lemon," she told him.

"I'm looking forward to it."

"Do you have plans for this evening?" she asked, getting back to their conversation.

"No. I am also hoping to have a quiet night. I want to work some more on a watch design I've been toying with, and the evenings are the easiest time to do so." He smiled at her. "I have neither my business nor my mother making demands on me."

She laughed and then happily dug into the ice that had been placed before her. She closed her eyes in bliss as the cold treat melted on her tongue, but when she opened them again, she found herself being stared at by two young ladies in the company of an older woman. The older woman turned to see who the younger ones were staring at. With a gasp, she turned both girls around and hurried them from the shop. "There is a fine example of what you should *never* become, girls," Elizabeth could hear the woman say as they walked away.

Elizabeth could only sigh.

"I don't suppose you can ever be free of this," Mr. Aldridge said softly.

She turned and looked into his sympathetic eyes. "No, I think not."

"At least not for the moment," he quickly corrected himself. "I'm certain that your reputation *will* be reestablished."

"But it will take a good amount of time," Elizabeth said, forcing a smile onto her lips. She appreciated his efforts at trying to bolster her emotions.

"Yes, but it will happen if you want it to."

"I can only hope, Mr. Aldridge." She did not want to give horrid people another thought, so she forcefully put them out of her mind. She turned to her companion and asked, "And how do you find the lavender-flavored ice?"

"It's much better than I had imagined."

She smiled. "So, you were just humoring me when you ordered it?"

"Oh, no! I truly wanted to taste it. And now I'm glad I did!"

Chapter Seventeen

~May 13~

Penelope was happily walking along with Bolton, Duchess beside Fluffy.

"I believe Fluff thinks she has a new pup," Bolton commented, looking down at the dogs as the older spaniel bumped the younger to put her back in line with the others. Duchess looked around to Penelope with a look that seemed to ask if she had to listen to Fluffy.

Penelope just laughed. "Yes, I do believe you're right. Well, I know she's already learned quite a lot from your pups."

"It's thanks to your dedication, bringing her out every day to walk with us," Bolton said, giving her a smile.

Penelope felt her face heat with his praise. "Oh, well, it's so kind of you to allow us to join you."

"It's no trouble at all to me. I'm here every day, weather permitting." He paused and then added, "Of course, the daily walk has become so much more pleasant now that I have human company."

"It's been quite lovely for me as well," Penelope added. "You always choose the quieter paths too, which I think helps Duchess. There aren't so many distractions." A strong breeze blew, ruffling the dog's long ears. Duchess shook out her head.

Bolton nodded but didn't say anything beyond, "A touch windy today, eh?"

"Yes, but not cold, happily," Penelope said. She paused and then spoke what was at the forefront of her mind. "May I... May I ask you a question?"

"I believe you just did, but go ahead and ask me another," he said with a little chuckle.

She laughed but then became a little more serious before she asked, "Do you ever attend society functions?"

"Society? As in the parties of the *haute ton*?" he asked. She noted his smile slip as he did so.

"Yes. I don't believe I've ever seen you at one," she probed.

"No, you haven't. I... I'm not a very social person. I'm afraid I prefer the quiet companionship of my dogs and that's about it."

"But going out to parties can be quite entertaining. You get to meet friends and—"

"Yes, well, I don't have many friends among that set."

"None at all?" she asked, wondering once again whether he truly was the gentleman he appeared to be. Since he'd never given her anything other than the one name and no title at all, she had no idea who he really was, and that was awkward.

He sighed. "I did, once upon a time, but I haven't exactly kept in touch with them. As I say, I've been living in the country for so long..."

"So, what did make you move back to the city?"

"My daughter," he explained too briefly.

"Oh dear. Do you not get along?"

"No. We do. It's just... I was in the way—well, me and the dogs," he explained.

"How were you in the way in your own home?" Penelope asked.

"Oh, well, she was, er, in the family way, you know. Her husband is off fighting, and so she's been staying with me. But when it came time for her to...er, you know..."

"Have her baby?" Penelope guessed.

"Yes. When it came to be that time, I figured it would be better if the dogs and I weren't about. All that female business, you know. And, er, babies. I was never one for babies."

Penelope laughed. "But you had her, and I presume other children?"

"Yes, there's Susan and Theo, but I made sure I wasn't around for a good bit when they came into the world. Returned when they were a month or so into life and had settled down."

"I don't understand why you wouldn't want to be there when your own children—or grandchildren—were born," Penelope mused.

"Had another one," Bolton said softly. "Abraham. Named after me—his mother insisted."

Penelope turned toward him curiously.

Bolton kept his gaze firmly on the backs of the dogs walking before them. "I was there for his birth. Only had the one dog then too. There was... There was an accident between me, the dog, and the baby."

"Oh, dear," Penelope breathed.

"Babies are damned fragile things, don't you know?" he said. He coughed a few times into his handkerchief before wiping his face with it.

"Did he...?"

"Died, yes. His mother blamed me, and rightfully so."

"I'm so sorry," she said, putting her free hand on his sleeve.

He gave it a little pat, smiling sadly at her. "So, you see, after that, I always made sure to stay out of the way when a newborn was involved. Better that way. And of course, I keep the dogs with me."

"Yes, I understand." The poor, poor man! Penelope's heart went out to him.

They walked on in silence for a few minutes, but Penelope couldn't leave her original idea alone. "Do you have no desire to meet your old friends again? Go to, perhaps, one of the quieter parties? A soirée or a dinner party?"

Bolton gave a little chuckle. "Don't know that anyone would remember me. There's no need, truly. I'm quite happy with my quiet life, and in another few weeks, I'll return home and see what my daughter has produced. I received a letter saying it was a boy."

"Congratulations on that. But I couldn't entice you..."

"No, no. Thank you, though."

He seemed to be absolutely set on avoiding society, which Penelope thought was such a shame. He was such a sweet man. She was sure he must still have friends among the ton, if he were to make an effort at renewing his acquaintances. But he clearly had no desire to do so. That baffled her more than anything.

She was mulling this over when she caught sight of Lord Rogan riding by. She had a hard time not exclaiming at his presence. It was a public park, after all, she reminded herself. There was nothing she could or should do but give the man a cold shoulder.

~*~

"Come along, Mummy," Matthew called as he raced ahead of Elizabeth onto the grass.

"Don't go too far," she called after him. She picked up her skirts and ran after the boy. "I think your kite will fly today."

He paused and looked up into the sky, as if looking for the breeze. "Do you fink so?" He didn't even wait for her to respond before taking off running, holding his kite into the air behind him.

"Let go of the kite, but hold the string tightly," Elizabeth instructed.

He did so, and amazingly enough, the kite took off.

"Mummy! Mummy, look!" he screeched as he both ran and watched behind him at the kite dodging this way and that in the breeze.

"Well done, Matthew!" Elizabeth said, laughing. She caught up with him but also kept her eye on the kite, hoping the child wouldn't let go of the string.

Neither one of them noticed the tree until a branch swooped down with the breeze and caught the kite amongst its leaves.

"Oh, no!" Matthew yelled. "The tree! It grabbed my kite! Mummy, do somefing! Do somefing quick before it eats my kite!"

"All right, Matthew, it's all right. We'll rescue your kite," Elizabeth said, trying to catch her breath. The words had just popped out of her mouth, but indeed, she had no idea how she was going to reach it.

She examined the tree, but the lowest branch was the one that had caught the toy, and it was well above her head and out of arm's reach as well.

Matthew started tugging at the string, trying to pull the kite free.

"No, no, if you pull too hard, the kite might rip or break," Elizabeth said, stilling his hand.

"But what are we to do?" he whined.

"I don't—"

"May I be of assistance?" a man's voice came from the road nearby.

Elizabeth turned and was horrified to find Lord Rogan watching them with a smile on his face. He was mounted on an enormous gelding.

"No—" Elizabeth started.

"Oh, yes, sir, please, can you reach my kite?" Matthew interrupted her.

"Of course, my boy, since you asked so very politely," Lord Rogan said. He slowly walked his horse under the tree. On top of the animal, he was able to reach up and extricate the toy carefully from the tree's grasp. He handed it down to the child. "Here you are," he said, smiling down at the boy.

Matthew took the kite, jumping up and down with joy. "Thank you, thank you, thank you! Look, Mummy, he got it, he got it!"

"Yes, I see that," Elizabeth said, giving Matthew a brief smile. It was gone from her face when she turned back to Lord Rogan. "Thank you, Lord Rogan." She would not model bad behavior for her child, no matter what her feelings.

"You are most welcome, Lady St. Vincent. I

didn't know you had a son," the man said, smiling at her with a lasciviousness that turned Elizabeth's stomach.

"Yes. Good day." She turned her back on him and took Matthew's hand. "Come along, my love. We need to return home."

"But can't I fly my kite some more? I'll stay away from trees, I promise, Mummy," Matthew whined.

"Not if you take that tone with me," she warned as she led him away.

"I won't. Please, Mummy?" Matthew softened his voice and tried his best to control the whine in it.

"Very well. We'll fly it back toward the gate, how about that?" Elizabeth relented. She just couldn't deny her sweet, little boy, no matter how sick she felt at being forced to accept a kindness from Lord Rogan.

She also couldn't help but be rather amazed at how very kind and, well, rather gentlemanly he'd been. She'd never seen the man behave that way. She was both grateful and a little confused that he was capable of such behavior when all she'd ever experienced was his horrid, lewd actions. She supposed even the most dreadful people had a touch of kindness in them—especially when it came to dealing with children.

~*~

"Charles, you are going to be so happy you came this evening," his mother said, smiling up at him.

He was pretty certain he *would* be happy he'd come, but not for the reason she thought. He did like making his mother happy, however, so he said nothing but smiled at her.

He was there to see Lady St. Vincent. His mother wanted to match him up with every other eligible girl present. It was going to be a dance in more ways than one. Only time would tell whether his mother would stay happy or if he would be the one to go home with a smile on his face.

Speaking of time... Charles pulled out his pocket watch. It was only half past nine. He didn't know if Lady St. Vincent was the sort to arrive earlier to a party or not. He rather hoped she was, otherwise...

"Oh, Lady Welles, Lady Colburne, you remember my son, Charles," his mother said, dragging him toward two young ladies he'd met a few times before. They were safe now that they'd both married. When he'd first met them last season, he could just see the calculations going on in his mother's mind, wondering which one of them might catch his attention.

"Yes, of course, we actually met last week at the park," Lady Colburne said, giving him a smile. "Did you and Lady St. Vincent have a pleasant stroll?"

"We did, thank you. You haven't seen her here tonight, have you?" He couldn't help but ask.

"No, not as yet," she said, narrowing her eyes ever so slightly while giving him a little smile.

He wondered if he'd given himself away already.

"I do hope she's coming this evening. I haven't spoken with her for a few days," Lady Welles commented.

"I saw her on Monday, but she didn't mention whether she would be here tonight or not," Charles admitted.

His mother turned to him. "You saw Lady St.

Vincent on Monday?"

"Yes, at the auction I went to, actually. I ran into her there," he said.

"Oh. You didn't mention it," she said, giving him a closer look.

He decided nonchalant was his best move and gave her a warm smile. "I don't tell you everything I do, Mother."

"No, of course not. You're a grown man," she said, turning back to her friends. He could see she was still thinking about it, though.

"So, you absolutely must tell me who Charles should dance with this evening. He is on the market, you know, and *very* eligible," she said to her friends with a broad smile. Or maybe she wasn't thinking about it anymore, he thought, correcting himself.

"Mother, I'm certain—"

"Well, he really should seek out Miss Poppinray," Lady Welles said at the same time. "She is quite lovely and such a sweet girl."

"And Miss Holdsbury," Lady Colburne added. "Her father is on the racing circuit with us, although I don't believe he's raced on the Continent like my father and I."

"Perfect," his mother said, clapping her hands together lightly. "Introduce us!"

"Mother—" Charles started. He most certainly did not want his mother being introduced to any young ladies. It was difficult enough that she was dragging him around like a prized piece to begin with.

Lady Welles giggled. "I have a feeling Mr. Aldridge would rather not be introduced with his mother in tow."

Lady Colburne laughed as well. "It does give a particular impression."

Charles's mother's eyes widened. "What sort of impression? That he has a loving, caring mother who just wants what's best for him?"

"Or perhaps, a slightly overbearing mother who can't leave his side and will make a nuisance of herself in any potential future household," he said as lightly as he could, adding a little laugh at the end in the hope that she wouldn't take offense.

The two other ladies clearly bit back comments as they shared a look of shock and laughter. Their response just confirmed his statement.

"Oh," was all his mother could find to say. She took in a deep breath. "Well, I wouldn't want to give *that* impression, certainly. I can imagine it might scare off a young lady."

"Exactly so," Charles said.

She gave him a nod and stepped back. "Very well, then, go on. I will see if I can find Lady Blakemore. I'm certain she'll be here tonight with her nieces.

"I believe I saw the duchess and Lady Margaret," Lady Colburne offered.

"Ah..." his mother hedged.

"You've become more friendly with the duchess since last week, haven't you?" Lady Welles asked.

"What happened last week?" Charles asked, happy to postpone the introductions to these young ladies.

"I had thought the Duchess of Kendell didn't particularly like me, but it turns out it's Duchess, my dog, who she doesn't like," his mother said.

"That makes sense. Not everyone likes dogs, no matter how adorable and loving Duchess is," he added, knowing his mother's devotion to her little pup. "But I can't see why anyone wouldn't like *you*."

He was rewarded by a loving smile from his mother.

"Precisely," Lady Welles agreed. "We were all rather perplexed by the duchess's animosity, but it turns out it was simply to Duchess—the dog," she added with a laugh.

"Oh, I see Miss Poppinray right over there, looking as if she'd like to dance, Mr. Aldridge," Lady Colburne said. "May I introduce you?"

"Er, thank you," Charles said, given that he really had no other choice in the matter. He bowed to his mother and Lady Welles but kept a sharp eye out for Lady St. Vincent as he and Lady Colburne made their way over to the young lady in question.

Quite before he knew it, he was leading the young lady out onto the dance floor. She wasn't disappointing like either of the young ladies with whom he'd had dinner recently, and for that, he was glad. Unless she turned out to be incredibly witty and clever, however, he was still going to keep an eye out for the one who he'd actually come to meet.

Chapter Eighteen

Unfortunately, he didn't spot her until he was half-way through a dance with Miss Holdsbury. It was only through sheer force of will and, ultimately, his manners that allowed him to pull his eyes away from Lady St. Vincent once he'd seen her.

She looked absolutely lovely this evening. For once, she wasn't in either purple or gray—the colors she favored, being still in half-mourning for her husband. Charles rather thought it had been more than a year since his death, but clearly the lady had held a great affection for him. Tonight, however, she wore blue. It was a deep, rich color in silk and made her eyes really stand out as they flashed with laughter at something Miss Kendrick said to her. Her laughter floated over to him as he executed a turn with the lady he was dancing with, and it was all he could do to keep his attention where it belonged.

"Do you also race horses, Miss Holdsbury?" he asked, determined to be polite.

"I do not, sir," she said. Her smile was tight as if she'd been asked that question too many times for her liking.

"I don't either. Don't particularly enjoy riding, either," he said with a teasing smile.

Her eyes widened, but the movements of the dance took them apart just at that moment, making it impossible for her to respond right away.

When they came back together again, she said with a laugh, "Don't ever let my father hear you say such traitorous words."

"I will be sure not to share that information with him. I do hope I can count on your discretion as well?" he asked.

She giggled. "I shall remain mum, I promise."

He concentrated on charming her for the rest of the dance, if only to keep himself occupied and not think about Lady St. Vincent, who he'd caught watching them at least once. His partner was positively glowing by the time he returned her to her mother. He bowed. "Thank you so much, Miss Holdsbury, for a most enjoyable dance."

She curtsied and replied, "No, sir, I must thank you. It was the most fun I've had for a while."

He gave them both a smile and walked off to find the true object of his interest. For a moment, his steps stuttered as he contemplated that thought. Lady St. Vincent was indeed the one woman who had caught his interest. At first, he had felt bad for her plight. No one should be so maligned, especially not when one was as innocent as she. But then, the better he'd gotten to know her the more he came to enjoy being with her. She was smart, interesting, and had a mind which she didn't hesitate to use. He appreciated that a great deal in a woman.

But dare he persist in this interest? She had already turned him down once. Of course, that had been before they'd actually gotten to know one another, but still... Well, perhaps it would be worth his time to find out. He continued toward the lady in question.

"Good evening, Miss Kendrick, Lady Blakemore," he bowed. He then turned and gave Lady St. Vincent a warm smile. "My lady, you are looking very nice this evening."

"I was just telling her that she should put off her half-mourning permanently," Miss Kendrick said. "That blue makes her eyes look so bright and pretty, doesn't it?"

Lady St. Vincent blushed prettily.

"Indeed, it does," Charles agreed. "May I be so rude as to steal you away from your companions for the next dance?" he asked.

At this she smiled. "I'm sure they would forgive you."

"Absolutely," Lady Blakemore said immediately.

"I suppose..." Miss Kendrick said with a giggle.

Charles held out his hand, and Lady St. Vincent ever so gently placed hers into it. Immediately, Charles felt a rush of heat and happiness. With her hand in his, nothing could go wrong in the world. She was with him, and he would defend her against all foes. Sadly, there were too many of those present as well, although they seemed to be holding themselves at bay just at the moment. For that, he was glad. He hated seeing her even the least bit unhappy.

~*~

Elizabeth smiled up at Mr. Aldridge as he stepped forward to bow to her at the start of the dance. "I have to say this is a very pleasant surprise."

"What is, my lady?"

"That you are here. I don't believe I've ever

seen you at a ball before," she said, turning with the movements of the dance.

He nodded. "I don't come to parties often, but my mother was insisting and..." He paused as the dance moved them away from each other.

"And?" she asked, when they came together again.

"And I was hoping to see you," he finished.

It was exactly what Elizabeth wished to hear. "You're just saying that to make me happy, aren't you?" she asked with a teasing giggle.

He chuckled. "I would do much to make you happy, but I assure you, I am merely telling you the truth."

"Honest *and* a lover of lavender ices. My, my, Mr. Aldridge you are determined to turn my head, aren't you?"

He just laughed.

Oddly enough they didn't talk very much after that, but Elizabeth felt they communicated very well through their movements. If anyone was watching them or had a word to say, she was oblivious to it all. She noticed no one but Mr. Aldridge for the entire dance—how handsome he was, how sweet and thoughtful, how intelligent... She could go on. He seemed to feel the same way because all he did was smile.

Best of all, though, was the fact that he treated her like an intelligent woman. He truly seemed to respect her for who she was. Oddly, when she was with him, she felt like she could just be herself and not have to worry about making a good impression—that impression was already assumed.

It was almost jarring when the music stopped,

and they suddenly found themselves in the middle of a crowded ball. Elizabeth felt as if she were waking up from a long nap. She laughed and had to keep herself from giving her head a shake.

"Are you warm? Shall we go for a stroll on the balcony?" Mr. Aldridge asked, offering his arm for her to take.

"That sounds lovely," she said, wrapping her hand around his sleeve.

And it *was* a lovely evening. Not too chilly so that she would have to send someone for her shawl, but not too warm either. A million stars shone overhead, twinkling their approval, and she could have laughed for sheer happiness in the evening.

"What makes you smile so beautifully?" Mr. Aldridge asked, turning to lean against the balustrade in a far corner where he'd led her.

"Nothing. It just seems like such a perfect night, that's all." She looked at him. "I'm happy and I feel like I haven't been this way for a very, very long time."

He took her hand in his. "I can't tell you how good it makes me feel, knowing that. I want you to be happy. You deserve to be."

Her smile wavered for just a moment as she wondered if he would make some sort of inappropriate move. She'd been in such a situation a few too many times to feel completely comfortable. Just to be safe, she moved to stand next to him, but faced the garden and looked out into the darkness of the evening. She could hear the rustling and giggles of other couples as they wandered the dark paths, but she was quite content to simply stand in the light spilling from the ballroom.

No, she had absolutely no desire to go for a walk. Instead, she looked up and admired the stars, reciting the constellations silently in her head as she saw them. Mr. Aldridge must have sensed her sudden unease for he, too, turned to face the garden and stare up at the sky.

The silence between them was the most soothing sound in the world. In front of them were the quiet whisperings in the garden, behind them the chatter and music of the ball, but she and Mr. Aldridge seemed to be in a silent, little bubble all their own.

Elizabeth relaxed.

"There they are just like I said. I told you that woman was a harlot. They're probably making plans for their assignation later this evening," the harsh voice of Lady Findlater interrupted the perfect evening.

"You are right, my lady. I have to admit I'm rather surprised not to find them *flagrante delicto* right here. Knowing her, I—"

"How dare you!" Mr. Aldridge spun around to face the women standing directly behind them. "Do you think that we can't hear you?"

"We are doing nothing wrong!" Elizabeth cried, turning around as well.

"You are outside alone with a man you are known to be having a relationship with—in public!" Lady Findlater snapped.

"First of all, I'm a widow. There are plenty of widows who have relationships with gentlemen," Elizabeth said. "Secondly—"

"What Lady St. Vincent does is none of your business," Mr. Aldridge said, interrupting her.

"Yes!" Elizabeth concurred. He'd taken the words right out of her mouth.

"Well, who our daughters are being exposed to and what sort of examples are being set for them most definitely is our business," Lady Wraxley retorted.

"Neither one of you have a daughter who is making her debut this year," Elizabeth pointed out.

"Perhaps not, but it most certainly is our responsibility to see that those of others are only exposed to the best sort of person," Lady Findlater said.

Mr. Aldridge snorted. "Well, if that's the case, you had better remove them to the countryside because they are not going to see anyone remotely resembling that description here in London."

Both women gasped in outrage.

He turned to Elizabeth. "I simply cannot see why these women's opinions matter so much to you, Lady St. Vincent. They are rude, nasty busybodies who are simply out to destroy your fine name."

"Ha! She doesn't have a fine name, there was nothing for us to destroy," Lady Findlater said.

"Never has, never will," Lady Wraxley added.

"I suggest the two of you slink back into your cesspool where you belong," Mr. Aldridge stated most firmly.

The two women gasped again before turned on their heels and stormed away.

"Oh, dear. I'm certain they are off to tell the world what a horrid, rude man you are," Elizabeth said, looking up at him with worry. "I'm so sorry you've become embroiled in my problems. I should never—"

"Please, my lady, stop right there. I have always been involved in this problem because it was mine as well as yours to begin with—if you will remember. I was feted by the idiots at Powell's for doing something which I did not do."

"Oh, yes," she said quietly, remembering what he'd had to endure as well.

"And secondly, I have no problem having my name bandied about because I don't care what anyone in society says about me, and I don't believe you should either. Truly, ma'am, what does it matter what these people think of you?"

"It matters a great deal!" Elizabeth argued. "It is society who decides who is a good person, who is respected, who is treated well, and invited to parties and...and so many other things. Perhaps it shouldn't, but it *does* matter to me." She could feel tears begin to prick at her eyes. "But perhaps you are right in that I should just give up even attempting to regain my good name. It's... It's useless. Those women are going to continue spewing their hate and maligning me." She blinked furiously in an attempt to stop the tears, then turned her face toward the garden so Mr. Aldridge wouldn't see. She just felt so hopeless. "I... I should just go," she said more quietly. "I should return to my estate—well, to St. Vincent's estate and...and stay there."

"Don't you dare!" Mr. Aldridge said, taking a firm hold of her hands, forcing her to turn toward him again. He gave her hands a shake. "Don't you dare give up, Lady St. Vincent. They don't deserve to win, those horrid women. Don't give them that!"

"But I can't... I can't fight them. I've tried.

You've tried. So many of my friends have tried to help me...but it's useless." She sniffed and pulled one of her hands free so she could root around in her reticule for a handkerchief. Thank goodness the tears had abated. At least she would not demean herself so thoroughly.

He was faster at finding his handkerchief and handed it to her.

"Thank you," she said. She took it and wiped her nose and then pressed it to her cheeks to be sure no tears had escaped.

"I will continue to try, Lady St. Vincent," he said gently. "And so will all of your friends, and you must as well. You are too good, too strong to give up now."

"Elizabeth," she said.

"I'm sorry?"

"Please call me by my given name. It's Elizabeth." She gave a watery little laugh. "It sounds odd for you to call me Lady St. Vincent when you are being so wonderful and supportive."

"Oh," he chuckled. "Then you must call me Charles. And I am merely telling you the truth. I think I've come to know you pretty well. Granted, not nearly as well as I'd like to, but still, there will be plenty of time for that because you are not going to run away and hide at your estate. Please. Stay in London. Stay and continue this fight. If you do, I promise you I will stay and fight by your side—as will your stepson, your brother, my cousin Ainsby, as well as all the ladies of the Wagering Whist Society. Elizabeth, you have many, many friends."

"I know. I am so blessed!" she said from her heart. Sadly, just that happy thought made her tears prick at her eyes once again, and she had to hold her breath for a moment to keep them at bay.

"Then you will stay?"

"I..."

"You are strong, Elizabeth. You can do this! *We* can do this together," he said vehemently.

She took in a deep breath and wiped at her face once again. "With your help...and the help of all of my wonderful, wonderful friends, maybe I *can*."

~*~

Later that evening as she was brushing out her hair and getting ready for bed, Elizabeth paused. Mr. Aldridge—Charles's words came back to her mind. Why *did* she care what other people thought of her?

Oh, she knew the answer she'd given him had been the correct one. It *was* important what society thought of a person, it *was* important that one was respected—and it wasn't just so she would be invited to parties; it was so both she and Matthew would have opportunities to be good people, to participate in philanthropic organizations, and be active, productive members of society. Even more importantly, she knew that her reputation, whatever it was, would color how her son was treated by society. Being the younger son of a viscount gave Matthew many opportunities, but he would still need to make his way in the world.

In the flickering candlelight, Elizabeth's pale face stared back at her in the mirror. She *was* a good person, and she had *not* allowed anyone to take liberties. She just had to prove that somehow. And yet, a tiny little voice in the back of her mind wondered if Charles was right. Was it possible she was seeking approval from the wrong people?

Chapter Nineteen

~May 14~

Mrs. Browning's drawing room was as spectacular as ever, Penelope noticed the moment she walked through the door. "Oh, Harriet! You do have the most exquisite taste in furniture. Did you have this room redone since the last time I was here?" Penelope asked, coming forward to take her friend's hands.

Harriet laughed as she gripped Penelope's hands. "It has been too long, Penny, too long. And yes, I did have it redone. I had just gotten tired of all that gold. I like this elegant blue so much better, don't you?"

Penelope looked around the room and nodded. "Yes, it is much more soothing," she agreed. The previous furniture in the room had been something to behold—gold damask material with all the wood painted stark white. The walls had been covered in a matching gold fabric, but that had now been replaced with a pale blue pattern with white diamonds. She couldn't figure out if the furniture was entirely new or if it had merely been reupholstered and had the paint stripped off it.

"I think so, too, but do come and sit down. Tea will be brought in momentarily." But even as she said it, there was a brief knock on the door. The maid came in pushing an adorable little tea trolley, which clattered lightly as she rolled it along the wooden floor, then onto the thick blue and gold carpet, which also looked new.

After Harriet had poured out for them, she sat back with a satisfied smile. Penelope was so glad. She'd somewhat worried it would be a bit awkward visiting her old friend now that she'd become so active in society and with the ladies of the Wagering Whist Society.

"Tell me how you've been," Penelope said. "It's been much too long since we've had a chance to sit down and visit."

"Oh, things are much the same with me," Harriet said airily. "But clearly the same cannot be said of you." She gave a little giggle. "You must be so happy your son is finally doing something!"

Penelope paused, her teacup half-way to her lips, before she lowered it again without taking the sip she had been intending. "Doing something? Charles has always helped his father run the business, and now that Mr. Aldridge is gone, he's taken over—"

"Oh, no!" Harriet laughed and waved her hand through the air. "I don't mean with his business—although, I do hear he has become quite active in the Company of Clockmakers, heading that committee. No, I meant with his search for a wife."

Penelope suddenly felt rather hollow. She carefully set her teacup down on the table in front of her. "I'm afraid I don't know what you're talking about. Charles hasn't said anything to me about—"

Harriet gasped and put a hand to her mouth. "Oh, no! I do hope I haven't spoiled some sort of surprise he was planning."

"What is it that you've heard and from whom?" Penelope asked, her throat feeling rather dry.

"Mrs. Foreman told me that he joined them for dinner last week to meet her little Honoria, and I heard from someone else that he had Sunday dinner with the Easts to meet their daughter as well," Harriet said, leaning forward as if she were divulging a great secret, which perhaps she was. Just the thought made Penelope feel distinctly unwell.

"Really?" Penelope asked, the word almost catching in her throat.

"Yes! I can't believe he hasn't told you! Mrs. Foreman said he was so very sweet to her Honoria, even though he did make it clear that he wasn't interested in the match—which is a shame—I hear she's a very good girl if a bit…well…" She didn't finish the sentence but just gave Penelope a polite smile.

She didn't know anything about the girl, so she had no idea what the smile indicated. In truth, she didn't care at all about the girl, so she instead asked, "And the East's daughter? Did you hear what he thought of her?"

"No! That's what I was going to ask you!"

Penelope sat back on the sofa. "I'm afraid I don't know. In fact, he didn't tell me any of this!" She was horribly embarrassed. Had she been paying too much attention to her friends to the detriment of her relationship with her own son? The thought of it was horrifying. Not only that, but she was furious when she thought that Charles had gone back to the watchmakers to find a wife when she'd expressly told him that she wanted him to find one among the young ladies of the *ton*. What *was* that boy doing?

"Well, fear not, I'm certain most young men don't share their matrimonial interests with their mothers," Harriet said consolingly.

"I'm sure *most* men do not, but you know I've always prided myself on the close relationship Charles and I have had," Penelope said.

"Yes, well... Boys do grow up, I suppose. Let me tell you what I've heard about Mrs. Silber—you won't believe!" Harriet said, undeterred. She always was a bit of a gossip, Penelope realized. Maybe it was just as well she didn't know anything of Charles's recent attempts to find a wife. She didn't want to be able to give her friend any more fodder for the gossip mill.

Still, it didn't make her any happier that Charles had kept this from her.

That evening, when she heard Charles would be spending the night at home, she decided she would do the same and sent around a note to Lady Ayres, apologizing for cancelling their plans at the last minute. They were to have attended Lady Weston's musicale together, but Penelope felt it much more important to spend the evening with her son.

Unfortunately, after sitting on the news all afternoon when she finally saw him, her hurt and anger simply exploded. "Charles, how *could* you?"

~*~

Charles had had a difficult afternoon trying to work with the other members of his newly formed committee. They needed to discover the extent of the problem—how many watches were being imported, how many of them were engraved with false "English" names, what they were being sold for, and any number of other details. Once they had the information, only then could they decide how they were going to tackle the problem.

The difficulty was in finding out the information, and none of the other men seemed to be able to agree on how to proceed. Should they go out and try to gather information on their own? Should they hire an investigator to do it for them? There seemed to be as many options and opinions as there were men on the committee. Now, Charles simply wanted to have a quiet, relaxing dinner, but clearly his mother had other plans.

He sighed heavily.

However, he was not about to get into an argument with her—not after the contentious day he'd just had. Instead, he finished pouring a glass of ratafia and handed it her. "I beg your pardon?"

"And so you should!" she pouted, taking the offered glass.

"I don't know what you're talking about, Mother. A little explanation would be helpful, if you please?"

"I met with Mrs. Browning this afternoon and learned you have been to *two* dinners with members of the Worshipful Company of Clockmakers to meet their daughters, *and* you have become more active in the guild? How is it that I know nothing about any of this?" she asked after taking a sip of her wine and making herself comfortable on the sofa.

He decided to tackle the easy query first, and perhaps he could distract her from the other. "Oh. Er, yes. I am heading up a committee to look into the sudden influx of watches from Switzerland.

They are cheap copies of many of the watches—"

"Charles! You know very well that is *not* what I am most interested in hearing about!" she said, clearly frustrated with his answer. No, he hadn't really thought it would be that easy.

He frowned at her for a moment and then downed his entire glass of wine. With another sigh, he said, "I didn't tell you because I knew you wouldn't be happy about it. I was hoping that I would simply be able to present you with a young lady who I'd chosen to marry, but sadly, I have not found the girl yet."

"But why are you looking amongst the watchmakers? You know I expressly asked you to find a girl from the *ton*," she said.

"Yes, but honestly, Mother, the young ladies of society are shallow, silly creatures. They do nothing but giggle and bat their eyelashes."

"Not all of them!" his mother protested.

"I have yet to find one who didn't," Charles stated.

"Lady Welles and Lady Colburne didn't."

"Which is why neither one lasted very long on the marriage mart," he pointed out.

His mother didn't seem to have an answer for that one, but she didn't look happy. Finally, she said, "Please, Charles, I want you to have all the advantages I never did. All the advantages your cousin now enjoys."

"Mother, you know even if I marry a girl whose father is a nobleman, it won't make me one. No matter what, I'm always going to be a businessman and a watchmaker," he said gently.

She frowned at him. "I know that! But it

doesn't mean you can't move in the best circles. A noble wife will give you that, at the very least."

"But I don't—" he started.

"I know you claim you don't care, but trust me, you will. Now just do as I say and look for a girl among the *ton*—please!"

He sighed again. "Very well. I will look, but I also won't rule out anyone. Personally, I think it more important that I'm happy with my choice of wife than which level of society her family inhabits."

"Well, of course I want you to be happy!" she said, her eyes widening.

"Then don't force me to limit my search."

She could say nothing to that, so he changed the subject and asked her, instead, about her friends. That topic kept her happily occupied for the rest of the evening allowing Charles to finally relax.

Chapter Twenty

~May 16~

Elizabeth was pleasantly surprised the following morning when a note from Charles was delivered. She smiled as she read it, remembering the wonderful time she'd spent in his company a few nights earlier.

"You look very happy," Paul commented from his end of the breakfast table.

She stood up, having finished her meal. "I have just been invited to go shopping with a friend."

"Ah!" He gave a little laugh. "Well, I hope you have a wonderful time."

"Thank you," she said. She gave his shoulder a little squeeze of affection on her way out of the room. She would spend the morning reading and deciding what to wear for her afternoon outing, she thought on her way up to her drawing room.

At precisely two, she was informed, with apologies, that Mr. Aldridge was outside waiting for her in his carriage. Since she was ready because he'd always proven to be a punctual sort of person, she simply put on her pelisse, gathered up her reticule, and headed out the door.

He was sitting on his phaeton's bench, waiting patiently, a young tiger holding his horse's head. He gave her a brilliant smile as he reached over to give her a hand up. "Thank you for not making the horse wait too long. I appreciate that a great deal. I'm afraid she's not the most patient animal."

Elizabeth laughed. "No problem at all. I've been looking forward to this since I received your note this morning."

"As have I."

"What is it we are shopping for?" she asked as he negotiated into the stream of traffic.

"Watches."

Now that confused her. "But don't you make watches?" she asked.

He nodded. "I do. Happily, I have a man who handles selling them to various jewelers in Town, so I won't be recognized when we go to the jewelers' shops. I prefer to oversee the actual craftsmanship."

"I see. Are we spying on him, then? Seeing if your watches are for sale for the right price, perhaps?" she asked, trying to guess at why he wanted to go watch shopping.

He gave her a bright smile. "No, although that's not a bad idea either." He lost his smile. "Unfortunately, we are going to be doing some reconnaissance of another sort, but I don't want to tell you exactly what it is so I don't prejudice you in any way. Just know I value your opinion and am looking forward to your thoughts on the watches we are going to see. Do you mind?"

"That you value my opinion? Not at all!" Elizabeth said with a laugh.

"Excellent. In that case, if we're asked, could we simply say we are shopping for a watch for your father or brother? I hate to ask you to lie, but..."

Elizabeth laughed. "That's perfectly fine. A little fibbing never hurt anyone and, actually, looking for a watch for my brother isn't a bad idea. I do want to buy him a wedding gift. I've already decided on what to get Bel and Bee, but I'd like to buy presents for Conway and Paul as well. Watches would be just the thing!"

"Excellent. We'll look for watches for them, in that case."

Their first stop was the infamous Rundell and Bridge, the favored jeweler of the prince. They explained the reason for their visit to the shopkeeper and were shown a very nice selection of watches. Charles didn't say anything as they looked at them but allowed Elizabeth to take the lead. It was such a lovely change of pace from the very few times that she'd been shopping with her husband.

He'd always taken charge of any situation when they'd been out. Most of the time, Elizabeth had been grateful for his expertise and command, but there had been times when she'd wished she could have had more say.

As they looked through the watches the jeweler had put in front of them, she questioned him on the advantages of each one and how much they cost. At his raised eyebrows she said, "I am more than willing to spend the appropriate amount, but I do need to be mindful of how much I'm spending."

"Of course, my lady," he said, his eyes shifting over to Charles.

The man just smiled but said nothing. Clearly, the shopkeeper was attempting to pull him into the negotiations, but Charles didn't seem to want to be pulled in. He was going to leave everything up to her. She was liking him more and more every time they met.

The shopkeeper gathered he wasn't going to get any assistance from the gentleman, so he turned back to her and began to explain in excessive detail about each of the most expensive watches he'd taken out for her perusal.

"And what of this one?" Elizabeth asked, taking up one of the other ones he hadn't told her about.

"Ah, that is a very good watch, my lady, you have an excellent eye," the man said. "It is, as you see, silver and very well made as well."

"And the price?" she asked.

He quoted an amount that was a third of the price of the others. Charles started to cough rather violently, making Elizabeth's skin prickle. Clearly, there was something about this watch and its price which had shocked him.

"Are you all right?" Elizabeth asked, putting her hand on his sleeve.

"Yes, yes. I do beg your pardon. Er, could you please tell us why that one is so much less than the others?" he asked.

"Yes, I was about to ask the same thing," she said, giving Charles a smile. He returned it, and she had a feeling he understood she had things well in hand.

"It is merely the simplicity of the watch, that's all, sir. I assure you, it is as well made as any of the others."

"May we see the maker's mark?" Elizabeth asked. They'd been shown the mark of a few of the more expensive watches, but the man hadn't opened this particular watch.

Charles gave her an approving nod, making her

feel stupidly happy.

The shopkeeper opened up the watch and showed them the maker's mark. Charles peered at it and then looked up at the man. "I don't know that watchmaker. Is it made here in England?"

"Of course, sir! Of course! All our watches are English," the man said, feigning offense.

"Ah-hmm." Charles gave the man a polite smile and then turned to Elizabeth. "Well, this has been most instructive. Would you be willing to look elsewhere?" He turned back to the shopkeeper. "Lady St. Vincent wanted to make a full survey before coming to any decisions, you understand, I'm sure." Since this was the first time he'd taken charge of the situation, Elizabeth had a feeling there was a very important reason. She stayed mum.

The man's eyebrows went up a notch, but he said, "Of course! Most wise. Most wise, indeed. I do hope you will come back once you've seen what other jewelers have to offer. I assure you, you won't find any as well-made and beautiful as what I've shown you."

"Thank you so much," Elizabeth said. "I'm sure you are right, but one does have to do their due diligence."

"Of course." He bowed them out of the shop and then watched as Charles signaled for his tiger to bring his vehicle forward.

Charles was silent for a few minutes as they started off again.

"Well?" Elizabeth said, eager for him to tell her what he was thinking.

"What did you think of that last watch?" he asked.

"It was very nice, but I do wonder at the price. It was much lower than the others. I can't help worrying that it perhaps wasn't as well-made, or perhaps the materials used weren't as good. What do you think?" she asked, giving him her honest opinion and hoping he would be open and honest with her as well.

"Oh, it definitely wasn't as well-made, of that I'm sure. I am also absolutely certain that it wasn't made in England. There is no watchmaker that I know of by that name," he said.

"Where do you think it was made then? And why would the shopkeeper have said it was, if it wasn't?" she asked, now very interested.

"It was made in Switzerland, and that watch is the very reason why I asked you to come shopping with me today," he told her.

"Ah ha! So, finally, we come to the heart of it," she said with a laugh. "Tell me more."

And so, he did. He explained to her all about the problems English watchmakers were having with the cheap Swiss imports beginning to flood the English market.

"But that's horrible! Not the least because we're being told that the watches are English made when they're not. Why don't they tell us the truth, I wonder?" Elizabeth asked.

"Because English watches are the finest in the world," Charles explained.

"And so, if we think a watch isn't English…"

"Then you'll know that it isn't as well-made as one that truly is," he finished for her.

"But that's deceptive!" she said, outraged.

"Indeed, it is. Not only that, but it's quickly

going to destroy the English watchmaking industry."

"*Your* business," she pointed out needlessly.

He gave a somber nod.

"Is there anything that can be done?"

He sighed. "I need to gather as much information as I can about what's happening and then, somehow, take it to Parliament and see what can be done about it. Whether it is tariffs, limits on imports, or legislation, I don't know, but something needs to be done."

"Well then, on to the next jeweler," Elizabeth said with enthusiasm.

Charles just laughed and did as she commanded, driving them on to another jewelry shop.

~*~

Penelope still wasn't happy about her conversation the night before with Charles. She'd allowed him to distract her with his questions about her friends, but she hadn't stopped thinking about his determination that all girls in society were empty-headed. She was certain it wasn't true, she just had to figure out how to convince him of this.

She was thinking so deeply about this while walking Duchess through the park, she almost missed Bolton.

"Mrs. Aldridge! I say, Mrs. Aldridge," Bolton's voice finally penetrated her thoughts. It was either his voice or the barking of dogs that finally caught her attention—she wasn't certain which.

"Oh, Bolton! I am so sorry. I didn't see you there," she said, coming to a halt next to him.

The dogs all began their greeting ritual, sniffing

each other most intimately as their owner simply stood there and laughed. "I'm standing in the middle of the path. How could you not see me?"

Penelope laughed and shook her head. "My mind was elsewhere."

"Well, that much is obvious. I do hope it was someplace more pleasant?" he asked, offering her his arm as they began to stroll along.

"I only wish it were, sir," she said, already feeling happier. He had a way of making her feel that way. She didn't quite know what it was, but he just made her feel content.

"Oh, dear. Perhaps you would feel better if you shared your concerns, then?" he asked gently, not pushing for her confidence if she didn't wish to share.

"Actually, you might be able to help," she said, as the thought appeared.

"Of course! I'd be honored to be of any service," he said.

"You are very good!" she gushed for a moment. "It's... It's my son."

"Ah! Children. They can be so trying," he said, understanding immediately.

"Yes. I just want what's best for him. I want him to be happy, yes, but more than that—"

"Now, wait a moment. You want him to be happy, you say."

"Yes!"

"But I feel as if you are about to tell me that you also want him to do something that *won't* make him happy," he said. He truly was a most astute gentleman!

"Well, but it might," she hedged.

He just looked down at her a little skeptically.

"I want him to find a young lady to marry, and I want him to look amongst the ladies of the *ton*. Is *that* so bad of me?" she asked.

"I don't know. Is he amenable to marriage, first of all?"

"Yes, he is. He has agreed to look for a wife."

"Then what, pray tell, is the problem? You have gotten past the biggest hurdle already." he said, smiling at her.

She couldn't help but smile back. "Yes, I suppose so. It's just that I learned yesterday he has been to the home of no less than *two* members of the Worshipful Company of Clockmakers to meet young ladies."

"The Company of Clockmakers?" Bolton asked.

"It's the clock and watchmakers guild," Penelope explained. "My husband was a member and Charles is now that he's taken over his father's business."

"I see." Bolton nodded. "So, he is looking for a wife amongst his peers."

"Yes, but I want him to look for one from society," Penelope explained.

Bolton paused in his perambulation. "But why?"

"Because he should become a member of society, and the easiest way to do so would be to marry a girl from society," Penelope explained. She found it necessary, then, to explain her background and all that she'd given up when she'd married Charles's father.

"I see," Bolton said, as they waited for one of the dogs to water a tree. "So, you believe your son should do better than you did."

"Yes! And I know he can. He is very close to his cousin, Lord Ainsby, and I am now a member of society thanks to both my sister and my involvement in the Ladies' Wagering Whist Society."

"But he has no interest, is that right?"

"He says he does, but that all the young ladies of society are empty-headed."

"Well, he's not entirely wrong. I mean, I'm sure there are a number of intelligent girls there, but finding them can sometimes be a challenge. But I think more than that, dear lady, is you need to have confidence in your son to know what's right for him. How old is the boy?"

"Two and thirty," Penelope told him.

He stopped at that and stared at her. He opened his mouth, shut it again, and then started to walk again. "You must have been but a child when he was born."

Penelope laughed.

"He is old enough to know his own mind, Mrs. Aldridge. Leave him be and have confidence that he will choose a woman who is right for him."

Penelope was sure he was right; she couldn't help but still worry. She was also just the tiniest bit annoyed that he'd taken Charles's side in this argument and not simply supported hers. Her husband had always supported her decisions when it came to Charles, knowing that a mother knew best.

She supposed Bolton didn't hold to the same belief. It was odd, but she did respect him enough to consider his opinion and not just dismiss it out of hand. He hadn't done that to her; she should not do so to him.

Chapter Twenty-One

~May 17~

Charles didn't know why he'd allowed his cousin to convince him to go for a ride at the height of the afternoon promenade. They both knew how slow going it would to be; they both knew they weren't actually going to have a pleasant ride. Charles quietly suspected there was a particular young lady his cousin wanted to "accidentally" meet, but he wasn't saying, so Charles wasn't going to ask. His cousin's romantic life was his own private business.

The afternoon was a fine one, however, and it seemed as if everyone in London thought so as well.

"I can't believe this. We haven't gone two hundred yards, and already my arm is getting tired from lifting my hat," Charles complained.

Ainsby laughed. "Clearly, you need to spend more time at Gentleman Jackson's, building up your strength."

"You know, I think you might just be right," Charles said, chuckling.

"Oh, look, isn't that Lady St. Vincent driving with the Kendrick twins?" Ainsby said, nodding toward a carriage a few equipages ahead of them.

"It does look that way," Charles agreed. "Shall

we try to catch up?"

Ainsby gave a nod, and they broke the line and urged their horses a little faster to overtake the few vehicles in between.

One of the twins—Charles had no idea which one—spied them and waved, causing Elizabeth and the other girl to turn around in their seats.

"Good afternoon, ladies," Charles said, coming alongside their carriage.

"Good afternoon, Mr. Aldridge. Lord Ainsby, what a delightful surprise!" Elizabeth said, smiling at them both. "You remember Miss Kendrick and Miss Bel," she said, indicating the twins.

"I don't believe I've been formerly introduced to Mr. Aldridge, although I've certainly heard a great deal about you," the girl next to Elizabeth said with a bright smile. Her bright red hair shone in the sunlight, its color made even more brilliant by her deep yellow spencer. "I'm Beatrice Kendrick."

"How do you do?" Charles asked, giving her a nod. He then turned toward her identical sister sitting opposite. She was in green, which made her hazel eyes shine. Elizabeth would probably look lovely in that color, too, he thought. "And you must be Miss Bel. It's a pleasure to meet you both."

"So, this is what the holdup is," a man's voice said as he approached on horseback. "Move along, now, or get out of the way. You are causing a great amount of distress behind."

Charles didn't recognize the gentleman with his pale blond hair and slender face. His companion, however, was Lady Sorrell, who he had met on a number of occasions. She was also a member of his mother's whist society.

"Well met, Sorrell," Ainsby said with a chuckle.

"Yes, yes, we'll move. I think we can talk and ride at the same time—at least I can. Aldridge?"

"I think I can manage it," he said with a laugh. He turned his mount around so that it was facing in the right direction, then allowed her to amble forward at the same pace as the ladies' carriage, which had begun to move once again.

"Good afternoon, Lady Sorrell," Elizabeth called from her seat in the equipage.

"Good afternoon, Lady St. Vincent, it is a lovely day to be out, isn't it?" Lady Sorrell said, riding alongside the gentleman.

"Indeed, it is!" Elizabeth said. She then narrowed her eyes at the gentleman beside her. "Mr. Aldridge, I don't believe you have met the Marquess, have you?"

"No," Charles said, turning to the gentleman.

"Lord Sorrell," the gentleman said, pulling his horse abreast of Charles's and reached out his hand.

"Charles Aldridge," Charles answered, taking his hand in a brief grip.

"Ah, Mrs. Aldridge's son?" the man asked.

Charles laughed. "Yes. Clearly, my mother's reputation precedes me."

"It is odd how we become known in various circles through our family members. Whenever I meet someone associated with the Ladies' Whist Society, it's always, 'Oh, you're Lady Sorrell's husband.' Anywhere else, and I actually have an identity of my own." He gave a little chuckle.

"That is precisely how I'm feeling," Charles said with an answering laugh.

"Lord Sorrell, have you heard of the

predicament being faced by the English watchmakers?" Elizabeth called out.

Charles was very surprised she'd brought up the subject. He turned and looked at her quizzically, but she just smiled and gave him a little wink.

"I beg your pardon, my lady? I have not heard anything about watchmakers. Why do you ask?" Lord Sorrell said, clearly very confused at the change in subject.

"Mr. Aldridge is a watchmaker. He owns a company that makes watches and sells them to jewelers. Yesterday, we went on the most fascinating shopping expedition to see the watches currently being sold. The English-made watches, such as the ones created by Mr. Aldridge's company, are being horribly undercut by imported watches made in Switzerland. The quality of the Swiss watches is not nearly as good, the materials not as fine, and yet they are being sold side by side with English watches. I'm sure this is something that Parliament should look into, don't you think?" she asked, smiling sweetly up at Lord Sorrell.

The man looked intrigued, much to Charles's surprise. He then turned to Charles and asked, "Is this true?"

"Yes, my lord," he answered shortly.

"I assure you, Lord Sorrell, Mr. Aldridge is right now as shocked as you are that I have approached this subject. He hasn't asked me to, but I thought it might be something you should be aware of and perhaps take an interest in," Elizabeth said.

Lord Sorrell gave Elizabeth and then Charles an understanding smile. "I was almost wondering if this was somehow pre-arranged.."

"It absolutely was not. I asked Lady St. Vincent to accompany me on a fact-finding excursion yesterday so it didn't look too obvious that I was gathering information. I did not expect, nor ask her, to take up the cause," Charles assured the man. "In fact, we're still gathering as much information as we can about the watches being imported—where they are being sold, for how much, and under whose name."

"Can you believe, they are putting fake English names on these watches to make them seem as if they were made here!" Elizabeth said from the carriage.

Lord Sorrell frowned, turning from her back to Charles. "Is this true?"

"I'm afraid so. And sometimes they are even using the names of well-respected watchmakers, even though I can easily see the watches are a completely different style than those made by that person."

"Have you informed the watchmakers whose names are being used?" Lord Sorrell asked.

"No, in the few cases that I've noticed, the watchmaker in question is either retired or dead," Charles said.

"My goodness!" He rode in silence for a moment and then turned to Elizabeth. "I am very glad you've brought this to my attention, Lady St. Vincent." He turned back to Charles and added, "I don't know what can be done, but it certainly sounds like something I'd like to know more about. I'd like very much to discuss the issue with you further. Do you have some time in the coming week? It sounds as if there should be a Parliamentary committee at the very least."

"Thank you, my lord. I do. Shall I be in contact with your secretary to schedule an appointment?" Charles asked. Never in his life would he have thought of discussing business while riding in the park. But Elizabeth had just given him an excellent connection, and he was grateful. Maybe something could truly be done after all.

~*~

Elizabeth knew she'd thrown Charles off-kilter with her intervention, but why shouldn't she take advantage of Lord Sorrell's presence to inform him about a matter that concerned Charles? It was, in fact, a serious problem facing a major English industry, and therefore, Parliament should be aware of it. And truly, she almost never saw Lord Sorrell, so she jumped at the opportunity when it presented itself.

She was actually quite pleased with herself. She'd never been much into politics, but she wondered if she wouldn't have made a very good politician's wife.

A few, minutes later, Lord and Lady Sorrell said their goodbyes and took a side path on their own leaving Charles and Lord Ainsby to continue alongside her carriage. Lord Ainsby was having some sort of silly conversation with Bel, and Bee was happily sitting quietly watching everything around them.

"Well, well, what a happy little group. How perfect it is that I should have come along just now. Lady St. Vincent, you are looking ravishing as always, but sadly alone, now that Lord Sorrell has taken his leave of you."

Elizabeth turned, her skin crawling merely at the sound of that voice—a voice that had haunted her dreams for the past few weeks. "Lord Rogan.

You can see I am not alone, and you are not welcome here."

"Tsk, tsk, tsk, Lady St. Vincent, you don't need to put on a show here and especially not now after I rescued your little boy's kite. You are among friends, they'll understand the depth of your feelings for me," he said, leering down at her, looking not so much at her as at her bosom.

"Indeed, we do," Bee said, frowning at the man. "She despises you with a greater intensity than I ever thought possible."

Elizabeth turned and gave the girl a grateful smile.

Lord Rogan just laughed. "That is what she wants you to think, my dear. In fact, it is all a ruse to hide the deep passion she feels. Truly, my lady, you only need to send round a note, and I will be at your home within moments, and then we can—"

"If you dare finish that sentence where I think it may be going, you will find yourself flat on your...back, in the dirt where you belong," Charles said, glaring at the man. He was clearly just barely holding on to his anger, and Elizabeth had a feeling he was censoring his language for her and the twins.

"And who might you be?" Lord Rogan asked, attempting to look down his nose at the taller man.

"Mr. Aldridge is a close friend," Bel said. Elizabeth wasn't so sure that disclosing his identity to Lord Rogan was such a good idea, however.

"Something you will never be," Bee added.

"Oh, really? So, *you* are Aldridge?" Rogan sneered. "And I suppose you think to continue to pull yourself up above your station by rubbing shoulders with your betters. First Lady St. Vincent and now Lord Sorrell. I do wonder that his lordship even had the time of day for a plebeian such as yourself, *Mister* Aldridge."

"If you must know, Lord Sorrell is going to help Mr. Aldridge by creating a Parliamentary committee," Bel said.

"Well, we don't know..." Elizabeth started.

"A committee, really? To do what, give cits—" Rogan started.

"To stop the import of Swiss watches," Bee answered, cutting off the odious man. "Something you couldn't possibly comprehend—actually working *within* the rules to do something good for English businesses."

Lord Rogan narrowed his eyes at the girl.

Elizabeth truly had no desire to antagonize this man any further. "Bee, Bel, I'm sure Lord Rogan—"

"I understand such things much better than you, little girl," Lord Rogan sneered. He then turned to Charles. "So, you think to get the assistance of Parliament for your own personal gain, is that it?"

"It is to help all British watchmakers," Charles said.

Lord Rogan's silence was more disturbing to Elizabeth than his retorts. After a moment, he turned toward her. "Lady St. Vincent, I can hardly believe you associate with this commoner, especially when my noble charms have been on offer for some time now."

"Your charms are of no interest to Lady St. Vincent," Charles said firmly.

"Did the watchmaker dare to speak? You may run along, little man, we have no interest in any watches today." Lord Rogan made a shooing motion with his hand.

"Mr. Aldridge is a friend," Elizabeth said.

"Is he now? How quaint. He may be a friend, but I..." He paused to leer down at her chest again. "I am so much more than that. Indeed, what would be the point of being a friend when physical charms such as—"

"Rogan, I believe it is *you* who should leave, now!" Charles cut in.

Lord Rogan turned back toward Charles, one side of his upper lip lifting ever so slightly. "How dare you tell *me* what to do. I told *you* to run along."

"I would never leave young ladies in company such as yours. I am—" Charles started.

"You are a nobody, and if you want to see your little committee to succeed, you will do as I tell you," Lord Rogan informed him.

"You don't have the power—" Charles started.

Lord Rogan burst out laughing, however. "Oh, don't I? Need I remind you that I am an earl and as much a member of Parliament as Lord Sorrell? He may suggest that a committee is formed, but I can stop it. No, if you want your committee to help your poor little watchmakers, you will sod off—now!"

"Charles," Lord Ainsby said softly, looking a little wide-eyed at Lord Rogan. "He does have the power to do that."

"There is absolutely no way I am leaving Lady St. Vincent and the Misses Kendrick alone in this man's company," Charles declared, not taking his eyes off his lordship.

Elizabeth's stomach began to cramp and her

heart to pound so loudly in her chest, she wondered whether the twins could hear it. They were both looking a trifle worried and nervous as well.

"We'll be perfectly fine—" Elizabeth started.

"No, Elizabeth, I appreciate what you are trying to do, but I do not trust this man. He is no gentleman, despite his title. And he is not to be trusted—not even in a public park," Charles said firmly.

Exultant joy mixed with dread in the pit of Elizabeth's stomach. Charles was being so strong. So noble. And such an idiot.

"Just bugger off, Rogan," Ainsby growled. "You'll do nothing to stop Lord Sorrell from forming this committee, and you're making a nuisance of yourself here."

"We'll see about that, Ainsby. Aldridge, say goodbye to your committee," Lord Rogan said. With that, he turned his horse's head in the other direction and kicked it into a trot.

"Oh, Charles, I am so sorry!" Elizabeth nearly cried both in fear for what Lord Rogan might actually do and in relief that he was finally gone.

"I am so sorry for even mentioning that committee. It was stupid of me," Bel said. She too looked as if she might succumb to tears.

"Now, now, ladies, please don't worry. It will come to nothing, I'm sure," Charles said, sounding much more confident than Elizabeth could have imagined after such a confrontation.

"I do hope you're right," Elizabeth said. The twins both nodded vehemently.

"As do I," Lord Ainsby said, almost too quietly for Elizabeth to hear.

Chapter Twenty-Two

~May 19~

Elizabeth was warmly greeted by the Duchess of Warwick as she entered that lady's private drawing room. It was a comfortable room, almost looking as if it belonged in another house entirely. The rest of the ducal residence was a study in opulence with soaring columns and an enormous golden chandelier in the foyer. This room, however, was warm with pale blue walls and mismatched, well-worn furniture.

Somehow, Elizabeth had managed to shove all the unpleasantness from her ride in the park the other day out of her mind. She could only hope that Lord Rogan was, in fact, too devoted to bettering British business interests that he wouldn't do anything to jeopardize Lord Sorrell's committee.

"I am so glad you could come," the duchess said, holding out her hands to Elizabeth.

"Well, since this gathering seems to be for my benefit, I could hardly send my regrets," Elizabeth said with a little laugh. Indeed, now was not the time to think of anything unpleasant, she was here to have fun.

"Your—" the duchess paused to think about it and then gave a laugh and shake of her head,

"Sister-in-law and daughter-in-law-to-be insisted we meet," she said with a giggle. "I assume those girls aren't used to having anyone say no to them."

"I'm beginning to get that impression as well. And yes, their relationships to me are going to be complicated in the extreme! Imagine, twins where one is the step-aunt of the other."

They both burst out laughing.

"You must tell us what's so funny!" Bel said, coming into the room followed by her sister.

"Oh, Bel, Bee! We were just laughing at the fact that Bel is going to be Bee's step-aunt soon," the duchess said, still giggling.

"Oh! Yes! We've had a good laugh at that," Bee said, smiling.

Bel giggled and nodded. But then she clapped her hands together and said, "But that's not why we're here! We are here for a very important reason!"

"Yes, indeed, we are," the duchess said, looking over at Elizabeth. "You, my lady, are starting a new chapter in your life. You are out of mourning, moving on from both your loss and the horrid things that have happened this season. This is the perfect time to revamp your wardrobe and show a new you to society."

Elizabeth sighed happily. "I couldn't agree more!"

Bel started clapping again in her excitement.

"Do you have the most recent journals, Tina?" Bee asked.

The duchess laughed and indicated the table in the middle of the room. It was completely covered with all the latest ladies' journals. "And I've got my sketchbook so we can design a few gowns for you that will be entirely new just for you."

"I can't tell you how much I appreciate this, Your Grace," Elizabeth said.

"Oh, my goodness! You can show your appreciation by calling me by my given name!" the duchess said, widening her eyes.

Elizabeth laughed. "Very well, Tina, and you will call me by mine."

"Excellent! To work, ladies!" Bee said, moving forward and taking a seat on the sofa.

Everyone else followed suit and began looking through the journals. They compared notes on what they liked and didn't like.

"What do you think of this?" Bel asked, holding up a fashion plate of a woman in a daringly low-cut gown.

"Too revealing for me," Elizabeth said.

"But you need something a little...you know, for a ball," Bel argued.

"No, I don't. A higher décolletage is better for both my figure and my age," Elizabeth said.

"Oh, come now, Elizabeth, you act as if you were forty instead of not even thirty!" Bee said, agreeing with her sister.

"Girls, with the reputation I am currently fighting, I assure you, if I could wear a gown that came up to my chin it wouldn't be modest enough," Elizabeth said.

"Oh, pish-tosh!" Bel said dismissively.

"I'm sorry, but it's true. I don't know what it is about me or my figure, but most men have a hard time controlling themselves around me. It's mortifying, but something I've been aware of ever since I was sixteen. Even my father warned me about it," Elizabeth said, confiding in her friends.

"I just don't understand why that is," Tina said, with a tilt of her head, showing she was thinking about this. "It's not all men, surely?"

"No, not all, but a good many," Elizabeth said. "And it's always been this way—ever since I grew into my current shape."

"Mr. Aldridge has no troubles controlling himself," Bee said with a teasing smile.

Elizabeth shrugged. "Perhaps he doesn't think of me in those terms. Maybe he thinks of me more like a sister."

"Ha! I doubt that!" Bel said.

"Oh, no, definitely not. Judging by the way he was looking at you Sunday afternoon, I'd say he most definitely doesn't look at you like a sister," Bee said.

Elizabeth kept quiet. She most sincerely hoped he didn't, because she was beginning to like him a great deal—and not in a brotherly way at all.

"I think you need a gown—perhaps not quite that revealing," Tina said, "but perhaps something like this?" She did a quick sketch and then showed it to Elizabeth.

"Yes! I like that very much," Elizabeth said.

"Add some embellishments, perhaps?" Bel commented.

"Perhaps just a little lace along the edges, but not much. Elizabeth should look refined and elegant—appropriate for her age and status," Tina said, adding some lace to her drawing.

"Thank you, Tina! You understand," Elizabeth said gratefully.

Tina gave her a bright smile.

"Good evening, ladies," a man said, coming into the room.

Elizabeth and the twins all rose and turned toward him at the same time.

"Oh, Warwick! I thought you were out at your club this evening," Tina said, giving him an affectionate smile. It was so clear that she was very much in love.

His returning smile showed he felt very much the same way. Even though they were only smiling at each from across the room, there was so much emotion in their faces. It was quite beautiful to see.

"I was. I just returned because I remembered you were hosting Lady St. Vincent and I felt it important that I relay some, unfortunately, disturbing information." He lost his smile and turned a somber face on to Elizabeth. "There has been a bit of an incident at Powell's," he started.

He had their full attention.

"Lord Rogan was in his cups," he told her.

"That's never a good precursor," Elizabeth commented quietly.

"No. When I left, he was shouting and carrying on. Nothing he said was good, kind, or in any way decent and, I'm afraid, it was all directed at you," the duke said. "It was disturbing enough that I felt you should become aware of this immediately. You need to be on guard, my lady. Please, do not go out unaccompanied. At the very least, you should have a footman with you at all times, if not a gentleman of your acquaintance who you trust to have the wherewithal to defend you should the need arise."

"My goodness, Warwick!" Tina exclaimed. "Is it

truly that bad?"

"I don't know, my sweet, but it's better to be safe than sorry."

"Thank you, Your Grace," Elizabeth said. "I will definitely take your warning to heart."

He gave her a nod. "I'm sorry to come bearing bad news. I didn't want to ruin your party, but—"

"No, this was important," Elizabeth said. "I appreciate it." She turned to Tina. "Perhaps that neckline needs to be a little higher, Tina."

"It will spoil the line of the gown. We'll have this made for you, Elizabeth, and you'll wear it once Lord Rogan is no longer a problem."

"As a celebration for him being taken care of," Bee said agreeing.

"When and how that will ever happen, I don't know," Elizabeth said, feeling almost hopeless that such a day would ever come.

"I'm certain it will," Bel said, reaching out and taking Elizabeth's hand.

Elizabeth could only hope she was right.

~*~

Meanwhile at Powell's...

Charles and Ainsby entered Powell's in time for a late dinner. It had taken some serendipity, but Charles had finally managed to find an evening when his cousin wasn't otherwise occupied. And yet, it had still taken the man over half an hour just to dress himself for an evening out.

"I just don't understand why it takes so long," Charles said, continuing the conversation they'd been having in Ainsby's coach on their way over.

"It's an art, Aldridge. I can't expect you to understand this," his cousin said, finally giving up his attempt at trying to describe precisely why and how it took him so long to get dressed.

"I'm sorry, but getting dressed is a chore, not an art."

"Then we must agree to disagree, old friend—" Ainsby didn't finish his sentence because of the commotion they were suddenly confronted with.

The normally peaceful reading room of Powell's Club for Gentlemen was filled with the reverberations of one man's shouts.

"Did she sleep with you, Touffy? I bet she did! Don't shake your head! You fucked her. I know you did. What about you, Fethington? You fucked her too! I can see it in your eyes!"

Charles and Ainsby stopped just inside the door. Lord Rogan was wandering the room, a glass in one hand, a bottle in the other, accosting men as they sat in their own little groups.

"She's a damned good fuck, isn't she? Isn't she?" he shouted at the top of his lungs. "I know it! I know! You know how I know it? Because she won't fuck me! Goddamn Elizabeth Fucking Saint Fucking Vincent!"

And then he stopped, his eyes widening as he caught sight of Charles.

"Oh, dear," Charles whispered.

"This is not going to be pretty," Ainsby agreed.

"Well, well, well," Rogan said, sauntering toward them, stumbling, and then sauntering some more until he stood directly in front of Charles. "If it isn't the little watchmaker." Charles did his best not to recoil from his putrid, rum-soaked breath. "Look gentlemen, it is the man who currently holds the keys to the lady's bedchamber—or so I've been told. Well, Aldridge, what have you to say for yourself? No, no, I don't give a damn. Don't tell me about you. Tell me about Elizabeth St. Vincent. How was she when you left her? Naked? Spreading her legs for you? Teasing you with her sweet—"

"That's enough!" Charles stated loudly and firmly.

"Enough? Oh, no, I don't think it is enough. I can tell you that it's never going to be enough. Not until I've had my fill of her and completely destroyed you and your silly business. *Then* it will be enough!"

"You're disgusting," Charles ground out between his teeth.

"If I don't get my turn with that bitch, I can tell you… I… I'll…" He seemed to have lost his train of thought for a moment. The alcohol must have been rattling his brain, but he shook his head and refocused himself. "Every man in London has had their turn with Elizabeth St. Vincent, and now it's mine, so step aside, Aldridge!"

"You know very well I can't do that," Charles said.

"If you don't—"

"There's nothing you can do, Rogan," Ainsby said, speaking up. "The woman is independent and wants nothing to do with you. Get over it and move on."

"I will not! Not until I've—" Rogan started.

"If you so much as touch a hair on her beautiful head—" Charles started.

Rogan burst out laughing. "Oh, it's not the hair on her head that I'm going to touch. No, no. It's the hair—"

"That's enough! Lord Rogan, you have clearly had too much to drink. I suggest you allow your man here to take you home before you say something you will truly regret," Lord Wickford, the proprietor of the establishment said, finally coming in the room. He turned briefly to Charles and Ainsby and then addressed the rest of the room as well. "My apologies, gentlemen. I had to be called away from an engagement, and it took me a few minutes to locate his man and his coach."

Charles gave Wickford a nod and stepped aside so Rogan's footman could attempt to guide his master out of the room. Of course, Rogan refused to go quietly.

"No! No! I'm not done! I *will* get back at you for stealing her from me, Aldridge. Your business is finished!" He stumbled and was caught by his man.

"Yes, my lord," the man said. "Let's get you home, Lord Rogan. You can tell us all about it at home." The man tried once again to get his master to move out of the room, but Rogan wouldn't cooperate.

"I don't want to tell *you* about it! I want to destroy that man and get an invitation into St. Vincent's bedchamber, and if I don't get one, I'm going to go in there myself and—" Rogan might have continued, but two of the footmen who worked for the establishment put themselves into position on either side of the gentleman and proceeded to physically pick Lord Rogan up by either arm and carry him from the room. "Hey! Hey! Unhand me!" he shouted all the way out.

"Again, my sincere apologies! Please accept a glass of rum courtesy of Lord Rogan," Lord Wickford said.

A few gentlemen laughed.

Wickford smiled and shrugged. "I'm sure he would have offered it himself if he was aware of what he was doing."

"And won't he be surprised by the bill he gets tomorrow," one man said with a laugh.

"It's okay, he won't remember a thing," his companion commented.

"He'll think he just lost it at the gambling tables," another said from the other side of the room.

"Common enough," Lord Wickford agreed. That set a number of gentlemen chuckling and nodding. Clearly, they'd either been present when Lord Rogan had lost large sums at the gambling tables or been among those who'd benefited from his losses.

Lord Wickford turned to Charles and Ainsby, who were still standing near the door. "Gentlemen, what can I get you?"

Chapter Twenty-Three

"We were actually here for dinner," Ainsby said good-naturedly.

"Excellent! Then please, allow me to show you to a table in the dining room." Lord Wickford turned and went out the door, turning toward the back of the establishment where the dining room was located.

"I think I might take you up on that drink, as well," Charles said.

Wickford half-turned as he walked and gave him a broad smile. "A full bottle for you and Lord Ainsby, Mr. Aldridge. I think that's the least Lord Rogan could do after his rude attack on you and Lady St. Vincent."

Charles gave a little laugh, while silently agreeing that it was, indeed, the very least he could do.

"How is your mother doing?" Ainsby asked soon after their dinner was served.

Charles looked up from his plate. "She's well, why?"

"What do you mean why? Should a dutiful nephew not ask after his aunt?"

Charles narrowed his eyes at his cousin. "Yes.

It's just that you see her more often than I do. Maybe I should be asking *you* how she's doing."

Ainsby laughed and popped a fork-full of food into his mouth. After a moment, he said, "I only see her at parties. I don't usually speak with her."

"Really? Isn't that rude?" Charles asked.

His cousin shrugged. "Not if she doesn't see me." He gave a sly little half smile before taking another bite.

Charles laughed. "Well, I don't know that she particularly wants to see *me* just now."

"Oh? Did you do something?"

"She found out that I've met a few young ladies without her knowledge."

Ainsby was about to take another bite of food but instead lowered his fork. "What do you mean? Who have you met, where, and when? I can't imagine your mother *wouldn't* want you to meet young ladies, coz."

Charles laughed at his cousin's sudden interest. "It's the *who* I met, not *that* I met them that upset my mother. I went to dinner at the homes of two different members of the Company of Clockmakers to meet their daughters. And before you ask, no, neither one of them interested me."

"Well, of course not!"

"What do you mean by that?" Charles asked, taking offense on behalf of the two girls—probably needlessly.

"Without having ever met either one of these girls, I'm one hundred percent certain neither one of them could hold a candle to Lady St. Vincent."

Now it was Charles's turn to lower his fork before he'd taken the food from it. "No, they couldn't, but how would you know that?"

"Because, my dearest cousin, you are a man in love. It's as plain as the confused expression on your face," Ainsby said before popping another bite into his mouth. He gave Charles a closed-lip smile as he chewed, looking awfully satisfied with himself.

Charles sighed. "I hate to admit this, but I've actually done a little thinking on this matter since we met Lord Rogan in the park. I'm beginning to wonder if you aren't right. But, please, no gloating," he added quickly.

It was too late, though, his cousin was already well into it. Ainsby chuckled. "How can I not gloat? Any man who would risk life and limb from the likes of Rogan..."

"I did not risk life and limb," Charles said, laughing.

"All right, but you did risk your business."

Charles sobered up immediately. "Well, yes, I did do that."

"I knew she was perfect for you," his cousin said with a self-satisfied grin.

"No, you did not. You never thought that."

"Oh, all right. I may not have, but I think it now. And won't your mother be happy? You will be marrying a society girl."

Charles frowned. "That's the thing. First of all, I don't know she *will* be happy because Elizabeth isn't exactly a girl. She a mature woman and widow, which is the main reason why I find her so very attractive. She isn't like any of those silly young girls my mother has been trying to foist on me."

"And secondly?"

"Secondly, I don't know that Elizabeth will have me. *I'm* not a member of society. If she wants to marry again, I'm sure it will be someone who is a peer. Why would she marry down?"

Ainsby frowned. "I don't think she's that petty. If she has feelings for you, it won't matter that you don't have a title."

"I would hope not, but considering how important society is to her, I honestly don't know."

Ainsby scraped his plate with his fork as he thought about this.

"Do you need more to eat?" Charles asked.

"What?" his cousin asked, looking up at him. "Oh, no. Although some pudding wouldn't go amiss." He lifted his hand and waved down one of the footmen. After putting in his order, he said, "You could give it a try."

"Give what a try?"

"Seeing whether Lady St. Vincent minds the fact you're not a nobleman. In fact, it couldn't hurt seeing whether she minds that you're a businessman."

"How would I do that?"

His cousin tapped an empty fork against his lips. "I don't know. If you just asked her, of course, she would say she didn't mind. But how she actually behaved in, say, a social situation might be a very different story."

Charles smiled. "Of course! You're brilliant, Ainsby!"

His cousin perked up a bit. "Of course I am, but what are you referring to now?"

"A social situation. I need to host a dinner party! I'll invite a few of my colleagues from the

Worshipful Company of Clockmakers and Elizabeth and see how she gets along with them—whether she looks down her nose at them or is perfectly pleasant."

"Ah! Yes, of course! That's, er, that's exactly what I meant." Ainsby blinked at him.

Charles didn't believe that for a moment, but he was willing to let it go because his cousin *had* given him the idea, and that was good enough.

~*~

Penelope knew something was happening the moment she walked into Lady Ayres drawing room for their weekly game of whist.

Lady Ayres, Lady Welles, and Lady Sorrell all had their heads together discussing something. Lady Moreton and the duchess were sitting on the opposite side of the room with Lady Blakemore, although they didn't look nearly as guilty as the first three when Penelope greeted them.

"Good afternoon, ladies," Penelope said, putting Duchess down on the floor so she could scamper over and greet everyone as she liked to do. Penelope watched happily as a number of the ladies reached down to pet her adorable little pup.

"Her manners have gotten a good deal better of late," the duchess said, giving the little dog a pat on her head. "Look, she hasn't even put her dirty little paws up on my knee."

Penelope smiled. "She's been getting a bit of training from another spaniel we met at the park. The older dog has quite taken Duchess under her wing, so to speak."

"You must be very happy," the duchess said approvingly.

"Sometimes it's the training from another dog

that sticks," Lady Colburne said from behind Penelope. She hadn't even seen the other lady come in.

"Yes, it appears so. And yes, I am extremely grateful for it. Since I'd never had a dog before, I didn't know *how* to train her."

"What made you get her?" Lady Welles asked.

"Before you answer that," Lady Ayres said, just as Penelope was about to open her mouth to answer her. "We completed our previous game last week."

"Oh dear! Who has lost this time?" Lady Moreton asked, looking worried.

"Not you, my lady, your secrets are safe for the time being," Lady Ayres said with a reassuring smile.

The lady relaxed ever so slightly.

"Although, you might want to mind your playing since you came in second-to-last," Lady Ayres continued.

Lady Moreton's eyes widened and she nodded. "I will certainly do my best."

"The lady with the least number of points this time is Mrs. Aldridge," Lady Ayres finished.

"Me?" Penelope asked, quite shocked.

"I'm afraid so," Lady Ayres said. "I've double-checked the numbers and asked Lady Sorrell to check them as well."

"Oh." Penelope sat down heavily on the sofa next to Lady Blakemore. "I'm just... Well, I'm surprised. I hadn't realized I'd lost so many hands."

"Would you care to take a moment to think of what you might like to share with us?" Lady Moreton asked gently.

"I do believe I would. But first, Lady Welles, I will answer your question," Penelope said, happy to momentarily put aside her momentous task. "And maybe some of you will be kind enough to count that as my secret."

A few of the ladies gave a little laugh at that.

"*I* didn't get Duchess," Penelope told everyone. "She was given to me by my late husband."

"Oh, how sweet," Lady Welles said.

"It's a bit more than that," Mrs. Aldridge said, giving the girl a smile. "You see, he knew he was dying, but he didn't want me to be lonely after he did so. He gave Duchess to me to keep me company. He'd always treated me as if I were a princess, and even called me his princess when we were alone. So, he felt it fitting to give me the same sort of dog favored by royalty and gave her a noble name."

"Oh, how very sweet," Lady Colburne said.

"That is, indeed, a touching story," the duchess said. "Why didn't he name her Princess, then?"

Penelope laughed. "I don't know. I'm glad he didn't, though, it would have been painful for me to call her princess when that's what he'd called me. Duchess is a much easier name for me."

"That makes a good deal of sense," Lady Sorrell said.

The thought of her beloved Mr. Aldridge made Penelope think of her happy marriage and led her to realize what "secret" she could divulge to her friends. "And now I believe I know what I'd like to share with you all."

"Oh, yes? Something else about your dog?" Lady Blakemore asked, frowning ever so slightly.

Penelope laughed. "Not about Duchess, but I suppose about me and my family." She paused and gathered her courage.

"Would you care for a cup of tea?" Lady Moreton asked, so kind and thoughtful as always.

"No, thank you," Penelope said, giving her a warm smile. She took in a deep breath and then said, "I know some of you"—she lowered her gaze so as not to look at anyone in particular—"have thought of me as... Well, as a mushroom. Someone who doesn't really belong in society but is trying to push her way in."

There was absolute silence in the room, so she knew she'd been right.

She looked up and around at them all. "Well, I have to tell you, the reason I have done so is not for my own betterment or, or to put myself forward in *any* way. In truth, it has all been for Charles, my son. You see, I didn't want him to pay the price for my own selfishness."

"What do you mean? In what way were you selfish?" Lady Welles asked gently.

Penelope smiled at the girl. "I married for love," she told her. "My parents had actually made arrangements for me to marry Lord Ainsby so I could become a member of the *ton*, but I had already met and fallen in love with Mr. Aldridge. Naturally, my parents were furious. They wanted the best for me, and I was spurning both their hopes for me and the difficulty they'd gone through to arrange this marriage."

"But you were in love!" Lady Colburne said.

"I was and nothing was going to stop me from marrying Mr. Aldridge. I told my parents they should give the groom they'd chosen for me to my younger sister because I wasn't interested." She gave a little laugh. "So, they did. Prudence was happily married to the gentleman for many years. I wouldn't have been, I know that. However, just because I chose to spurn an excellent match, shouldn't mean my son should suffer the consequences. It was *my* choice. Truly, he should be a part of society. So, I wrote to my sister and asked her if she would allow Charles to use our connection to become a member of society." She smiled around at the ladies listening to her tale. "She is such a sweet thing, and she refused to allow Charles to come without me. She knew I would enjoy being a member of society. If I joined in and went to parties and such, then that would pave the way for Charles and make it easier for him to do so as well. Honestly, I don't mean to be pushy or an upstart, I just want what's best for my son."

"Well, I, for one, don't believe you are pushy or an upstart," the duchess said with sniff.

The way she said it, as if she were the queen, made Penelope laugh. "Thank you, Your Grace," she said. She'd nearly said Your Majesty but caught herself just in time.

"No, you're not pushy at all," Lady Welles agreed. "And I see no reason why you shouldn't be a part of society. You do have the connections after all."

"I do, and I very nearly married a nobleman. My father was a gentleman farmer as wealthy as any nobleman—possibly even more than some," Penelope admitted. "All he lacked was the title, but as he knew, that could be bought with his daughter."

"It is a time-honored way to enter society," Lady Blakemore said. "Quite a number of people join society through marriage. In your case, it is through your sister's marriage."

"And hopefully Mr. Aldridge will do so as well," Lady Sorrell commented.

"I do hope so!" Penelope said with feeling. "I don't know for certain, though. He has been looking among the daughters of other watchmakers for a wife, which I have to own, quite frightens me. I have been told I should leave well-enough alone. He is a grown man and should be able to make up his own mind, but..."

"You've gone to a lot of trouble to provide him with the opportunity to marry someone from the nobility," the duchess said with a nod. "He *could* show his appreciation by following through."

"He could. On the other hand, I do want him to be happy," Penelope said.

"Well, then, I suppose you're just going to have to wait and let him make up his own mind, in that case," Lady Ayres said.

"I do. It's probably the most difficult thing for me to do. Now, I have to say, I know *exactly* how my parents felt when I told them I was going to marry a man other than the one they chose for me," Penelope said. She picked up Duchess, who was sitting at her feet looking as if she were following the conversation as well as anyone. Penelope put the dog on her lap and began to stroke her soft fur. She was such a comfort. Penelope just didn't know what she would do without her little dog.

Chapter Twenty-Four

~May 20~

Charles had thought his cousin's idea to hold a dinner party to see how Elizabeth got along with his watchmaking colleagues was a good one... Until he realized it would involve telling his mother. He couldn't very well have a dinner party without her. But how he was going to tell her, and why, was *not* going to be easy.

He'd thought about it for two nights in a row, practically unable to sleep. He'd spent countless hours in his room, pacing back and forth, going over all the different ways he might tell her and preparing counter-arguments to her possible responses.

"Charles, out with it!" his mother said, barging into his room.

He stopped short, staring at her. "Out with what?"

"Whatever it is that has you pacing," she said in a most exasperated voice. "You do know that your bedchamber is just across the hall from mine. I can hear your pacing as if it were in my own room. You paced back and forth all last night *and* the night before and half of the day already today. Just tell me what it is, and we'll figure out a way to solve it, or remedy it, or do whatever needs to be done."

Charles could feel his face heat with embarrassment. He had no idea she could hear him! "I do beg your pardon, Mother—"

"Don't. Just tell me what is bothering you," she said coming forward and taking his hands in hers.

Instead of telling her, though, he simply puts his arms around her, holding her close. He was over thirty years old, and it still felt good to hug his mother. She gave him such comfort and happiness. He could only hope that he didn't upset her too much with what he had to say.

"Goodness, Charles, is it that bad?" she asked.

"No, truly it isn't. I just love you, that's all," he said, giving her a gentle squeeze.

"I love you too," she said, pulling back a little so she could look up at him. "And I hate for you to be upset or worried over anything. You know whatever it is, I will do everything I can to help you."

He smiled at her. "I know." He gave a little sigh. "Very well. Come and sit down."

"Oh dear, it really is bad isn't it?" she said with a quivering little laugh.

He chuckled. "No, actually, it's not bad. I think it's very good, but...but you may not."

She sat down at the edge of his bed, and he took his place next to her, still keeping hold of her hands.

"I... I am in love."

She gasped, her brow furrowing. "It's one of the watchmaker's girls, isn't it? Oh, dear, please don't let it be the Foreman's daughter. That girl is as simple as a field mouse, isn't she? Very sweet, to be sure, but I honestly don't think she'll make you happy, Charles. You need someone who you can talk to. Someone who's not just a pretty face."

He laughed. "No, it's not Miss Foreman. She is, indeed, a little too, er, simple for my tastes. You're absolutely right about that."

"Oh, good," she sighed with relief. But her eyebrows went up again almost immediately. "But then, who is it?"

"Elizabeth St. Vincent," he said.

"Elizabeth... Lady St. Vincent?" His mother's face lit up. "You're in love with Lady St. Vincent? But why would I be upset about that? She's a wonderful girl! She's clever and sweet and... I know you don't put any store by this, but she's a member of society."

"I know, but she's also an older lady and a widow, and I worried that you wouldn't like that," he told her.

She sobered a bit. "Well, she hasn't just made her debut, that's very true, but she's not so very old. How old is she?"

"I don't know. A gentleman never asks such a thing," he said with a chuckle.

"Oh, no, of course not. Well, she can't be above thirty, for certain. She still has many prime childbearing years left," his mother said, thinking about it. "And has already proven herself quite capable in that area."

He looked at her with a tilt of his head, not knowing what she was referring to.

"She has a son, did you not know?" his mother said, her eyes widening.

"Oh, yes. She mentioned that to me once."

"I hope that doesn't change your mind about her," her mother said, beginning to wring her hands.

"No, no, it doesn't. In fact, I look forward to meeting him some time." He thought about it for a moment, but could find no reason why he wouldn't be happy with a woman who already had a son. It might even move him one step closer to having that person his mother was hoping would help with his business. Although, Elizabeth might have something to say to that.

"Do you know if Elizabeth reciprocates your affections?" his mother asked, getting back to the point of their conversation. "Have you asked her for her hand yet?"

"I don't know and no, I haven't. Before I do so, I want to be sure she'd be happy married to a businessman. She is a delicately bred woman. I'm sure she's only ever socialized with members of *ton*. I don't know how she would react to my colleagues in the Company of Clockmakers. Some of them can be rather..."

"Oh, yes, I see what you mean," his mother said, nodding. "But she is a lady, a true lady. I'm sure she would do fine."

"Oh, I'm sure she would behave with grace and dignity, but would she behave with too much grace and dignity? Would she put the other ladies to shame? Or look down her nose at them? I want to be sure before I propose, so if you don't mind, I'd like to host a dinner party. I'll invite the Easts and Mr. and Mrs. Browning, as well as a few other people I know from Company. And I'll invite Elizabeth," he finished.

"Yes, but you can't *just* invite her. She's very

clever and would know immediately what you were up to," his mother pointed out.

"Hmmm, your right," Charles said. He hadn't thought about that. "Well, we could also invite a few of your Whist Society friends, in that case. Who do you think would do well in such company?"

His mother's gaze wandered away as she thought. "What about...Lord and Lady Welles? It would be nice to have some more young people there. And...oh, of course! Lord St. Vincent must be invited as well," she said, turning to him with a smile.

He returned it, saying, "Excellent! So, I'll invite three couples and you invite two—the Welles and the St. Vincents. With the two of us, that will make twelve, which is a nice number for a dinner party."

His mother gave a little clap of her hands. "Oh, how wonderful! I've been wanting to host a party for so long! It would have been best to invite all the ladies of the Whist Society, but that will have to wait for another time—perhaps after Lady St. Vincent has accepted your proposal?" she asked with a laugh.

He smiled. "We'll see."

~*~

"I am so happy you are doing well. Things seem to be getting easier for you as well, aren't they?" Mrs. Aldridge asked, smiling at Elizabeth as she sat across the tea service from her.

"Indeed. I think your campaign has definitely worked. People are hardly speaking of me anymore, and I've begun receiving invitations again," Elizabeth agreed.

The older lady sighed happily as she took another bite of her seed cake and gave a nibble to her dog, who was sitting at her feet looking at her hopefully. After she'd cleared her mouth with a sip of tea, she said, "Of course, I do have another reason why I've come to visit today."

Elizabeth gave a little laugh. "I suspected you did."

Mrs. Aldridge returned the smile. "And yet, you've been patiently waiting, indulging me by listening to my prattle for the past quarter of an hour." She gave a little laugh. "Well, I shall make you wait no longer. The reason I came, my dear Lady St. Vincent, is because I am going to be hosting a little gathering of friends for dinner on Tuesday, and I was wondering if you were free that evening."

"Oh, how very kind of you to think of me!" Elizabeth exclaimed. "It's rather short notice, but I don't believe I had anything much planned for that evening. I believe Lady Musgrove is hosting her annual musicale, but it wouldn't be any great loss if I were to miss it."

"Oh, my goodness! Miss Musgrove isn't planning to sing, is she?" Mrs. Aldridge asked, sounding a little horrified.

Elizabeth laughed. "I do believe she is."

"Oh, dear! No, no, no. You *must* come to my dinner party instead. Send your regrets to the Musgroves."

"I believe I shall," Elizabeth giggled.

"So, this is going to be a very small party," Mrs. Aldridge continued, warming to her subject. "It's just going to be some friends of mine and Charles's from his business circles—you are all right with this, aren't you?" The lady looked at her with widened eyes, almost as if there were more to the question than what was on the surface.

"Of course!" Elizabeth said immediately.

"I *knew* you would be!" she said with some relief. "And—"

"Was there any doubt?" Elizabeth asked, interrupting her. She couldn't help it; she was suddenly very curious.

"Oh, not on my end, I assure you. Charles was a little worried you might feel awkward socializing with watchmakers, but I assured him you wouldn't."

"Oh," Elizabeth said, a little taken aback. Did he think she thought herself above his business colleagues? "I do hope I haven't given him the impression that I think better of myself."

"No! No, of course not!" Mrs. Aldridge protested immediately.

"Then why would he think it would be a problem for me to socialize with his colleagues?"

"I have a feeling he believes you to be rather...innocent, shall we say, when dealing with people of other classes. You haven't had a great deal of experience doing so, that's all." Mrs. Aldridge said.

"But I have. I lived for six years at my husband's estate where my only friends were the local gentry and the villagers. Although I do *aspire* to be a prominent member of London society, I am also quite proud to call many others, not part of the *ton*, my friends."

Mrs. Aldridge smiled broadly at her. "I was certain that was the case, my lady. Charles will know it very soon as well, I can assure you." The lady paused to take a sip of her tea.

"So, is that all who will be there? Mr. Aldridge's colleagues?"

"No, no. I would be honored if you would bring your stepson, Lord St. Vincent, and I'm also inviting Lord and Lady Welles," she finished before taking another bite of cake.

"Oh! Lydia will be there? How lovely!" As Elizabeth thought about Charles's colleagues, a thought occurred to her. "Of Mr. Aldridge's colleagues, are these the people who are on his import committee?" she asked.

Mrs. Aldridge tilted her head a little to the side as she thought about it. "I do believe so. Why do you ask?"

"Oh, no reason. It would make sense for him to become a bit closer, to socialize with them so as to smooth the way for the work they're doing together on this problem of Swiss watches."

Mrs. Aldridge just blinked at her for a moment, so Elizabeth explained further. "Rather like when a member of Parliament invites other members to their home to encourage them to work on a particular project or vote a particular way. It's not overtly political, but it achieves the same ends in a more pleasant and relaxed atmosphere."

A broad smile grew on the lady's face. "You know, I hadn't thought of it that way, but you may have just hit the mark. That is probably *precisely* why Charles wanted to invited these people."

Elizabeth nodded, immediately feeling much better about this invitation. She also knew exactly what she must do. "So, the dinner will begin at seven?" she asked.

"Yes."

"Do you figure we'll sit down to eat about eight,

then?" she pressed.

Mrs. Aldridge looked at her, little confused. "That's exactly what I was planning, is there a problem with that?"

"Oh, no! Not at all. I was just curious," Elizabeth said. "Would you care for more cake?" She picked up the cake plate and offered it to the lady, a plan taking shape in her mind.

Chapter Twenty-Five

~May 26~

Charles handed his mother a glass of Madeira before any of their guests arrived for their dinner party. He needed a bit of Dutch courage and thought his mother might as well.

"Oh, thank you, my dear," she said and then downed nearly half the glass.

Charles could only laugh as he pulled out his pocket watch to check the time.

"I can't imagine anyone will turn up right on time," his mother said, looking at the clock on the mantel.

Charles checked to be sure the time on the clock and that on his watch matched. Naturally, they did. Every clock in the house was precisely set every day.

Just to prove her wrong, a knock was heard at the front door. Charles laughed and replaced his watch. "Who do you think that is?"

"The Brownings would be my guess," she said with a little laugh. "They always were a little gauche."

Much to their surprise, Lord and Lady St. Vincent were announced a moment later.

"I do hope you won't think it too forward of us to show up so early," Elizabeth said as she came in giving Charles a warm smile. It sent heat rushing through his veins—that, along with how incredibly beautiful she looked in her pale pink gown, just reinforced all his feelings and every wonderful thing he'd been thinking of her.

"I tried to hold her back, honestly, I did," Lord St. Vincent said with a laugh as he bowed over his hostess's hand.

"He did! He took so long to get dressed—and men are always complaining how long it takes a lady to prepare herself for an evening," Elizabeth said, also laughing.

"My apologies, Aldridge, I can't imagine what you must be thinking of us," he said, taking Charles's outstretched hand.

"I was just so eager. Anxious, perhaps?" Elizabeth said, looking to Charles as if for forgiveness. "And I could just imagine Charles looking at his beautiful pocket watch."

Mrs. Aldridge burst out laughing. "You do know my son!" She sobered a moment later after everyone had had a bit of a laugh and asked, "Now, what's made you so anxious, my dear?"

"Oh, I just want... I want to make a good impression on Charles's colleagues, I suppose," she admitted, wringing her hands adorably. "I have been worrying almost without end since we spoke, Mrs. Aldridge. Worrying that I come across as too... Oh, I don't know, particular? Or, or high and mighty?"

"What? No! Why ever would you think that?" Charles exclaimed.

"It might have been something I said," his

mother admitted. "But I assure you, Lady St. Vincent, you do not come across that way at all. You are the sweetest young woman. So very thoughtful."

"Do you really think so? I worry sometimes, especially lately, that I've been a little self-centered—what with this scandal and so on. I can assure you, I usually don't give a thought to how other people see me or what they think. It's just…"

"You've had a rather hard time of it, lately," Lord St. Vincent said.

"Yes. Extraordinarily so," Charles agreed. "I assure you, Elizabeth, we think you've been extremely brave in facing down your detractors. You've been very strong in standing up for yourself. But the wonderful thing about this evening is that no one here will have heard any of what's been going on among the *haute ton*. You should be completely at your ease tonight. The only people who will know are the Welles."

"And they are such good friends and know the truth of what actually occurred, you need not worry about them," his mother finished for him.

Elizabeth gave them both a warm smile and let out a breath of relief. "Thank you. You are both too kind. And Mrs. Aldridge, you must call me by my given name! I should hope we are close enough by now that you would feel comfortable doing so."

"Oh, you are so sweet. Of course!" his mother said with a little giggle. She was about to say something else in response when the footman came in once again and announced Mr. and Mrs. Browning.

Charles and his mother exchanged a little look and a laugh but greeted their guests warmly. He couldn't help but notice that somehow Elizabeth had placed herself at his side as he made the introductions. He looked down at her as she reached out and offered her hand to Mrs. Browning in a friendly gesture. She looked so right just there, next to him. He knew at that moment, without a doubt, that she was the woman he wanted to spend the rest of his life with.

She was so warm and kind, intelligent and clever, and wonderful to be with. He wanted nothing more than to wake up with her by his side, discuss the issues of the day with her over the dinner table, and spend his nights... He had to keep his mind centered on what was going on around him, or he'd quickly get himself into trouble, he sharply reminded himself.

The rest of the guests joined them, and soon, the drawing room was filled with laughter and the hum of voices. Elizabeth had managed to stay by his side, making him feel comfortable and his guests welcome.

A footman came around with a tray of wine glasses. Charles took one for himself and handed another to Elizabeth. He turned to her and quietly said, "Thank you."

She took the wine and widened her eyes at him. "For what?"

"For being here. For being so warm and welcoming and wonderful."

She laughed and shook her head, the color rising in her cheeks, making her look even more adorable. "I've done nothing yet."

"You've done a lot already," he argued.

"Just wait, and then we'll see if you still feel this way." Her smile faltered for a moment, but she moved away before he could ask what she'd meant.

His attention was claimed by Mrs. East.

"Oh, Mr. Aldridge, this is such a lovely party," the lady gushed.

"Thank you, ma'am. I do hope your daughter is well?" he asked, so glad that his mother hadn't extended her invitation to include the girl as well. He didn't quite know how she'd managed to do that, but he was grateful.

At precisely eight o'clock, the butler announced dinner, and they all progressed into the dining room.

"Mrs. Aldridge," Lady Welles said, as the pudding was placed on the table, "this meal was incredible. Please don't tell Margaret or Tina I said this, but I think it was even better than the dinner before Lady Ayres's wedding ball."

Charles's mother's cheeks turned bright red. "Oh, Lady Welles!" she giggled. "You are too kind. Now *that* was a feast! This was merely a simple dinner for good friends."

"Here's to friends," Elizabeth said, raising her wine glass.

"To friends!" everyone replied, also raising their glasses.

Charles gave her a grateful look. She responded with a wink and a little smile. She knew! Somehow, she knew that the conversation could have taken a very difficult turn at the mention of Lady Ayres's ball and the dinner before it. Her toast effectively turned the conversation.

He didn't like boasting about his mother's connections to the *haute ton* and knew that she would never do so either. It was an innocent comment by Lady Welles that could have become something awkward if Elizabeth hadn't stepped in with such grace.

His thoughts were interrupted when the butler bent down next to him and whispered in his ear, "Sir, there are three gentlemen here who wish to have a word."

"What? Why are you interrupting me with this in the middle of a dinner party?" Charles whispered back fiercely.

"Because they are the Marquess of Sorrell, the Viscount Stenford, and the Earl of Gorling," the man whispered back.

Charles could feel the color drain from his face.

"Charles, is there something wrong?" his mother called from the other end of the table.

"Er, no, Mother. Not at all." He stood up. "If you would simply excuse me for a moment." He bowed to everyone assembled and followed the butler out of the room.

He'd put the three noblemen into the drawing room.

"My lords," Charles said, coming into the room.

"Ah, Aldridge. So sorry for taking you away from your party."

"It's my fault," a woman's voice said from the doorway.

Charles turned to find Elizabeth there, looking at him with worried eyes.

She came farther into the room and curtsied to the three gentlemen. She then turned to Charles. "It was perhaps very wrong of me, but I asked Lord Sorrell to come and bring whoever he felt should be here—presumably the gentlemen on his committee if he's had a chance to create it yet."

Charles was momentarily speechless. She'd

invited people to his party? That was beyond rude, awkward, and well, downright odd.

"Your mother told me that the gentlemen you were going to be inviting this evening would be members of your committee on the importation of Swiss watches," Elizabeth said. "I thought that if you and the other gentlemen could meet with Lord Sorrell and the members of the committee, perhaps you could work together to...to do something, or start doing something." She looked from Charles to Lord Sorrell.

That gentleman started as if he'd suddenly realized it was his turn to speak. "Er, yes, well, I have started speaking to men who might be interested in forming the committee, my lady. So far, I've spoken with Lords Stenford and Gorling who were kind enough to join me this evening to learn more. Lords Rogan and Kershawn, unfortunately, were not able to join us tonight... previous engagements, I believe."

"Lord Rogan? You asked Lord Rogan to join the committee?" Charles asked. If that man was on committee he was done for. It might as well not exist at all—or worse.

"Actually, he overheard me speaking with Gorling and asked to join. I couldn't very well turn him down." Lord Sorrell had the grace to look a little uncomfortable. "I, er, believe you know him."

Charles winced. Clearly the man was aware of the scandal. "I can't imagine he would be a helpful person to have, my lord, if you'll excuse my plain speaking."

"Oh, I don't think he would allow his personal feelings to get in the way of business," Lord Stenford said, jumping into the conversation.

"I should hope not!" Lord Sorrell agreed.

Charles had absolutely no confidence in Rogan's ability to keep his personal life and business separate, but there didn't seem to be anything he could do about it.

"Well, this is all a little awkward," Charles started.

"Lady St. Vincent explained the situation earlier when she asked if we would come. We did so, knowing it would be deuced awkward, but had to agree that the opportunity wasn't one to be missed. We need to learn more about the situation and what we might be able to do about it. What do you say, Aldridge? Would you mind very much taking some time from your party to talk business?" Lord Sorrell said.

Charles nodded. Lord Sorrell was right. Elizabeth was right. He just didn't like the way she'd gone about it. He turned to her. "I agree that this *is* an excellent opportunity, I just wish you'd said something to me first."

She nodded. "It was one of those situations where I felt it would be better to ask for forgiveness rather than permission."

Charles had to give her a little smile at that one. He himself had done that quite a few times when he'd been at school. "Right. Well, gentlemen, would you care to join us in the dining room for port? I'm afraid we've just finished dinner."

"Ah, then our timing is perfect," Lord Gorling said with a laugh.

They all followed Charles back into the dining room. Introductions were made, and then the ladies excused themselves to retire for tea in the drawing room while the men got down to business.

Chapter Twenty-Six

~May 27~

Penelope rushed out the following afternoon to the park with Duchess. The silly dog kept stopping her to smell things, however. It was most annoying! She had someone to meet and important things to discuss. She didn't have time to wait while her dog smelled some other animal's feces.

"Oh, do come, Duchess. Honestly!" Penelope said, finally giving up on patience and just yanking the dog forward.

She rushed through the park as quickly as her legs could carry her and was nearly out of breath when she reached the area of the park where she always met Bolton and his pack of King Charles Spaniels. Strangely, though, he was nowhere in sight.

Had they missed him? Was he simply not coming?

It was true, it wasn't the nicest day—to be honest, it looked as if it was going to rain any minute. But the weather had never seemed to stop him from coming out before. Why, he had even teased Penelope for not coming out in the rain once. "The dogs still need to be walked whether it's raining or not," he said, laughing at her.

"True, but we don't like getting wet," Penelope had explained to him.

He'd just chuckled and shrugged. It seemed neither he nor his dogs cared one way or the other about the weather. They went out no matter what, he'd told her.

But then, why wasn't he here today, she wondered.

She and Duchess wandered around the area for a quarter of an hour, both looking around anxiously whenever they heard another dog or someone coming down the path. Penelope was ready to give up and go home with a very heavy heart when they heard a few yips coming toward them. They both turned around eagerly to find all four of Bolton's spaniels dragging the poor man behind them in their eagerness to reach her and Duchess.

She could only laugh as their master tried in vain to keep the dogs in check, but he was completely outnumbered. One little spaniel was difficult enough to control, but four of them would have required a much larger, stronger man than poor, dear Bolton.

As they neared, he was nearly dragged off his feet as the four dogs tried to run the last distance to them. When they were finally all together and the dogs were happily sniffing each other in greeting, he pulled out his handkerchief and swiped it across his sweating brow.

"Oh, you poor thing," Penelope said, not able to contain her laughter.

"My word, but they were determined," he said, beginning to chuckle himself. "This is what I get for being a few minutes late." He gave her a slight bow. "My apologies, madam, if I made you wait."

"That's perfectly all right. I'm just so happy that you came. I *was* beginning to worry we'd missed you, or you had befallen some ill," she said, smiling up at him.

"Oh, no, no," he said, smiling broadly at her. "I'm afraid a meeting with my solicitor just ran a little longer than anticipated. That's all."

"Well, I *am* glad you made it." She looked down at the dogs, who were now all waiting patiently for their walk to begin. "And it looks like they are too."

"Indeed," he said, laughing. "Well, shall we?"

He offered her his arm, and they began their stroll, the five dogs leading the way.

"So, you missed me, eh?" he said, looking down at her, his eyes twinkling with happiness.

She laughed. "I did." Even as she said it, she could feel her cheeks heating, so she quickly changed the subject. "I have excellent news."

"Oh?"

"Charles is going to marry!"

"Ha! Excellent! My felicitations to you both. Who is the lucky girl? Did he go with one of the young girls you wanted or a miss from a watchmaking family?"

"Neither! He has fallen in love with Lady St. Vincent—and she with him, judging by the way she looked at him throughout dinner last night," Penelope said.

"Lady St. Vincent? I don't know who she is," he said, turning his head in thought.

"She is a young widow—I can't imagine she is past thirty—and a very sweet girl. Very clever and thoughtful. She's going to make Charles a wonderful wife," Penelope said with satisfaction.

"You are clearly very happy. I assume the bride and groom-to-be are as well."

"Oh, well, Charles hasn't actually proposed quite as yet," Penelope admitted.

Bolton stopped walking. "He hasn't proposed? But you are already planning the wedding."

"Well..."

"Has he even told you whether he's planning on proposing to the young lady?" Bolton asked, starting their stroll once again.

"Well, not..." Penelope hedged.

"Woman! You cannot assume such things," he said, sounding rather annoyed, much to Penelope's surprise.

"Why are you so upset about this? I know he's thinking of proposing, it's why we held a dinner party last night. He wanted to see how she would behave with his colleagues from the Company of Clockmakers," she said in defense.

"And he *said* he was thinking of proposing? Told you as much, in so many words?"

"Yes! He said he wanted to propose to Elizabeth but needed to be sure she would fit in with all the different sorts of people he socialized with."

He settled down a bit. "Well, all right, then. And I assume she did get along with them."

"Most wonderfully! She was so kind and considerate, not at all condescending or haughty. I tell you, she is a gem of a girl," Penelope said.

"That's very nice."

"And not only that, she invited some noblemen

to join us after dinner so they could work with Charles and his colleagues on creating a committee or something in Parliament."

Bolton frowned at her. "Why do they need a committee?"

"Oh, something to do with imported watches. I don't know the details. But the point is that Charles had discussed the issue with Elizabeth—that is, with Lady St. Vincent—and she was thoughtful enough to use her influence to help Charles."

Bolton pursed his lips and nodded. "Sounds like she'll be an excellent political wife for him."

"Yes. I don't know how often he'll need such assistance, but if he does, she is clearly not afraid to make sure he gets it. I am *very* happy."

Bolton smiled down at her. "Well, if you are happy, then I am happy." He tucked her hand closer to his body making Penelope smile. A warmth and sense of comfort she hadn't felt in a rather long time overcame her. She felt cared for and protected.

She looked up at Bolton. "You are a very good man, Mr. Bolton."

He looked down at her, chuckling. "And you are very sweet woman, Mrs. Aldridge."

"You make me happy," she sighed, momentarily resting her head on his shoulder.

"Good. You deserve to be happy. You deserve all the happiness in the world."

~*~

Elizabeth couldn't help herself as she brushed back Matthew's hair, which hung perilously close to his eyes. She smiled at her boy as he moved his little tin soldiers into place for the grand battle about to take place on the nursery floor.

"Mama," he whined, waving her hand away. "You're supposed to be putting your men into position."

"I'm sorry. You need to have your hair trimmed," she said, smiling at him.

"You said you would play with me," he pointed out with a seriousness to his expression that belied his few years.

She laughed. "Yes, I did." She turned back to the solders laying helter-skelter in front of her on the floor and began to dutifully stand them up in formation. A man would probably have a great deal more fun with this game than she. She knew what to do—she'd played toy soldiers with Edward when they'd been children—she just thought a man, a father-figure, would enjoy it more and perhaps be able to teach Matthew things she simply didn't know or had never bothered to learn.

A father-figure. Like Charles.

She'd felt so good, so right standing next to him, greeting his guests the night before. Perhaps she should introduce him to Matthew. She just wasn't sure when. Should she wait until Charles had proposed, if he would? Or should she do so before, so he could gracefully back out if he realized he didn't want to marry a woman with a child of her own?

Her heart stuttered at the thought.

Surely, he wouldn't end their relationship because of Matthew, would he? She would be happy—more than happy—to give Charles sons of his own. Maybe it would be better for him to meet Matthew before he considered proposing to her. There wasn't anyone who met the child who didn't immediately like him. He was a very sweet, lovable boy.

"Mama," Matthew said, reminding her that she was supposed to be paying attention to the game.

But she simply couldn't stop thinking of Charles, of their relationship, of how sweet and wonderful he was. Of how handsome and gallant. Of how intelligent and...

"Mama!"

"Yes, Matthew, I do beg your pardon. I will do better. I will pay attention," she said, brushing his hair back again. Charles should definitely meet her sweet, adorable, demanding child.

But again... How would she arrange it? She would have to think on this.

~*~

"Ah, Aldridge," Lord Wickford greeted Charles as he walked into the reading room that night.

"Evening, Wickford." Charles gave the man a smile.

"Are you alone tonight?"

"Yes. Just thought I'd come and, er, escape the female presence if you know what I mean?" Charles said with a little laugh.

"As are so many here!" Wickford said with a chuckle. "Say, do you know Lord Rossburke?" His lordship began guiding Charles toward the far side of the room.

"No, I don't believe I do, but I'm always happy to meet new people."

"Excellent. He doesn't know too many here either, but he's an old school friend of mine." Wickford stopped in front of a rather large blond gentleman with impressive shoulders reading the newspaper. "Rossburke, I'd like you to meet Mr. Charles Aldridge."

The man put down the paper and stood up, extending his hand as he did so. "A pleasure."

Charles shook his hand as their host explained, "Rossburke is an artist. A painter. He did some of the pieces we have on display in the entry hall."

"Really? They're quite good," Charles said, smiling at the man.

"Thank you. You don't actually need to say that, though," Rossburke said with an embarrassed laugh.

"Not at all. Have you ever done miniatures?" Charles asked.

"Mr. Aldridge is a watchmaker by trade," Wickford informed his friend.

"Really? That's fascinating. Now that is quite an art in itself," Lord Rossburke said, indicating for Charles to take the seat next to him.

"I'll send over a bottle of rum," Wickford told them before he made a graceful exit.

Charles and Rossburke were having a very enjoyable discussion on art, and the possibilities to be had within the confines of a pocket watch, when Lord Sorrell stopped just in front of them.

"Good evening, Mr. Aldridge," his lordship said. He nodded toward Rossburke but clearly didn't know him so Charles made the introductions.

"Very pleased to meet you," Lord Sorrell said, shaking Rossburke's hand. He then turned back to Charles and asked, "Er, might I have a word?"

Charles stood. "If you'll excuse me for a moment?"

Rossburke gave a nod of assent, and Charles

stepped away with Lord Sorrell's guiding hand on his back.

"I'm afraid I have some bad news," his lordship started.

Charles stomach began to tighten. "It's Rogan isn't it?"

"I'm afraid you were right to be worried about him."

Charles let out a breath and turned to look the other way. Lord Sorrell had the power to destroy his business or save it. He didn't want to seem ungrateful or to be rude in any way, but he *had* warned him.

"He's doing everything he can to stop this committee from doing its job," Lord Sorrell said, sounding very frustrated.

"Is there anything I can do?" Charles asked, turning back to him.

"I don't know. Right now, he's saying we need more evidence of wrong-doing on the part of the Swiss. Have you been able to gather more information?"

Charles frowned. "Actually, something came to light just today. A watch with *my* name engraved on the inside. I was thinking that perhaps I might trace where it actually came from."

"Where it came from? Did the jeweler selling the piece not know?"

"He knew who he bought it from—not me, obviously—but I was unable to track the supplier. He's apparently returned to the continent, possibly to get another shipment of these fake watches from Switzerland."

Lord Sorrell's eyes widened. "But then you've

got to go! You need to go to Switzerland and follow this trail."

Chapter Twenty-Seven

~May 29~

Elizabeth was a little surprised a few days later when her footman informed her that Mr. Charles Aldridge was at the door and asking whether she was at home.

"Yes, of course!" Elizabeth said, putting a hand up to her hair to be sure it was still in place. She wondered if he was going to propose. The connection they'd felt at his dinner party had been unmistakable. The entire evening she'd felt it, and she was pretty certain he had as well. When she'd stood by his side greeting his guests, it had felt so right. She had stood there, wishing with all her heart that she was indeed his hostess, his companion...his wife.

For a moment, she wondered if she was ready to get remarried. She laughed at herself. Of course she was! She had never had deeper feelings for her husband. He knew that and didn't expect anything else. Charles, on the other hand, was the most wonderful man, and she knew she was in love with him. Oh, yes, she most definitely would accept his proposal should he offer for her.

"Mr. Aldridge, my lady," Frank announced a few minutes later.

Elizabeth schooled her face into a polite smile rather than the silly grin that had probably been there a moment before.

Charles came into the room and bowed. She rose and gave him a slight curtsy. "What a lovely surprise, Charles. Please, do come in." She indicated he take a seat as she sat back down on the sofa.

Much to her surprise, he sat next to her instead of in one of the chairs. She would have taken this as an excellent sign, except he was also looking rather upset. His brow was furrowed, and his eyes looked worried.

"What is it? Has something happened?" she asked with concern.

"I'm afraid I have rather bad news," he said.

"Is your mother all right? I do hope she hasn't suffered any ill effects from the other evening's dinner."

"No, no. Thank you. She's fine." He reached into his pocket and pulled out a watch. It wasn't the one he ordinarily carried and, she noticed, it wasn't attached to his watch chain. "Mr. East found this watch a few days ago at a jeweler's on Pall Mall." He turned it over and opened up the back of it, showing her the mechanism inside.

She looked at it and then up at him. "I don't know what you're showing me, I'm afraid," she admitted.

He shook his head. "Look at the inscription, the maker's mark, there." He pointed with the tip of his smallest finger.

Elizabeth squinted and could just make out some tiny flourishing letters scratched into the gold dial. "C. Aldridge, London," she read out. She looked up at him. "C. Aldridge. That's you!"

"Yes, but I didn't make it." He frowned.

She widened her eyes. "It's a forgery?"

He nodded. "And not even a very good one. The workmanship is shoddy, the materials are not of the quality that I, or any British watchmaker, would use and... Well, I could go on. Needless to say, it is not a watch I would be proud to have my name on."

"But that's terrible, Charles! Who would have done this?"

"It came from Switzerland. I bribed the jeweler who sold it to give me the name of the man he bought it from as well as his direction. I went to confront him but learned he'd already left for the continent. I have managed to procure a ticket to Calais on a ship leaving tomorrow afternoon. I am going to find those who are making these watches."

"You're going to Switzerland?" she asked, knowing even as she said it, it was a silly question.

"Yes. Lord Rogan is demanding more evidence before the committee even begins its work on the issue. This will get us the information they'll need."

She took in a deep breath and did her best to remain calm. Lord Rogan. He was behind this as always. The man was determined to destroy everything in her life. "I see." But what about *her*, she wanted to scream at Charles. What about *them*?

Just a few minutes ago, she had been all but certain he had been coming to her with a proposal of marriage, not to tell her that he was leaving the country.

"How long will you be gone?" she asked, hoping her voice wouldn't give away just how upset she was.

"I don't know. Certainly a month, perhaps two. It depends on what I find once I get there."

She gave a nod, no longer even trusting her voice. A month! He was leaving for at least a month. Tears began to prick at her eyes. She blinked and turned away so he wouldn't see. She needed to be strong. He couldn't know how upset she was. She wouldn't put that burden on him, not when he was going on such an important mission. She was sure his business was dependent on his finding out where these watches were being made and by whom. He needed to do his best, be at his best, to stop this counterfeiting.

She knew this, but it didn't make it any easier.

She gave a little sniff and swallowed hard at the lump in her throat. "Well, I certainly hope you find whoever is making these cheap watches. You *must* get them to stop!"

He seemed to be watching her reaction closely, but he hadn't lost the frown between his eyes. "Yes. Yes, indeed." He paused and snapped closed the watch in his hand, putting it carefully back into his pocket. "Will you be all right while I'm gone?" he asked tersely.

A sob caught in her throat, but she swallowed it down and gave him the smile she knew he needed to see. "Of course! I've got my brother here and St. Vincent, of course. All the ladies of the Wagering Whist Society, naturally—your mother not the least of them." She forced out a laugh. "Why wouldn't I be all right?"

She might have all those people, but not one of them made her feel as safe and protected as he did. Not one of them made her happy like he did. Not one of them made her tingle just by being in the same room. Not one of them was *Charles*—the man she loved with all her heart.

"Very good, then," he said, frowning even more fiercely. He cleared his throat and stood. "Well, I should go. I have a lot to do before leaving as you can imagine." He seemed to be angry. Perhaps it was just that he was thinking of all he had to do before he left and then on the journey itself. She was certain it wouldn't be easy. Perhaps he was upset about seeing his name on a watch not of his making. Yes, that had to be it.

"Yes! My goodness. I'll...er, I'll see you when you get back. And if... If you wouldn't mind writing, I will be eager to hear how things go," she said, also standing.

He gave a little nod as a smile flitted on and off his lips. "I will most definitely do so."

He bowed and then strode out of the room.

Elizabeth didn't move. She couldn't as she watched the door close behind him. She could barely breathe.

Chapter Twenty-Eight

Charles stormed into the drawing room, slamming the door with a satisfying bang.

"Oh! Charles! Must you?" his mother protested.

He hadn't even seen her sitting there on the sofa. He hadn't seen his cousin either.

"What are the two of you doing?" he snapped.

"Good afternoon to you, cousin," Ainsby said amicably.

"No, it is *not* a good afternoon. What are you doing in my house?" Charles retorted.

"Charles!" his mother protested once again.

"I thought I'd come and see if you were free this evening, but clearly you don't seem to be up for company," his cousin said. "Perhaps an outing to Gentleman Jackson's Saloon would be more appropriate just now? Although, to be honest, I don't think I want to lift a fist to you when you're in this sort of mood. Who knows what sort of damage you might do to me?"

"Thank you, no. I cannot go out. I've got to pack," Charles said, trying to be more polite.

"Pack? Where are you going?" his mother asked.

He finally turned to her. "I need to go to Switzerland." He pulled out the watch Mr. East had bought and handed it to her.

She simply held it her hand, ignoring its presence. "Switzerland? You can't go to Switzerland! You're needed here. What about Elizabeth? What about me? You can't just leave us!" His mother was becoming nearly hysterical. Tears began to fall from her eyes, and her lower lip trembled. She looked for all the world precisely the way a woman surprised and upset about his upcoming journey *should* look.

"I don't believe Elizabeth needs me, nor cares," he told her.

"No! I don't believe that for a moment," she said, as tears began to slide down her soft cheeks.

"Mother, look at yourself. You're crying and upset because I'm leaving," he pointed out.

She pulled her handkerchief out of her sleeve. "Of course I am! You're leaving me here alone. And poor, dear Elizabeth! Her situation is greatly improved, but there are still—"

"Elizabeth didn't cry," he said, interrupting her. "She hardly looked upset at all when I told her just now. In fact, she smiled and told me not to forget to write!" He nearly growled he was so angry.

"No!" his mother said, looking up at him with wide watery eyes.

"I thought you said she cared for you," Ainsby argued. "You were going on about how perfect she was at your dinner party—which you did not invite me to, but that's all right, no hard feelings there."

"You would have thrown our numbers off," Charles's mother said. "I explained that to you, Quinten."

"I thought she did care for me. I'd thought we shared something that evening, and before then as well. In fact, I was so certain of it, I didn't just go over to her this afternoon to tell her I was leaving, I went to propose." He pulled a jeweler's box from his other pocket and showed his mother the ring he'd purchased when he'd gone to the jeweler for information on the watch.

His mother gasped. Ainsby got up and took a closer look at the ring.

"She turned you down?" he asked, turning the diamond and sapphire ring this way and that so that it caught the light.

"No. I never asked. She was so blasé about the fact that I was leaving, I decided not to propose. Why should I ask a woman to marry me when she couldn't care less if I'm leaving for two months?"

"But you love her!" his mother protested.

"I do. But she clearly doesn't reciprocate the feeling."

"Oh, no, I don't believe that!" she said. "She *must* care for you. I saw the way she was looking at you at dinner and before."

"Well, if she does, she does a damned good job of hiding it!" Charles said.

"So, you didn't propose and now you're going to leave?" His mother's lip began to tremble once again. "Are you sure now is a good time to go?"

"Why are you going anyway?" his cousin asked.

Charles pointed to the watch still in his mother's grasp.

She wiped her eyes, then finally took a look at the watch. She examined the front and opened the back to look inside at the mechanism, noticing his name inside. When she looked up at him again, she said, "It's got your name in it! I take it you didn't make this?"

"No, I didn't." At least his mother had the good sense to immediately realize the problem, although he really couldn't blame Elizabeth for not understanding right away. She knew nothing of watches or watchmaking. His mother had lived with a watchmaker for over thirty years.

"Is that one of the cheap forgeries you told me about?" Ainsby asked.

"Yes, but this time it has *my* name on it. I'm going to trace the supply chain back to Switzerland and find out who is making these watches and, hopefully, get them to stop," Charles said.

"Must *you* be the one...?" his mother started.

"It clearly doesn't matter one way or another to Elizabeth whether it's me or someone else," Charles said bitterly.

"I'm sure that's not true," Ainsby responded immediately.

Charles just glared at him. "You didn't see how well she took the news."

"There was no reaction on her part?" his mother asked.

"Perhaps there was a slight shine to her eyes for a moment, but that could have just been a reflection of the light from the window. So, no. There was no reaction. She doesn't care," Charles said. "So, clearly, it doesn't matter if I go or not, and honestly, I'd like to get the whole business with these Swiss watches sorted out. I bought a ticket on a ship to Calais. I leave first thing in the morning for Dover."

"But that's so soon!" his mother protested.

Charles sighed. "Perhaps, if I can go quickly, I can return quickly."

"All the way to Switzerland and back? It's going to take months!" his mother cried.

"Not months, Mother. Switzerland isn't all that far. It's not like going to India. I should be able to return in a month, maybe two, depending on how things go."

"I don't like it, Charles," his mother said, clearly becoming resigned to the idea.

"I know, Mother. I only wish Elizabeth felt as you do."

~*~

Elizabeth had finally found her breath after Charles had left, but it didn't last for long. Too soon she lost it again as the sobs wracked and rattled inside her chest, stomach, and throat.

"Elizabeth!" Edward's shocked voice came as if from far away.

Warm arms surrounded her, and her brother's strong chest was there for her to lean her head against. His presence didn't ease her crying any, but at least she wasn't entirely alone with her tears.

When she'd finally cried herself dry, she found his large white handkerchief in her hand, so she used it to wipe her face and nose.

"If this was Rogan who drove you to such tears, I swear—" he began.

"No, it was Charles," she hiccoughed.

"Aldridge? I thought you liked him! I thought he was a good fellow," her brother protested.

"He *is*. It's just...he's leaving. He needs to go to Switzerland on business," she explained.

"Oh! But he'll be back," he said, beginning to sound confused.

She nodded. "It's just... It's stupid, but he came to tell me he was leaving, and when I heard he had come, I thought he had come to propose."

"Ah, I see," Edward said with a nod. "It's more a matter of dashed expectations."

"Well...yes, and also the fact that he's leaving. Edward, he's going to be gone for the rest of the season," she said. "How am I to go on? How am I to continue going to parties and entertainments when I'm missing the man I love?" She buried her face in the handkerchief and let her sobs overtake her once again.

Edward rubbed her back and held her until her tears subsided once again. "I... I hate to ask this since you are clearly upset about Aldridge leaving, but well, just humor me here."

She looked up at him expectantly.

"Are you certain—absolutely certain—that he's the right one for you?" her brother asked.

Elizabeth's jaw dropped open. How could her brother even ask such a question?

"Now, Elizabeth, hear me out," he said quickly. "I know that Aldridge is Mrs. Aldridge's son, and she is a trusted member of the Ladies' Wagering Whist Society, but what else do you know about the man? He's a cit. He's... He's a watchmaker, for God's sake! Do you really want to marry and spend the rest of your life married to a watchmaker?"

Fury rose up in Elizabeth's breast. "How could you? Edward..." She paused to take in a deep breath. "You of all people... You, who lived with an opera singer of low birth... You are questioning whether I am serious about marrying a well-respected businessman?"

Her brother had the grace to pale slightly. "I just want to be sure you know what you're doing. That he's the right man for you. You don't want to get into another loveless marriage. You don't need to marry at all, Elizabeth. St. Vincent left you well enough off that you can live comfortably for the rest of your life—not in luxury, granted, but comfortably enough."

"No, I don't need to marry. I *want* to marry. And not just anyone. I want to marry Charles," she told her brother, pulling away from him. "I love him."

"I understand that you *think*—"

"Edward Manning, I am not a child!" Elizabeth finally exploded. "Charles is the only man—the *only* man—I've ever known who has treated me with respect. He doesn't look at me like I'm easy game. He speaks with me about his business, about his interests, about everything. He acknowledges my intelligence—unlike a certain brother I could name."

Edward winced. "I'm not questioning your intelligence, Elizabeth, I questioning whether he's the right man for you."

"He is. End of discussion."

~May 30~

Lady Kershaw's annual ball was an event very few of the *ton* missed, and Elizabeth wasn't going to be one of them. After allowing her emotions to rule for a full day, she was determined to live her life to the best of her ability.

She was so very grateful for the support of both Edward and Paul. Even little Matthew had realized something was upsetting his mother and had insisted they go out to play. She knew he'd meant to cheer her, but it had taken all her fortitude to go out and try to be happy for the sweet, well-meaning child. Indeed, by the end of an hour with his infectious laughter and good cheer, it was impossible not to at least be a little happier.

With Matthew's cheering that afternoon and the escort of both her brother and stepson, she managed to show a good face at the ball that evening. The fact that the two men stayed by her side for a good quarter of an hour as they greeted friends and others helped a great deal as well.

Lady Sorrell had just excused herself when Elizabeth saw Mrs. Aldridge come in with her nephew Lord Ainsby. Elizabeth wasn't far from the door, so she was certain the lady must have seen her, and yet she turned and went in the opposite direction.

"Did Mrs. Aldridge just cut you?" Paul asked, also watching the lady.

"I can't imagine why she should, but strangely yes, it did look that way," Elizabeth responded. "I'm not inclined to just let that be. Excuse me, I'm going to have a word with her."

Paul gave her a nod, and she headed straight for the lady, who had just been abandoned by Lord Ainsby. Perfect.

"Good evening, Mrs. Aldridge," Elizabeth said, approaching her.

"Good evening," the lady responded coldly, not even giving her the slightest smile.

"I do beg your pardon, but what have I done to offend you?" Elizabeth asked, beginning to feel a knot growing in the pit of her stomach.

Mrs. Aldridge finally turned and looked

directly at Elizabeth for the first time. "Do you feel nothing, my lady? Do you have emotions?"

"What? Of course, I do!"

"Ah, then it's simply that you don't actually care for my son despite that I—and he—had thought otherwise," she said with an angry sniff.

Elizabeth opened her mouth but didn't know what to say for a moment. Finally, she whispered, "I love Charles very much. I... I don't know why you—and he—would think that I don't."

Mrs. Aldridge turned back to her again. "If that is true, then how could you smile and happily send him on his way when he told you he was leaving?"

"Because I didn't want him to feel bad about having to leave. Because I believed that's what he needed to see and hear. He was upset about the counterfeit watch and pre-occupied with his business interests. I didn't want to be a nuisance, a distraction, when he needed to focus on his work."

Mrs. Aldridge just blinked at her, perhaps debating whether to believe her or not.

"My husband, may he rest in peace, hated it when I showed my emotions. He said it showed weakness and was irritating to a gentleman who had more important things to deal with. He hated it when I became emotional about anything. I learned... I learned not to do so. Charles shouldn't have to deal with me when he has much more important things that he needs to take care of," Elizabeth explained as calmly as she could. She wasn't going to cause a scene in the middle of a ball.

Mrs. Aldridge reached out and took her hand. "Oh, my poor, poor dear. Your husband was clearly not the kindest or most understanding of men, was he?"

"I can't say that he was," Elizabeth said, feeling tears prick at her eyes. She quickly blinked them away. "I may be struck down for saying this, but I also can't say I was horribly upset when he died. That was one time when I didn't need to suppress my emotions, for I simply didn't have any except, perhaps, relief."

Mrs. Aldridge gave her hand a consoling squeeze. "I am so sorry. We are not used to such behavior, and I'm afraid we read your lack of emotion in the wrong way."

"I do hope Charles didn't leave thinking I didn't care!" Elizabeth said, horrified.

"I'm afraid he did."

"I will write to him! I will tell him exactly how I feel and why I behaved the way I did. Oh, Mrs. Aldridge, I'm...I'm..." Elizabeth felt almost overcome. She prayed she hadn't destroyed the one good thing that had come into her life. She couldn't bear that. Before she could say anything more, however, there was a commotion at the door.

Chapter Twenty-Nine

Charles had been on the road for three hours sitting in the mail coach bound for Dover. Three hours of thinking. Three hours of wondering whether Elizabeth loved him. Three hours of mulling over exactly how much he loved her.

He had been lucky enough to get a seat inside the coach, but it didn't make the tedious journey any easier—not when he had nothing to do but think. He realized now he should have just ridden his horse, but then he would have had to arrange for a change of mount along the route, and he would have been exhausted by the time he arrived.

So, instead, he'd sat there, swaying with the movement of the coach, staring out the window, thinking. He'd gone over his last meeting with Elizabeth again and again, and yet the more he thought about it, the more certain he was that those had actually been tears in her eyes when she'd turned away from him.

Was it possible she had turned away so he couldn't see her tears? But why would she want to hide them? Why wouldn't she simply show him how upset she was? Why hide her emotions?

It just didn't make any sense to him. He shook his head and heaved a heavy sigh.

"My word, you poor man, you look like you've lost your greatest love," said the kind-looking young woman sitting across from him. She looked like she might be a governess on her way to a posting. Her dress and hat were sensible. Not exactly ugly, but certainly not flattering to her round face and large brown eyes.

"I may have," he admitted.

"Ugh, I'm sure it can't be that bad," she said, giving him a smile.

He noticed their conversation had attracted the attention of the other occupants of the carriage. He truly had no desire to air his private business in public, but, on the other hand, maybe this gentle woman could shed some light on Elizabeth's reaction. His mother certainly hadn't been able to, but then she had always been one to wear her emotions on her sleeve.

"I don't know," he admitted. "I, er, I have to go to the continent on business," he told her. "I told this to a young lady with whom I have been quite close of late. She simply smiled and told me not to forget to write."

"Not the reaction you were hoping for, I take it?" the woman asked.

"No," Charles said. "I had been planning on proposing, but with a response like that, I reconsidered."

"Oh, how very sad! I *am* sorry!" She tilted her head and looked at him as if he was a boy who'd just lost his puppy.

"I just don't understand it. I thought she loved me," he admitted quietly.

"Are you certain she doesn't? Could she have, perhaps, been hiding the fact that she was upset?"

"That's what I'm now wondering. There was a moment when I thought I might have seen tears in her eyes, but she turned away from me before I could be certain."

"Well, there you have it. I'm *sure* she was upset and just didn't want to show it for whatever reason."

"I can't help feeling that I've missed something...something important."

"It sounds as if you have. You missed your opportunity to have a happy life with this lady. What would you do, if while you were away, she found another gentleman?"

He shook his head. "If she loved me, she would wait."

The woman nodded. "Perhaps. Perhaps not."

"I can't imagine... No, I'm not worried about her falling in love with anyone else. I'm worried... I'm worried for her. For us. Even, perhaps, for me. I don't fall in love easily, but this lady is very special."

"Then why don't ya just go back to 'er?" asked the man sitting next to Charles.

"I need to see to some business—"

"And yer business is more important than yer young lady?" the woman next to the governess asked, sounding rather horrified.

Charles opened his mouth, but he didn't know what to say.

"Will ya lose yer business if'n ya wait another month or two to go?" the man next to him asked.

"That's a good point," the governess said. She then looked at him as if she expected an answer.

Charles paused to wonder what Lord Rogan would do if he didn't provide his evidence right away. Would Lord Sorrell be forced to dissolve the committee? Could it be created once again? He wondered if some time passed whether Rogan wouldn't simply forget his about objection to Charles and allow the committee to do its work. "No, I wouldn't lose my business. I'm going on a fact-finding—"

"Fact-finding? And those facts won't be there later?" the man persisted.

"I suppose they will," Charles admitted. And Rogan might have a cooler head if allowed to just sit and calm himself for some time.

"Well, then, can you postpone your trip? I'm certain she's put off things for you, or given up something so she could be with you, hasn't she?" the governess asked.

Charles thought about it. He was certain she had, even if no examples immediately sprung to mind. "Well, she did introduce me to some people who will be able to help me with my business, actually. I'm certain..." He paused. If Elizabeth hadn't had her social connections, she would never have been able to introduce Charles to Lord Sorrell or invite him to Charles's home. She wouldn't have known his lordship.

Charles gave a little laugh. He'd been arguing with her that society was completely useless, and here he was, proven wrong. If he was wrong about that, was it possible he was wrong in thinking she held no feelings for him?

"You're thinking about this thing she did for you, aren't you?" the governess asked, watching him.

He nodded.

"Well, then, might you want to reconsider

going on this journey? Instead of sitting here wondering whether this young lady loves you, you should be in London *asking* her," the governess said.

"Yes," he agreed. "Yes, you are absolutely right—all of you." Charles looked out the window for any signs of a village. "Do you know if we're going to be stopping any time soon?" He pulled out his watch and looked at the time. It was half-past eleven. Surely, they would stop for something to eat and for the passengers to stretch.

"I imagine we will at about mid-day," the governess said with a little smile.

Charles nodded. "Thank you. I may... I may return to London at that time and see if I can't speak with her." He turned to the man next to him. "You are right, sir, my business *can* wait, but this lady cannot."

The man nodded with satisfaction. "That's the way to do it. Ya go after what you want, and people are always more important than business."

When they did stop, Charles shook the hand of everyone who had been with him inside the coach. "Thank you. Thank you very much for your good advice. I greatly appreciate it."

He managed to hire a horse and sped back to Town as quickly as possible. Still, it was late when he reached Mayfair. He took one look at his watch and knew that both Elizabeth and his mother would most likely be at a party. He only needed to query his butler to find out which one.

He didn't even bother changing his clothes. He had a terrible, nagging feeling he needed to get there quickly.

~*~

"Where is the bitch!" a man's voice could be heard shouting. "Get your bloody hands off of me!"

Elizabeth was horrified to see Lord Rogan stumble into the room.

"Where is my woman? Where is she—ah! There you are my beauty." He changed direction and began to weave toward Elizabeth. "You're mine. Do you hear me? You are mine, Miss Elizabeth Manning, Miss High-And-Mighty."

Elizabeth began to back up but found herself bumping against other people, all staring in shock at Lord Rogan. There was no escape.

"Lord Rogan, you are drunk," she said. "Would someone please remove this gentleman?" she pleaded to someone, anyone, before there was even more of a scene that she most definitely did not want to be a part of.

Lord Brentley tried to approach Lord Rogan, but to everyone's shock, Rogan swung around, planting a facer on the man. He was knocked onto his backside where he stayed. No one else made another attempt.

"You can't stop me," he told the fellow. "You...you're Brentley! Trying to protect what was once yours, eh?" Rogan gave a bitter laugh. "You may have had her once, but now it's my turn, I tell you. My turn!" he shouted, pointing to himself.

"I...I never!" Lord Brentley protested.

"Oh, don't pull that with me. I know. You were bragging about swiving her. Told everybody. I heard you. Others did too. Well, now it's *my* turn."

There were horrified gasps around the room. Elizabeth thought she was going to be sick.

Lord Rogan spun around to her. "You are not

going to escape me, my sweet. I know you want me. You've wanted me ever since...ever since..."

"Lord Rogan, you are mistaken," Elizabeth said, trying to keep her voice from trembling.

"No, I am not! Stop telling me that! I know you've shagged him. I know you've tupped at least five, ten, dash it all, how many *have* you had relations with?"

"None!" Elizabeth cried. "This is all in your imagination."

"You are not my imagination. You want me!" He stopped shouting and then actually smiled at her. "You came to me. At the Welles's party. You came to me in the library." He sniggered.

"You tricked me! You sent a message saying my stepson wanted a word."

"Yes," he laughed cruelly. "And you fell for it— such a gullible little... But once you were there... You would have enjoyed it. You *will* enjoy it. When I get you into my bed..."

"My lord, it is *never* going to happen! You *must* believe this," Elizabeth said, standing up to him even as he advanced on her. She was trembling worse than anything, but she would *not* show her fear. She was certain if she did, he wouldn't believe her, and she *had* to make him believe her. She had to get through to him. She simply could not continue allowing this man to destroy her life.

"It will, my sweet. I am going to get under those pretty little skirts. We are going to make the beast with two backs, and you are going to enjoy every single—"

"My lord, stop this!" she protested. "I didn't have relations with anyone. Not with Lord Brentley, not with Mr. Aldridge, no one!"

Rogan started to laugh. "Aldridge, that naïve imbecile. Got rid of him, didn't I? No, I can believe you didn't sleep with *him*. You've got better taste than that. But everyone believed you did, didn't they? They believed me when I told them you'd spent the night with him." He laughed, but quickly became serious again. "You have better taste than that in bedfellows. You're going to be mine."

He lunged at her, and suddenly, everything slowed and the world went silent.

One moment Elizabeth was standing up to Lord Rogan in front of Mrs. Aldridge and any number of other people. The next, he was reaching for her, grabbing a hold of the back of her neck. She shoved her hands into his chest to push him away, and suddenly, he was moving backward much faster than her push would have caused.

Charles's fist swung in a wide arc, smashing into Lord Rogan's jaw, sending him flying to the floor where he landed like a sack of flour. His body bounced with the force of his fall, his limbs flopping. The man didn't move after that.

And then Elizabeth was in Charles's arms. It didn't last long enough, though. Her stomach rebelled too soon. She pushed away from Charles's warm, comforting arms and went running for the door. She shoved her way through the party-goers before she cast up her accounts on the beautiful, useless people who were all still just standing there watching the show.

It almost would have served them right. The idea was in the back of her mind as she vomited just outside the front door. That and the horror of all that had just happened. The horror of standing there in the street being sick, knowing that everyone had been watching her. Watching Lord

Rogan. Listening to all his filth. His lies. The horror of knowing she was crying in public. Knowing that her reputation was entirely ruined. Knowing that she could never, ever show her face in public again.

And yet...and yet... Charles!

She spit one more time and then found a handkerchief being pressed into her hand. She used it to wipe her face, then stood and looked to make sure she hadn't imagined him.

No, Charles was there. He was standing next to her, looking worried and concerned.

"Charles, you're here? You were to have left," she said between her tears.

"Are you not pleased to see me?" he asked, beginning to frown.

"I..." After all that had happened, he was questioning whether she was happy he was there? She couldn't take this. The man she loved more than anything else in the world had just witnessed her public humiliation, and he wanted to know whether she was happy to see him? Her stomach revolted once again.

She turned away, heaving at nothing. There was nothing left inside of her to spit out, but still her stomach rebelled.

"Elizabeth! My God! Oh, Aldridge, er, you have things in hand?" Elizabeth could hear her brother ask.

"I think it might be best if you took her home," Charles said as Elizabeth put his handkerchief to her mouth again.

"Oh, yes, yes of course," Edward said. He put his arm around her. Somehow her coach was right there. He led her to it and assisted her to climb in.

She caught a glimpse of Charles standing there on the pavement, watching, as they pulled away.

All she could feel was a great, gaping hollowness inside of her as if she had spit out more than just her dinner. Somehow, she seemed to have lost everything, but *everything* that was important and dear to her.

Chapter Thirty

~May 31~

Penelope was at sixes and sevens the following morning. She paced this way and that and simply could not settle down. Duchess had paced with her, the dear pup, but even *she* could do nothing to calm her mistress.

Penelope had tried to eat but had no appetite. She tried to sit and read but couldn't concentrate. Even her knitting couldn't distract her. She couldn't go out for her regular walk with Duchess, she just couldn't imagine facing anyone from society, and she couldn't risk missing Charles. She needed to speak with him.

She had seen him flatten that awful Lord Rogan, but then he'd left immediately afterward. She didn't know if he'd taken Elizabeth home or had simply come home alone. All she knew was that he was in his room.

So, she did nothing all morning but wait for Charles and pace, taking short breaks every so often to sit anxiously and pet her dog. Why did the boy not come down for breakfast? Why did he not appear to go into his workshop? Why did he not—

"Ma'am, there is a gentleman here to see you," the footman announced as she paced back and forth in the drawing room.

She spun around hopefully. "Who is it? Is it Lord St. Vincent? Lord Conway?"

"No, ma'am. He said his name was Bolton—just Bolton," the footman said, clearly as confused as she had ever been.

"Oh, Bolton!" She went running from the room, Duchess barking at her heels.

The man was standing in the entryway, all four of his dogs standing anxiously around him. They answered Duchess's barks with yaps of their own. They all clearly knew something was wrong—even Bolton.

As she hurried down the stairs, he dropped the dog's leads and rushed forward. "Mrs. Aldridge, my dear woman, what's wrong? Are you all right? What has happened?"

"Oh, Bolton," she wailed, throwing herself into his arms.

He just stood there holding her for a good minute before putting some space in between them and looking her over. "Please, madam, do not keep me in suspense. What has happened?"

"It was awful!"

"Are you hurt?"

"What? No! No, not at all. Come upstairs and I shall tell you everything. I am so upset. I haven't been able to eat, sit, walk, nothing. I... I..."

"Wait just a moment," he said, pulling her to a halt as she was about to climb the stairs again. "You haven't eaten yet today?"

"No, I couldn't. Charles—"

"Don't worry about Charles. He's a grown man and can take care of himself. You, however, clearly need someone to take care of you. Come along, now, you need sustenance." He turned to the footman. "Bring your mistress some breakfast in her drawing room and take the dogs—all of them—outside into the garden. We don't need them underfoot just now."

"Yes, sir…or…ma'am?" he asked, looking to Penelope for confirmation that he should follow these orders.

"Yes, yes. Do as he says," Penelope said, so happy to have someone take command. She turned and continued up to the drawing room.

She spent the next fifteen minutes detailing the entire previous evening for her friend. He was, as to be expected, happy that Elizabeth did care for Charles and then shocked and horrified no one had managed to stop Lord Rogan from attacking the poor girl.

"So, it took Charles to finally down the man?" he asked, as Penelope began to dig into the food the footman had brought up to her.

"Yes! But immediately after he did so, she ran outside—honestly, I believe she was ill, not that I blame her one bit. Charles followed her, but then neither one of them returned. I believe her brother went out as well," Penelope said, now that she thought back.

"And did he return?" Bolton asked.

"No."

"So, we must assume that at least one of them escorted the lady home," Bolton said, always so practical.

"Yes, precisely. But I don't know who, and Charles has not emerged from his room as yet. I've been waiting and waiting. I am sorry I missed our walk, but you must understand—"

"Of course! You couldn't leave without having spoken with him," Bolton said.

"Yes," she said, so very grateful he understood.

He gave her a consoling look. "It's quite all right. Now that I know you're all right and taken care of, I'll take my leave. I'm sure Charles will come out when he's ready. It sounds as if he had quite a difficult day yesterday as well."

"Oh, yes. Thank you, Bolton. It was so sweet of you to come and check on me," she said, standing as he did.

He paused and took her hands in his. "I want... I *always* want to be here for you. Please never hesitate to call for me." He leaned down and gave her a light kiss on her lips before leaving.

She stood there, a little stunned for a moment, and then realized she had no way of knowing where he lived. She didn't even know whether Bolton was his name or his title. How could she send for him if she did need him? At least he had come and, clearly, he cared.

~*~

It took all of Elizabeth's will to get herself out of bed the following day, and even then, she didn't manage to do so until well past ten. Normally, she was an early riser, but she just couldn't get herself going.

She didn't know if there would be any breakfast still, but her stomach insisted she at least take a look. She was surprised to find her brother and Paul sitting together, sharing the meal.

"Elizabeth!" Edward said, rising as she came in. "I'm surprised to see you here."

She gave him a little smile. "I live here,

remember?"

He frowned at her. "I didn't expect to see you at breakfast."

"Well, I'm afraid my hunger insisted," she said, sitting down at her place. A footman approached, and she ordered an egg and toast as well as a fresh pot of tea.

"You are looking remarkably well," Paul said.

"Am I? I don't feel particularly well," she said in the most off-hand way she could.

"You're not crying, I count that as looking remarkably well," he said, giving her a smile.

She gave a little laugh. "Oddly enough, I'm not." She took stock of her emotions. "No, I don't seem to have any tears at this point. Perhaps I'm still in shock."

"That is possible," Edward agreed.

"Honestly, I hardly feel anything. I mean, nothing. Absolutely nothing." She let her gaze wander toward the paintings on the wall. "I feel rather as if my insides have all been ripped from my body—my heart, my lungs." She gave a little laugh as the footman placed a plate in front of her. "Everything except my stomach."

Both men frowned at her, looking much too worried. She decided to ignore their concerned looks and focus instead on eating, since she could.

"Do you have plans, Paul?" Elizabeth asked after a few minutes of silence, during which she kept her eyes firmly on her plate so she wouldn't see the concerned looks the two men were sharing.

"Plans? What sort of plans?" her stepson asked.

"Well, I was thinking that I should probably return to St. Vincent, but I'm not quite comfortable going alone. Would it be a very great imposition for you to escort me?" she asked, finally looking up at him.

"So that's it? You're just going to run away?" Edward asked.

She lowered a full fork back to her plate as she looked over toward her brother. "Do you really think I have any other choice?"

"I don't know. *I* think you've been exonerated. Rogan admitted to everything last night, didn't he?" Edward said.

"I don't believe society is going to see it that way," she said, picking up her fork once again.

"If you can wait a day or two, I should be able to clear my schedule," Paul said.

"Excellent. I appreciate that." She gave him a fleeting smile and turned her thoughts to packing.

~*~

Elizabeth found she couldn't concentrate—not even on something so simple as deciding what she would take with her. Her mind kept going back to the previous evening. It had been horrible. No, worse. It had probably been the worst experience of her entire life, and that was saying something, considering she'd practically been run out of town after she'd made her debut.

Now that she thought about it, though, it was more her mother who dragged her back home rather than anything anyone had said directly to her. But she hadn't exactly known what they were saying about her. She hadn't found that out until they'd gotten home, and her mother had had to explain it all to her father.

This time, though, the humiliation had been complete, and it had been public. Was there truly any recourse other than to run away again? She honestly didn't know.

She needed to think and to do that, she realized, she needed to go out. She had absolutely no desire to see anyone she knew, but she definitely needed a good long walk. Perhaps she could walk along the lesser followed pathways through Hyde Park.

She was just putting on her hat and pulling on her gloves when Matthew came bounding down the stairs, his governess rushing along behind. "Oh, please, Master Matthew, you mustn't," she called after him.

"Mama! Where are you going? Can I come?"

"I'm just going for a walk," she told him.

"I'd like to go for a walk. May I? Please?" the child asked, looking up at her like a little angel.

"Well..."

"Please, Mama, please. I've finished my lessons for the day, isn't that right, Mrs. Reed?" he said, turning toward the governess who was hovering in the background.

"Well, yes, but—" she started.

"See? Please, may I come?" the child asked again.

"Will you promise to be good and not jabber my ear off? I'm going out so I can do a little thinking," Elizabeth told him.

"I won't. I'll be so quiet you won't remember I'm there," he said. It might have been her imagination, but it looked as if he had batted his eyelashes at her.

Oh, goodness, how could she resist such a sweet face? "All right. Come along, then."

Chapter Thirty-One

The day was bright and clear, Elizabeth found as she stepped out of her house, Matthew's hand safely tucked into her own. It was odd that the weather was so fine when her mind was in such a fog. Perhaps, she thought, some of that clarity would seep in.

Sadly, there was no other way to get to the smaller paths in the park except to go in the main gate. They had crossed the street and were headed that way when Elizabeth was horrified to see Lady Findlater and her now constant companion, Lady Wraxley, approaching her. What could those two women be doing out at this time of the morning, Elizabeth wondered.

She briefly contemplated ducking her head or crossing back to the other side of the street, but then she'd never thought of herself as a coward. What sort of example would that set for Matthew? No, there was no other choice; she simply had to walk past the two ladies with her head held high.

Elizabeth could see the moment the two women spotted her. Lady Findlater did a double take with her eyes widening as soon as she saw Elizabeth. The two women leaned toward each other, whispering something, but strangely they didn't look away. They didn't turn away. They did nothing but continue walking toward her as she did toward them.

"Lady St. Vincent," Lady Findlater said, nodding her head as they walked past.

Lady Wraxley nodded as well but said nothing.

Elizabeth was so shocked, her head nodded in response, but it hadn't been intentional. It was more of an automatic reaction. She said nothing, however, and her feet simply kept moving.

"Who was that?" Matthew asked, turning to look back at the two ladies.

"No one," she said. "They were no one of any import."

There was a bench not too far from the park gate. Elizabeth was grateful it was unoccupied for she sorely needed to sit down. Her heart, strangely enough, was beating a rapid tattoo inside of her chest.

Very slowly, she lowered herself onto the bench and then just sat there staring toward the gate where the most vocal, most cruel gossip in all of London society had just acknowledged her. How had that happened?

"Are you all right, Mama?" Matthew asked. He was looking at her with such concern in his eyes.

"Yes. If you could, please, just give me a moment."

He nodded and sat on the bench next to her, holding her hand. Never was she more grateful for that small show of support from someone so sweet and innocent.

The acknowledgement couldn't have been a mistake, Elizabeth thought. Lady Findlater had clearly discussed it, even if momentarily, with her friend. No, it was most definitely deliberate.

But how could that be? After last night when Lord Rogan... Elizabeth found that she could hardly recall what Lord Rogan had said, nor what she'd said to him. Was it in any way possible that he *had* somehow exonerated her?

She vaguely recalled him admitting to tricking her into meeting him in the Welles's library. Could that have been enough to change the mind of Lady Findlater? Was there anything else Lord Rogan had said that had changed her mind? And most importantly, if Lady Findlater's mind had been changed, did that mean all of society now thought different of her?

Elizabeth got up again and continued her walk, Matthew silently staying by her side just as he'd promised. Mindlessly, she walked straight down Rotten Row thinking about all this. Trying her best to recall exactly what had been said the night before.

There weren't many other ladies and gentlemen of the *ton* out so early, but there were a few. She recognized a face here and there among both those walking the path or riding by. Each one nodded to her, some with a slight smile, others more solemnly, but they all nodded!

She was halfway down the road when she suddenly realized that while this was completely unexpected, she honestly, truly *didn't care.*

The thought almost stopped her in her tracks.

She didn't care!

She didn't care if Lady Findlater and Lady Wraxley acknowledged her. She imagined what she would have done if they hadn't. She would have felt, perhaps, a momentary stab of disappointment or hurt, but then... Then it would have gone away. If no member of society had acknowledged her on this walk, would it have upset her? Truly made her unhappy? Hurt?

No, it wouldn't have.

All of a sudden, she felt so much better. So much lighter. The pace at which she was walking increased, and she added a slight spring to her step.

She didn't care if society acknowledged her or not.

She looked down and shared a smile with Matthew.

"Are you feeling better, Mama?" he asked.

"Yes. Yes, I am. You see, I just needed to think for a bit," she told him.

"And it's easier to think when you're walking?"

"Yes."

Charles had been absolutely correct, she realized, still allowing her thoughts to churn. It didn't matter what other people thought of her. She didn't need them. She didn't care about their appropriation. She knew who she was. She knew what she had and hadn't done. Why should she care what others thought?

So why was she leaving London?

Ah, that made her pause.

"Did you think of something else?" Matthew asked, looking worried.

"Yes, but I don't know it's a bad thing. In fact, it might be quite good," she told him. "I had thought we would have to leave town and go back to St. Vincent, but...now I'm not so sure."

"That's good. I like it here," Matthew told her.

There really was no reason for her to leave, and Matthew liked it here. If she was or wasn't invited to society events, she didn't care. She knew she would be invited to a few events by those who were her true friends. That was most certainly enough for her. She didn't need to go out every night. She wasn't looking for a husband, just some pleasant social interaction with friends.

The thought of Charles and a husband did bring her down a touch. She'd been so upset when Charles had left, and so shocked when he'd come back. She wondered what had made him return. It would be too much to think it was her, wouldn't it? Was it simply wishful thinking that maybe, perhaps, he'd returned for her?

She silently cursed society's rules that said that a woman couldn't call upon a man because she most definitely wished she could call upon him right now and find out. Instead, she would simply have to wait until he came to her. She could only hope he wouldn't take very long. Thank goodness, she had Matthew to keep her occupied.

~*~

Penelope was still nibbling at her toast when her son wandered into the drawing room.

"Ah, you have something to eat! I went into the dining room, but there was nothing laid out," he said, looking longingly at her nearly empty plate.

"Charles! How are you feeling? What happened last night? How is Elizabeth?" Penelope said, jumping up.

He gave her a little smile. "Do you think I could get something to eat before the interrogation?"

"Oh! Of course," Penelope said. She rang for the footman and asked him to bring a plate for her son.

"Two eggs, ham, toast, jam, and coffee," Charles elaborated. "I'm famished."

The man bowed and went off to do his bidding.

"Now will you tell me everything? What made you come back from Dover?" Penelope asked, sitting back down.

Charles took a seat across from her and gave a little shrug. "I realized it was more important that I find out how Elizabeth feels about me…about us rather than simply coming to my own conclusion. She is more important than this trip. The trip can wait."

"Oh, Charles, I'm so happy!" Penelope said. She was so tempted to tell him everything that Elizabeth had told her about being forced to learn to keep in her emotions, but then thought perhaps it was better that Elizabeth tell him herself. It was her story to tell, not Penelope's. It was probably more important that it come from her.

"The thing is," Charles continued, "I *still* don't know how she feels. The whole way back I had decided that I had, in fact, seen tears in her eyes when I told her I was leaving, but then…"

"Then? What happened?"

"Then last evening she looked up at me after I took her outside." He paused and looked out the window across the room. He gave a little shake of his head. "I don't know. I guess I expected her to throw her arms around me and tell me how happy she was that I was back. Or say something like 'Thank God, you're here! I missed you! I needed you.' Something along those lines. Instead, I got 'What are you doing here? I'd thought you'd left.'" He turned his attention back to Penelope. "She didn't seem all that happy I was there. More surprised and worried than happy."

"Oh, Charles, she'd just been horribly attacked—in public! You can't expect her to immediately turn her attention to you and how she feels for you. That would have been quite an abrupt turnabout. No one is capable of that—not after what she'd just been through. She was probably horribly embarrassed at what had just occurred."

Her son sighed and nodded. "I suppose you're right. I just... I was really hoping for some sign of happiness. I had, after all, just saved her from being hauled out of there by that rogue."

"And I'm certain she was extremely grateful. Why don't you allow her to show you her gratitude today?" Penelope asked, an idea forming in her head. "I was thinking of going over this afternoon to check on her. Come with me."

"Oh, no! I don't think..."

"Charles," Penelope said. She was sure if she asked the right way he would do as she wished, and she was one hundred percent certain that all Elizabeth and Charles needed was a chance to talk, and everything would be worked out.

He gave her a little smile. "I can tell from your expression that you're not going to accept no for an answer, are you?"

"Not at all," Penelope agreed. "We'll leave around three."

~*~

Elizabeth was discussing household arrangements with the housekeeper, now that she'd decided not to leave town, when Frank knocked and then entered the drawing room.

"I beg your pardon, my lady, but you have

visitors. Are you at home this afternoon?"

"Who is it?" she asked, curious as to who would seek her out after last night's debacle.

"Lady Welles and Lady Colburne."

"Oh! Of course, I am home to them. I am at home to any of my close friends, Frank," she informed him.

"Very good, my lady. I shall show them up." He bowed and left the room.

The housekeeper curtsied after he left, saying, "We can finish this later, my lady. I'll prepare a tray of tea and cake for your friends."

"Yes, thank you." Elizabeth wondered whether Lydia and Diana would be able to tell her what occurred after she'd left the ball last night. Considering the experience she'd had while out for her walk earlier, she was very curious.

"Oh, Elizabeth!" Lydia said as she practically ran into the room. She came forward and gave her a big hug, which felt better than any words could have.

"Thank you so much for coming," Elizabeth said.

"Of course! We had to see how you were doing," Diana said, coming forward. "I nearly brought Andrew just in case you were still ill."

Elizabeth smiled at her dear friend. "How wonderful it is to have a physician for a husband! Thank you, but really, I'm fine."

"Are you?" Lydia asked as they all sat.

Elizabeth nodded. "It wasn't easy getting out of bed this morning, but I managed. I have to admit, I've been wondering about what happened last evening after I left."

The girls looked at each other, but before they could answer, Frank was back.

"Lady Blakemore and Lady Ayres," he announced, showing the two women into the room.

"Oh! Lady Welles, Lady Colburne, but of course you two are already here," Lady Ayres exclaimed with a laugh as she came in the door.

Lady Blakemore came forward and took Elizabeth's hands, giving them a warm squeeze. "How are you, my dear? We were all so worried," she said with feeling.

"Thank you, my lady, you are too kind. Both of you," she said, turning to include Lady Ayres.

They hadn't even had a chance to sit down properly when Frank was back. "Lady Moreton, my lady."

Elizabeth stood to greet her new guest. She didn't know Lady Moreton very well, but knew her to be a very kind and empathetic person. Of course, she was a member of the Ladies' Wagering Whist Society, so she was probably fully aware of Elizabeth's predicament.

Within half an hour, all the women of the Wagering Whist Society were seated around Elizabeth's drawing room. Noticeably absent was Mrs. Aldridge, the one person Elizabeth would have expected to be the first on her doorstep.

"Ladies, you are all so kind to have come to check on me," Elizabeth said, looking around at them all. "I cannot tell you how much your show of support means."

"You are one of our own, Lady St. Vincent," Lady Sorrell said.

Chapter Thirty-Two

"It's true. You don't need to be an actual member of the Whist Society to be one of us. Perhaps one day we will expand our group, but for now, please know you are cared for as much as anyone within it," Lady Ayres said.

"Thank you," Elizabeth said, putting a hand to her heart. Truly, she felt...wanted. It was the best feeling in the world to be part of this group of thoughtful, caring women. She was truly touched. Nothing was better than friends.

"Do you truly want to know what went on after you left?" Diana asked.

Elizabeth turned to her. "I...I think so. Should I not?" she asked with some trepidation.

"You might," Lady Blakemore said.

"It isn't as bad as you might have imagined, actually," Lady Moreton said. "Personally, I was rather surprised."

"Why, what happened?" Elizabeth asked, now eager to know. Before anyone could answer her, however, Frank was back.

"Mr. and Mrs. Aldridge, my lady."

Mrs. Aldridge and Charles came into the room and all talk ceased as all the ladies either rose to greet the newcomers or nodded in their direction as befitting their station. Elizabeth also noticed a few of the women looking rather closely from her to Charles and back again—clearly curious as to their relationship. Frankly, Elizabeth was wondering about that herself.

Mrs. Aldridge rushed over, taking Elizabeth into her arms and holding her to her ample bosom. "My poor, poor, dear Elizabeth! I had wanted to be the very first to see how you were doing, but I felt it more important that I bring Charles with me. You will please forgive us for being so late."

Elizabeth smiled down at her. "You aren't late, and I appreciate that you've come. You as well, Charles," she said, looking up at him. He was still standing a little awkwardly by the door.

"I do beg your pardon. I had some correspondence that had to be seen to immediately, before I could leave," he said.

"Of course. You must have had quite a scramble after cancelling your trip," Elizabeth said.

He nodded his agreement.

"Please come and join us. I was about to be informed of what occurred after I left," Elizabeth said, indicating an unoccupied chair. Lydia shifted over on the sofa making room for Mrs. Aldridge.

"Very simply, once Lord Rogan was picked up and carried away by some footmen—" the Duchess of Kendell began once they were all settled.

"I do hope they simply threw him into the gutter where he belongs!" Lydia said with vehemence.

Elizabeth giggled. It was terrible, but she couldn't help it.

The duchess gave Lydia a look as if to say that, while her interruption was rude, she might have agreed with the sentiment. "As I was saying, after they removed Lord Rogan, there was some chatter for a little while, but then the orchestra began playing, and everyone went back to dancing and the party."

"I'm sure it was the topic of discussion, though, wasn't it?" Elizabeth asked, rather surprised.

"Oh, I'm sure it was on everyone's tongues, but that didn't mean they were going to allow it to stop them from having a pleasant evening," Lady Colburne said with a touch of dismay to her voice.

"I did hear a number of people refer to you as 'poor, dear Lady St. Vincent,'" Mrs. Aldridge commented.

"Really? So… It is possible that people *don't* have a further disgust of me?" Elizabeth asked. This seemed to confirm what she had actually experienced while out for her walk.

"Disgust? Definitely not!" Lady Ayres said with certainty.

"Not in the least," Lady Moreton agreed.

"All the talk I heard was in your favor," Lydia commented.

"Lord Rogan showed his true colors," Lady Sorrell said. "He outright said he had tricked you into coming to the Welles's library and made up the story about you going home with Mr. Aldridge." She paused to give the gentleman an apologetic look.

"So he *did* say that? I wasn't sure," Elizabeth said. She shook her head. "I have to say, it's all rather a bit of a blur to me, exactly what he said, how I responded. I was just…just in shock, I believe."

"Of course you were!" Lydia said.

"The odd thing, I believe, that had the most impact was when he said you actually didn't even need to have done anything, and still people would have thought the worst of you," the duchess commented thoughtfully.

"Yes! I can tell you, that got a number of people talking," Lady Blakemore said in agreement.

Elizabeth gave a sad shake of her head. "It's why I've always been especially careful about my behavior and my clothing choices. I never wanted to give the wrong impression."

"And yet gentlemen still jumped to wrong conclusions about you," Lady Moreton said with a frown. "Present company excluded, I'm sure," she added quickly, looking to Mr. Aldridge.

"Oh, that's quite all right. I agree that men can sometimes be rather idiotic when it comes to women who are as beautiful as Lady St. Vincent," he commented in such a matter-of-fact way Elizabeth could feel her face heat with embarrassment.

"Oh, no, Mr. Aldridge..." she began to protest.

Some of the other women giggled.

"I assure you, however, Lady St. Vincent, that my respect for you far outweighs everything else," he added quickly.

Elizabeth couldn't even look him eye, she was so mortified by the turn the conversation had taken. "You are too good, sir." A thought occurred to her in the moment of silence that followed. "I wonder..." she started. "Perhaps it is because I have been behaving as if I had something to hide that there has been so much talk."

"What do you mean?" Lady Colburne asked.

"After Lord Rogan's first attack, we all worked very hard to give the impression that I was respectable. What if we tried too hard?" Elizabeth asked.

"You mean like in that Shakespearean play? 'The lady doth protest too much, methinks'?" Lady Welles asked, quoting. "Which one was that?"

"Hamlet," Lady Sorrell supplied. "But I have to disagree, Lady St. Vincent. You were attacked, first physically by Lord Rogan and then by all those who believed his and Lady Findlater's lies. You did what you needed to do to reestablish your good name. I don't believe it was too much."

"No, indeed," Mrs. Aldridge concurred. "You did what was necessary, and you did it with strength and fortitude."

"And a positive attitude," Lydia added with a smile.

"Yes, indeed, Lady Welles! A great deal can be said about the way you've handled this whole ordeal, Lady St. Vincent, but that you did too much? No, I don't believe so either," the Duchess of Kendell said.

"You don't think that if I had simply behaved innocent as I truly was—absolutely not guilty of any wrongdoing—that perhaps Lord Rogan's assertions wouldn't have gone the way of any other outlandish tales?"

"No, I'm sorry, you did what you needed to do," Lady Blakemore said with finality.

The talk happily turned to other subjects, and before too long, all the ladies began to excuse themselves. Soon it was only Charles, his mother, and the Duchess of Kendell who were left.

The duchess stood to make her departure, but before she could begin to do so, Mrs. Aldridge spoke up. "Duchess, if you are leaving, might I ask you to give me a lift home? I have a feeling Charles and Elizabeth have some matters they might need to discuss." She didn't even look over to her son to see if that might be the case, Elizabeth noticed with some amusement.

"I would be very happy to do so," the duchess said. She nodded to Elizabeth and Charles. "Lady St. Vincent, I am so happy you are doing well. I'll look forward to seeing you again soon."

"Yes, indeed. Thank you for coming, Your Grace," Elizabeth responded with a curtsy.

As she closed the door behind her last two guests, she turned to see Charles standing in the center of the room waiting for her. Her heart seemed to speed up, and her stomach clenched ever so slightly in anticipation.

"Well..." she said.

"Yes, well."

"Would you care to go for a walk in the garden? I find I'm suddenly in need of some fresh air."

"That sounds lovely," he said.

~*~

Outside, they walked side by side, along a path bordering the flower bed, awkward with each other for the first time in weeks. Charles knew he had to begin; he just wasn't sure where. Finally, he simply threw all caution to the wind and said, "I'm glad to see you're doing all right. I was worried we'd find you abed, unable to rise at all."

Elizabeth gave a nod. "Oddly enough, I *was* able to get up—a little later than normal, but..." She sighed and then said, "I managed."

"I'm happy you did so, and hopefully, this entire episode is at an end," Charles said.

"Yes, indeed, and I have to say, seeing all the ladies here today has only reinforced something which I was thinking when I went out for a walk this afternoon."

"And what is that?"

Elizabeth turned to him. "I have come to realize that it is truly only the good opinions of those who I like and respect that matter to me. So long as I have that, I don't care about the rest. While it is important that no door be closed to my son because of me and my reputation, on the whole, I don't need everyone in society to like to me. I certainly don't need a huge stack of invitations to feel good about myself. Simply having a few good friends is enough for me."

"I'm happy to hear this. On the other hand, society is *important,* and you shouldn't simply dismiss it out of hand," he said.

She gave a little laugh. "Since when did *you* think the *ton* was important? You hate society. You think it's silly and frivolous."

"I don't hate it. I *did* think it silly, that's certainly true, but I don't any more. A wise woman showed me how very important it is to be a part of society."

"Your mother?" she asked, smiling up at him.

He laughed. "No. You."

That took her by surprise. "Me? I'm certainly not wise."

"But you are. And very clever. You introduced me to Lord Sorrell, which made it possible for me to speak with him and explain the situation with the

Swiss watches. You may have saved the British watchmaking industry."

"You are certainly exaggerating," she said with a wave of her hand he found rather amusing. "But what about Lord Rogan? With him on the committee, I thought..."

"Yes, he is impeding things but I... I don't know. I'm still hopeful we might be able to get past him," Charles admitted.

"It's entirely my fault that he's even there. That he's doing this. I don't see how you could possibly even be speaking with me, considering all the harm I've done to you and your business," she said with a frown.

"Elizabeth, you are not responsible for Lord Rogan's bad behavior." He paused and put a finger under her chin, forcing her to look at him. She blinked up at him. "The point is, *because* you're a respected member of society, you were able to start this entire process. Yes, I think parties are a bit of a waste of time, but they have their purposes too. Being on good terms with the members of Parliament is a very good thing. No, I don't like that we should be reliant on what other people think of us, but it does *help* to be well thought of. What I'm trying to say is you were absolutely right."

She shook her head. "I'm honored that you think so. I don't know how well respected I might be now, but I'm—"

"You don't know that. You certainly earned my respect last night—well, you'd already had it, but if you hadn't, you certainly would now." He took her hands in his own and faced her. "You were incredible last night. You were so amazingly brave and strong... It still takes my breath away."

She blinked a few times but looked up at him, slowly shaking her head. "I can't imagine what you mean."

"You stood up to him, Elizabeth. You stood up to Lord Rogan even as he was making all those horrid accusations about you. You were clever and got him to admit to everything he did, and when he did so, you didn't faint or swoon or do anything most other ladies would have done. No, you stood there and fought back, telling the truth in the face of his lies."

Elizabeth had pulled her hands from his and turned her head away while he'd been speaking. He realized she was doing exactly the same thing that she'd done when he'd told her he was leaving. He reached out and turned her face toward him once again so she was forced to look at him. Her eyes were filled with tears! He'd been right. "You're crying!"

She gave a sniff and quickly wiped away a tear that had leaked from one eye. "I beg your pardon. I...I..." She paused and shook her head, turning her gaze downward.

"Elizabeth, it's all right! You can cry," he said.

She shook her head, then seemed to stop herself. She gave a sniff and looked up at him. "Your mother told me that you were upset I hadn't... I hadn't shown you my emotions the other day when you told me you were leaving. She told me you're not used to women concealing their feelings. My husband... He couldn't stand a show of emotion. I learned to hide them."

He frowned at her. "But why? Emotions are normal. They're natural."

"Yes, but he found them overbearing, useless,

and distracting, especially when he had work to do. So, when I knew you were pre-occupied with your work and needed to leave to attend to it, I didn't want to burden you with how upset I was." She gave a little shrug. "So, I hid it."

Charles frowned. "Your husband was an idiot. I'm sorry for speaking ill of the dead, but that's truly the most ridiculous thing I've ever heard."

"You... You *truly* don't mind?"

"Not in the least. How am I to know when you're upset if you don't show me or tell me so?"

She shook her head.

He was silent for a moment, just watching her. "Elizabeth, no matter what your emotions were the other day, I want you to know I'm proud of you. In fact, I'm rather in awe of how you've handled this whole situation and...and I love you."

She smiled through the tears still lingering in her eyes. "Thank you. I love you! And I was *truly* upset you were leaving. I... I can't stand the thought that you would go away at all, let alone for two months or more!"

"Good. I mean, I'm sorry you were upset, but in another way, I'm glad because when I thought you didn't care. I didn't ask what I'd meant to ask you. I didn't say what I had come to say."

She looked up at him, her eyes widening, but she said nothing.

He smiled at her, enjoying the sensation of all the wonderful emotions he'd been feeling for the past few weeks all coalesce together inside his heart. Everything came together in a rush of joy and happiness that he didn't *want* to contain any longer. "I love you, Elizabeth St. Vincent. I love you with all my heart, and I want to spend the rest of my life with you." He lowered himself onto one knee before her. "Elizabeth, would you do me the great honor of marrying me?"

She gasped and giggled, but tears streamed down her cheeks, and she didn't even try to stop them or look away, which made him so very happy. "I love you so much," she whispered. "And I would be very happy to marry you. You don't mind..."

"Don't mind what?"

"What people will say? What society might think?" she asked. Her lips trembled. She covered her mouth with her hand to hide the fact that she was crying indeed.

He stood up and took her in his arms. "I don't mind because I don't think anyone is going to say anything negative. After last night, they know all the rumors and gossip weren't true, and we will tell everyone what *is* true—because of the rumors, we met and got to know one another and fell in love."

She gave a little sob against his shoulder. He hoped they were happy tears.

He reached into his pocket and pulled out his handkerchief and handed it to her, all without letting her go. He couldn't. He wanted her close. Needed her there.

She gave a little laugh and wiped away her tears. She then settled her head more securely against him, and he felt as if time stood still.

Chapter Thirty-Three

~June 2~

Charles and Mrs. Aldridge joined Elizabeth and Paul for a small, family celebration of the engagement before they all attended Lady Midton's ball. All the ladies of the Wagering Whist Society agreed they would be in attendance to support Elizabeth should anything untoward occur. It was unlikely, however, as the knocker on Lord Rogan's door had been removed making it clear that he had finally decided that retreat was his best option.

"You look beautiful," Charles told Elizabeth quietly soon after he'd come into the drawing room.

She laughed "Why, thank you." She did a graceful turn so he could admire her from every angle. "This is a new gown Tina, the Duchess of Warwick, designed for me. What do you think? Not too daring?"

The gown's décolletage was lower than anything she'd worn in years, and she was, frankly, feeling a little exposed. But the deep blue silk underdress was beautiful and flowed with her every movement. It was topped by a lighter silk half-dress of a paler version of the same color and trimmed with white lace along all the edges and stretched across the neckline. Without that, there would have been a great deal more flesh to be seen and Elizabeth was nervous enough as it was.

"It is certainly much more revealing than you usually wear, but at the same time, it's very elegant. It teases rather than blatantly showing off what you have," Charles said, clearly admiring all he could see.

"Oh, dear, it *is* too revealing! I knew it!" Elizabeth cried. "I should go up and change before—"

"Don't you dare change. You look stunning, and you are not showing anything that any number of ladies don't show on an average day."

"But you just said—"

"I said that it is more revealing than what people are used to seeing *you* wear. That doesn't mean that it's indecent in any way."

"Are you certain?" she asked hesitantly. It was going to be difficult enough once they got to the ball. She didn't want to make it more so with her dress.

"Absolutely." He smiled at her. He seemed to lean toward her as if he were going to kiss her, but then shot Paul and his mother a guilty glance. They weren't paying any attention to them, but he seemed to think better of the idea, anyway.

Elizabeth felt momentarily disappointed, but knew that before too long they would have plenty of opportunities for stolen kisses.

"Have you decided when you're going to put the announcement into the papers?" Paul asked turning toward Charles. Perhaps he was watching after all, Elizabeth thought with a little laugh.

"I thought I might do so tomorrow or the day

following. I didn't want to do anything to make anything more difficult for Elizabeth this evening," Charles answered.

"It's definitely going to be interesting to see how people react," Mrs. Aldridge said.

"I'm sure it will be fine," Paul said, calm as always.

"Oh, most definitely! I didn't mean to imply otherwise," Mrs. Aldridge said quickly.

"I hate to change the subject, Elizabeth," Charles started. "But I was wondering if it was possible that your son was still awake?"

Elizabeth was surprised by the question but said, "I did say goodnight to him just before you arrived, but I imagine he is. Why?"

"I thought it might be nice to meet him, that's all. And, er, I brought him a little something," Charles said.

"How sweet! I've been wondering when I might introduce the two of you," Elizabeth said. Her heart, already filled with such happiness, felt like it would burst with joy that Charles would think of her son. "I'll just go and see. If you'll excuse me for a moment."

She ran lightly up the stairs to the nursery where she was not surprised to find Matthew still awake in his little bed. "I have a surprise for you," she told him after peeking into the room.

He immediately sat up. "What?"

"A good friend of mine is downstairs, and he'd like to meet you. He said he had a present for you," she said to entice him even further. She hadn't yet told Matthew about Charles, unsure of how to even broach the subject of her marrying again. This seemed to be the perfect opportunity, though.

"Can I get dressed first? I don't want to go down in my pajamas," Matthew said, climbing out of bed.

"Of course!"

Elizabeth helped him to dress quickly. While they were busy at it, Mrs. Smithy, Matthew's governess came in. "May I help with something, my lady?" the confused woman asked.

"Oh, no... well, yes. I am sorry to disturb your routine but I have a special guest downstairs who wanted to meet Matthew. Could you join us?" Elizabeth asked.

"Of course, my lady." The woman bent down and helped finish getting Matthew dressed and even combed his hair quickly.

Elizabeth then took Matthew's hand to ensure that he didn't go bounding into the drawing room as he usually did.

Charles was sitting on a chair which put him at a good height to meet the little boy and his welcoming smile was all the invitation the child needed to approach him.

Elizabeth realized she'd forgotten to remind Matthew of his manners before they'd come in, but she was very proud to see that he remembered on his own. He walked straight up to Charles and waited for Elizabeth to make the introduction.

"Mr. Aldridge, may I present my son, Matthew Alder?" Elizabeth said.

Matthew bowed properly saying, "I am pleased to meet you."

"I am very pleased to meet you, Matthew. Er, may I call you Matthew?" Charles asked, seriously.

The boy smiled and nodded, clearly thrilled at being treated like an adult.

Charles looked up at Elizabeth and asked, "Have you..."

"No. I haven't, but I think now would be a perfect time," she said, understanding that he was asking if she'd told Matthew about their engagement. She knelt down next to her son. "Matthew, Mr. Aldridge is more than just a friend of mine."

Matthew looked at her quizzically.

Elizabeth took in a deep breath. "He's going to be your new papa."

Matthew frowned, looking from her to Charles and back again. "Because my papa went to heaven you are giving me a new one?"

"Yes, that's right. Mr. Aldridge and I, er, like each other very much. He and I are going to marry and then he'll become your papa."

"Oh," Matthew said, still frowning. Clearly, he was still trying to work this out in his mind.

"I know it sounds very strange right now, but I do hope that we will quickly become good friends," Charles said. "And to that end, I did bring you a small gift." He pulled a small lumpy brown paper package from his pocket and handed it to Matthew.

For a moment, the boy looked to Elizabeth. She gave him a little nod, and he tore off the paper. Inside was a beautiful little metal toy soldier with a little drum affixed to him. In his hands, drum sticks were poised over the instrument.

"Ooh. I have some toy soldiers but I don't have a drummer," Matthew said, examining it.

"This one is special," Charles said. He turned it

over in Matthew's hands. Sticking out the back of the toy was a key. "You see, you can wind him up and he'll hit his drum."

Matthew's jaw dropped open.

"Do you want to see?" Charles asked.

Matthew nodded and handed the toy over. Charles twisted the key a few times. As he did so, gears could be heard winding up. He then placed the soldier on the floor, and they all watched in amazement as its little arms moved up and down hitting the drum with a little *tink-tink-tink*.

"My word! That's fantastic," Paul said, coming over to watch the soldier as well.

"Charles is so clever with mechanical objects," his mother gushed.

"You made that?" Elizabeth asked, quite surprised.

"Yes. I always have extra gears and materials from my watchmaking," Charles said with a little shrug.

Matthew had picked up the soldier and was winding it up again. He struggled a bit with the key but managed to turn it a few times and set the toy down on the floor to watch it play.

"Matthew, what do you say to Mr. Aldridge?" Elizabeth said, reminding her son who was absolutely fascinated with toy.

He grabbed it in mid-stroke and ran at Charles throwing himself into the man's arms. "Thank you, thank you! You are going to be the best papa I ever had!"

Elizabeth found herself having to blink back a few tears.

Charles laughed. "Oh, no, I don't think that

could be possible. I'm sure your real papa was quite wonderful. But I do hope we can become good friends. And I'll even teach you how to make toy soldiers if you want when you're a little older."

"I want! I want!" Matthew said, jumping up and down a little.

"All right, then. But you do need to go to sleep now so you can grow big enough," Charles said.

Matthew deflated a little but nodded.

Mrs. Smithy came forward and took Matthew's hand.

"Good night," Matthew told Charles, Mrs. Aldridge, Paul.

Elizabeth knelt and gave him a kiss. "Sleep well, my love."

He gave her a one-armed hug, his toy soldier clasped tightly to his chest.

After he left Elizabeth turned to Charles. "That was so kind of you."

"Oh, it's nothing. I had a number of wind-up soldiers my father made me when I was young. I had a drummer and some that could even walk. I wish I knew what happened to them," he said with a little shrug.

"They're in the attic. I know where they are," Mrs. Aldridge said. "You don't think I would have thrown them away, do you?"

He laughed. "I should hope not!"

"We'll find them and you can oil them and make sure they're all still working," she told him with a broad smile.

Elizabeth was almost sad to leave the comfort of their little party to go to the ball after dinner.

Chapter Thirty-Four

Their hostess greeted them as soon as they'd walked into the ballroom. "Why, Lady St. Vincent, what a lovely surprise. I almost thought we wouldn't see you here this evening."

"Thank you, Lady Midton. I am very happy to be here. I'm looking forward to a very pleasant evening," Elizabeth said, giving the woman a slight curtsy. She then moved on before the lady could say anything else. She was determined to behave as normally as possible.

"Lady Ayres, Lydia, good evening," she said, approaching the two ladies who were standing close to the door.

They both turned as one. Lydia gasped before her face was covered in a broad smile. "Good evening, Elizabeth. What a stunning gown!" she said.

"Thank you. Tina designed it for me."

"Of course she did," Lady Ayres said with a little laugh. "She is so very talented in that way. It is just right for this evening."

"I sincerely hope so," Elizabeth said.

"Good evening, Mr. Aldridge, Mrs. Aldridge," Lady Ayres said, turning to greet Elizabeth's companions. "I was wondering whether I'd see the announcement of your engagement in the papers this morning," she said pointedly to Charles.

He gave her a little smile and said, "I thought it would be better if Elizabeth were to have this evening first, and then I'll put the announcement in the papers."

"That's very thoughtful of you," Lydia commented with a nod. "She does need this one night to see how her reputation fairs."

"I hope it all works out as we thought," Mrs. Aldridge said. She was looking a trifle nervous but seemed to be hiding it well enough.

The orchestra began to play the introduction to the first dance.

"Would you care to dance, Elizabeth?" Charles asked, putting out his hand.

"I would, thank you," she said, smiling up at him. Not only did she enjoy dancing with him, but this would give everyone in the room a chance to see her. She allowed him to escort her into the center of the room.

They were laughing at something silly soon after the dance had ended, and were about to head back to where they'd last seen Charles' mother, when Mrs. Aldridge's voice rose above the crowd. "Bolton!"

Charles rushed forward with Elizabeth close behind. They both stopped to see an older gentleman in a brown coat and matching knee breeches bow to Mrs. Aldridge. "My dear lady," the man said.

"Bolton? Is that you?" an older lady said from nearby. She walked toward him as if she wasn't certain if he was a figment of her imagination, one hand reaching out toward him.

"Ah, Lady Fareham. It has been some time, hasn't it?" he bowed toward her.

"Some time? Your Grace, it has been at least twenty years!" the lady exclaimed.

"Has it really? And here you are, looking hardly a day older than the last time I saw you," he said, giving her a smile.

The lady giggled, putting a hand to her bosom. "Oh, Your Grace, you have not changed! Not one whit."

"Your... Your Grace?" Mrs. Aldridge asked hesitantly.

The man turned toward her, his cheeks turning rather pink. "Ah, yes. Perhaps, Mrs. Aldridge, we should have a word? In private?"

"Not before you introduce us," Charles said, interrupting.

"Oh, Charles!" his mother exclaimed, suddenly noticing him.

"Ah! You must be Aldridge. A pleasure to meet you. I've heard all about you. And you must be Lady St. Vincent. An honor, my lady," His Grace said, reaching out a hand toward Charles even as he nodded toward Elizabeth.

Charles took his hand but said, "And how, may I ask, do you know my mother?"

"Haven't told him, have you?" His Grace asked, turning and giving Mrs. Aldridge a wink.

"Told me what?" Charles demanded.

"Nothing! Nothing at all. It's just... Bolton and I have been walking our dogs together in the park for some time," Mrs. Aldridge started.

"Some time? For about two months now," Bolton said with a little laugh.

"He has *four* King Charles Spaniels," Mrs. Aldridge said with a little awe. "They are so well behaved. They've quite shown my little Duchess how to go on." She gave a nervous little laugh.

"Really? And why haven't you mentioned this to me, Mother?" Charles asked.

"Yes, why *haven't* you mentioned it?" Bolton repeated.

"I, er, I, well… I didn't see the need. And I didn't know you were a duke!" she frowned at the gentleman accusingly. "You didn't mention that to me. You simply told me your name was Bolton. What an *awful* trick to play on me, Your Grace."

"It wasn't a trick. My name *is* Bolton and I, well, I didn't see the need to—"

"You've been meeting for walks in the park for two months, and you never happened to mention your title?" Elizabeth asked with a little laugh. "And it sounds as if you've grown to be rather close, er, friends?"

"I had thought so," Mrs. Aldridge said, still looking rather upset.

"Well, I'd like to think we're closer than just friends," His Grace said, looking to Mrs. Aldridge. "But before we get into that, I do think we should have that little talk." He took her unresisting arm. "If you'll excuse us."

Elizabeth and Charles watched them walk off toward the garden.

She turned and looked up at him. "What are you thinking?" she asked, seeing the confusion and concern on his face.

"I don't know. I just… I can't believe my mother has been meeting a man on the sly."

Elizabeth laughed. "Well, he sounds absolutely perfect for her. *Four* spaniels? And they look to be of an age," she added.

"Yes. I just wish she'd told me, that's all. I could have found out who he was. Learned earlier that he was a duke." He turned toward Elizabeth, his eyes wide. "My mother has been courted by a *duke*!"

Elizabeth laughed. "And it seems as if she hadn't even known it."

~*~

"I can't believe you didn't tell me!" Penelope snapped at Bolton the moment they were out of earshot on the balcony.

"Would it have made a difference if I had?" he asked with a slight tilt of his head.

"No! Of course not," she huffed.

"Then why should I have told you?"

Penelope opened her mouth, but she didn't know what to say. She just felt hurt, as if she'd been used, which was ridiculous actually because he hadn't used her, not in the least. "It would have been a good thing for me to know," she said finally.

"Would you have treated me differently if you'd known?" he asked, cocking his head a little.

"Yes, of course! You're a duke, you *should* be treated differently."

"I beg to differ. I'm a man, duke or not. Being a duke is not who I am. It's a title I inherited from my father. It's a responsibility and an occupation. It's not...*me*," he said taking her hands. "The person you met and came to know, that's me."

She looked up at him, understanding. "It's you who I've come to...to love," Penelope admitted

"And I'm honored you've allowed me to get to know you, to become friends with you, to spend time with you. It has been the most precious time I've spent all season."

He gave her a little smile. "You sound as if it's going to end."

"Isn't it, though? The season is nearly at an end. You probably need to return to your estate and your responsibilities." She felt her throat tighten at the thought.

"Actually, I'm just as able to see to my work from London as I am from my estate—more easily, in fact. I was thinking I might just stay, what do you think?"

A smile grew on Penelope's face. "I'd like that very much."

"Do you know what I'd like?"

She shook her head.

"I'd like to stay with you... Or, more precisely, I'd like you to stay with me. Charles is going to be getting married and his new wife will, presumably, be moving into his house. Why don't we do the same?"

Penelope blinked a few times, parsing out his words. "Are you asking me to marry you?"

He nodded, smiling. "I am, in a rather ham-handed way, yes." He ran a hand down her cheek. "I love you, too, Mrs. Aldridge. I love your silliness and your concern. I love your thoughtfulness and how you look out for and try to mother everybody. And I think I'd like to spend the rest of my life with you, if you'll have me."

"Penelope," she said.

He looked at her blankly for a moment.

"My name. It's Penelope. Some people call me Penny, but I prefer my full name if it's not too much of a mouthful," she said.

"Ah. Penelope is a lovely name. My given name is Abraham, but I've been called Bolton for so very long, I don't know that I'd even answer to it," he said with a laugh.

She giggled. "Abraham is a very nice name, but yes, I think I'll continue to call you Bolton."

"And will you do me the great honor of calling me husband?" he asked. He winked at her. "You still haven't answered that one."

"Oh!" she laughed. "Yes, Abraham, Duke of Bolton, I would be honored to become your wife."

~*~

"You're what?" Lady Welles nearly screeched when Penelope shared her news with the ladies at their next meeting.

"Congratulations!" came from a couple other ladies.

"You must tell us who the lucky gentleman is! Why, I don't believe we've even seen anyone pay court to you," Lady Blakemore said. "I have to admit I've been rather pre-occupied this season, but I think I would have noticed," she added with a laugh.

Penelope giggled. "Actually, we've been meeting nearly every day in the park. He has four King Charles Spaniels," she said as she petted her own sweet dog, who was sitting in her lap. "Duchess just loves them, and they love her."

"But that's perfect! How wonderful," the duchess said, nodding her approval.

"So...?" Lady Colburne said.

"So, what?" Penelope asked, turning to her.

Lady Sorrell gave a laugh. "Who is the gentleman?"

"Oh! It is the Duke of Bolton," Penelope answered. She was still getting used to referring to him by his title. It was so out of place for her in her life—or, at least it had been before she'd met and became a member of the Ladies' Wagering Whist Society.

"The Duke of Bolton? I know him, of course, but he hasn't been in town for years," the duchess said.

"He was at Lady Midton's party the other night," Lady Welles said. "Mrs. Aldridge introduced me to him."

"Yes, indeed he was. But no, he generally doesn't go to parties. He doesn't like being social. And, you are right, Duchess, he has been out of town at his estate for many years. His daughter just had a baby, and he wanted to give her some space, so he came to Town for the season," Penelope explained succinctly.

"That makes perfect sense," Lady Moreton said.

"Well, congratulations," the duchess said, giving her a warm smile.

"And soon we'll have two duchesses in our group, isn't that impressive?" Lady Ayres said with a laugh.

The duchess gave her and then Penelope a tight smile but said nothing, which just made Penelope burst out laughing. "Don't worry, Duchess, you will still take precedence. I won't insist on being called duchess or any such thing," Penelope said, trying to reassure the lady.

"Oh, it makes no difference to me," the woman said quickly. "Actually, after I marry Lord Gosling, I will no longer be a duchess. I'll be renouncing that title and will become a mere countess."

A number of the ladies laughed at the idea of "merely" a countess.

"But you *will* be a duchess, Mrs. Aldridge, and so we shall address you," Lady Blakemore commented.

"Well, I think we've done very well this season, ladies, what do you think?" Lady Colburne asked, looking around the room.

"Indeed! We have succeeded in arranging four marriages—the Kendrick twins, Lady Margaret's, and Lady St. Vincent's—and will be celebrating another two from our own ranks on top of that!" Lady Sorrell said.

"Personally, I can't wait until next season," Lady Ayres said, rubbing her hands together. "We have gotten rather good at these affairs of the heart, don't you think?"

"Indeed," Penelope agreed. And all around her the other ladies nodded their agreement as well.

About the Author

Meredith Bond's books straddle that beautiful line between historical romance and fantasy. An award-winning author, she writes fun traditional Regency romances, medieval Arthurian romances, and Regency romances with a touch of magic. Known for her characters "who slip readily into one's heart," Meredith's heart belongs to her husband and two children.

Meredith loves connecting with readers. Sign up for her monthly newsletter at http://meredithbond. com/blog/newsletter-sign-up/ to receive free short stories and get all her news before anyone else. And don't forget to find her online:

Website: http://www.meredithbond.com
Facebook: https://www.facebook.com/meredithbondauthor
Twitter: https://twitter.com/merrybond
Pinterest: http://www.pinterest.com/merrybond/
Amazon: http://www.amazon.com/Meredith-Bond/e/B001KI1SNE
Instagram:
   https://www.instagram.com/meredith_bond/
Bookbub: https://www.bookbub.com/authors/meredith-bond
Newsletter: http://meredithbond.com/subscribe/

Please don't forget to leave a review wherever you buy books.

Follow all of the women of the Ladies' Wagering Whist Society

1806 Season
A Hand for the Duke
Featuring Christianne Norman, Lady Norman
The Jack of Diamonds
Featuring Miss Lydia Sheffield
The Games She Played
Featuring Miss Diana Hemshawe

1807 Season
A Trick of Mirrors
Featuring Claire Tyne, Lady Blakemore
A Bid for Romance
Featuring Alys Russell, Duchess of Kendell
An Affair of Hearts
Featuring Mrs. Penelope Aldridge

1808 Season
Love in Spades
Featuring Cynthia Montley, Lady Sorrell
coming: Spring, 2021
A Token of Love
Featuring Ellen Aston, Lady Moreton
coming: Spring, 2021
Bonus
The King of Clubs
Featuring Joshua Powell, Lord Wickford
coming: Spring, 2021

Other Books By Meredith Bond

The Merry Men Series
An Exotic Heir
A Merry Marquis
A Rake's Reward
A Dandy in Disguise
My Lord Ghost
My Gentleman Thief
Under the Mango Tree
A Spanish Dilemma
When Hearts Rebel

The Storm Series
Storm on the Horizon
Bridging the Storm
Magic in the Storm
Through the Storm

The Children of Avalon Trilogy
Air: Merlin's Chalice
Water: The Return of Excalibur
Fire: Nimuë's Destiny

Falling
Falling for a Pirate

Chapter One: A Fast, Fun Way to Write Fiction
Self-Publishing: Easy as ABC
"In A Beginning", a short story featuring Lilith

Made in the USA
Coppell, TX
05 March 2024